THE RAILWAY DETECTIVE'S CHRISTMAS CASE

THE RAILWAY DETECTIVE'S CHRISTMAS CASE

EDWARD MARSTON

Allison & Busby Limited
11 Wardour Mews
London W1F 8AN
allisonandbusby.com

First published in Great Britain by Allison & Busby in 2022.
This paperback edition published by Allison & Busby in 2023.

A CIP catalogue record for this book is available from
the British Library.

10 9 8 7 6 5 4 3 2 1

ISBN 978-0-7490-2739-1

Typeset in 11.5/16.5 pt Adobe Garamond Pro by
Allison and Busby Ltd.

By choosing this product, you help take care of the world's forests.
Learn more: www.fsc.org.

Printed and bound by
CPI Group (UK) Ltd, Croydon, CR0 4YY

To George and Toni Demidowicz,
our dear friends, wonderful guides
to the Malvern Hills and its surrounding areas

CHAPTER ONE

1864

A cold December wind was scouring the platform but the hundred or more passengers waiting at the railway station were impervious to its bite. They were in such high spirits that nothing could trouble them. They had enjoyed a free cooked breakfast with a cup of hot tea to wash it down. By the time they reached the station, everyone was buzzing with excitement. Thanks to the generosity of their employer, the workers and their families were being rescued from the stink and smoke of the Black Country and taken to the scenic beauty of the Malvern Hills. It was a day they would never forget.

Presiding over the excursion was Cyril Hubbleday, the

works manager, a big, solid, middle-aged man, impeccably dressed and wearing the tall, shiny top that set him apart from anyone else on the platform. Hubbleday was making his way through the waiting throng, beaming at children, smiling politely at their mothers, and nodding at the employees whose work lives he controlled.

Derek Churt saw him coming and braced himself. Arm in arm with his wife, Agnes, he had his other hand on his young son's shoulder.

'Say nothin', Aggie,' he warned his wife.

'We ought to say thank you,' she argued.

'Do as I say, woman.'

'Why?'

'It's not him as is paying for all this – it's Mr Appleby.'

'Ah, yes . . .'

Like her husband, Agnes Churt was short, thin and wiry. She had lost the youthful bloom that had attracted him to her years earlier, and now had pinched features and rounded shoulders. Like her husband and son, she was wrapped up warmly and wearing a scarf and gloves she had knitted. It was not long before Hubbleday came right up to them.

'Good day to you!' he said, raising his top hat.

'Same to you, sir,' replied Churt, dutifully.

'Unless I'm mistaken, you work in a paint shop, don't you?'

'I do, sir.'

'That's right. Chort . . . Chart . . . something like that?'

'Churt, sir. Derek Churt.'

'Then you must be Mrs Churt,' said the works manager, running an eye over Agnes. He bent over the child. 'And who do we have here?'

'It's our son,' explained Churt. 'Peter.'

Hubbleday grinned. 'Hello, Peter.'

'Mornin', sir,' said the boy, responding to a nudge from his father.

'Have you been to the Malverns before?' asked Hubbleday.

'I been nowhere, sir.'

'That's what most of the children say.' He patted the boy on the head. 'You look like a bright lad, Peter. Let's hope you follow in your father's footsteps and work for us one day. Would you like that?'

'Yes, please, sir.'

'Make it your goal in life.'

After patting him on the head once more, Hubbleday moved on to the next family and distributed a smile among them. Agnes waited until the works manager was out of earshot before making a comment.

'Will there really be a job for our Peter?' she whispered.

'Doubt it,' grunted her husband.

'Mr Hubbleday said there would be, and he seems such a nice man.'

Churt curled a lip. 'You don't know him as well as I do.'

When the train steamed into the station and came to a halt, the passengers climbed into the compartments allotted to them with shrieks of pleasure. Hubbleday waited until they were all aboard then clambered into the compartment closest to the locomotive. Like all the other employees of the Oldbury Railway Carriage and Wagon Company there, the works manager was proud of the fact that they had built the carriages in which they were about to travel. Given the nature of the event, it was highly appropriate.

Peter Churt, meanwhile, did what all the other children were doing and stared out of the window of his compartment in sheer wonder. He had never been more than five miles from his home. Until the train was steaming along, he was unaware that, once they had emerged from the permanent dark haze under which they lived, they entered open countryside. The boy had to shield his eyes against the unexpected glare of sunshine. Other delights scudded past every second. He missed nothing. Worcester was a particular revelation to him. Against a clear sky, it looked quite beautiful. As they thundered over the bridge across the River Severn, Peter could see narrowboats moored along the banks and caught a glimpse of the racecourse nearby. The majestic cathedral drew a gasp of delight from him.

'Why can't we live here, Dad?' he asked, innocently.

'Because we can't,' muttered Churt.

'Why not?'

'We're Oldbury folk, born and bred.'

'It looks so clean.'

'You heard what your father said,' Agnes told him.

But her son's attention had already shifted to something

else of interest and he forgot that his parents were even there. It was a journey of discovery for the boy, and he wanted to relish every second of it.

Alone with his companion in their private compartment, Hubbleday removed his top hat and scratched his bald head. He had lost all trace of his former geniality and resorted to a snarl.

'I'm starting to hate these excursions,' he admitted. 'It's one thing to give the workers an occasional reward, but Mr Appleby takes it to extremes. An Easter Outing, a Whitsun Treat, a Summer Celebration and now this Christmas Party – we're spoiling them.'

'I agree,' said Drake, quietly.

'When the men are given an unnecessary holiday, we lose production.'

'Mr Appleby believes that it helps morale.'

'I'd prefer to keep their noses to the grindstone,' said Hubbleday, 'and I daresay that you feel the same.'

'I do, Cyril,' said Drake. 'Far be it from me to criticise Mr Appleby, but we are a manufacturing concern. Workers are there to work – not to be given days off.'

Ernest Drake was the company accountant, a tall, anxious man in his fifties with eyes glinting behind rimless spectacles. Across his lap was a ledger that contained the names of all those on the excursion. It had been his job to allocate the compartments on the train.

'At least we don't have to travel with them,' said

Hubbleday, scornfully. 'That would be unbearable. The men stink of mothballs, the women reek of cheap perfume and their ugly, snotty-nosed children have no idea how to behave themselves.'

'It was wise of you to insist on a private compartment,' said Drake.

'We deserve some privileges, Ernest.'

'I'm grateful to you.'

'We're managers. They need to be reminded of that.'

Settling back, he stretched out a hand and absentmindedly stroked the top hat beside him as if he were fondling a favourite cat. He soon went off into a reverie. Drake, meanwhile, opened his ledger and took out a copy of the seating plan he had devised. He unfolded it with care. On arrival, they would all be taken on a ride through the Malvern Hills before arriving at Appleby Court. The visitors would then be shown to their places in the dining room by Drake. He had inked in every name with care. As befitted their position, he and Hubbleday would be seated at the top table with the Appleby family.

When they eventually entered a series of cuttings, daylight was replaced by dark shadows and the stunning vistas disappeared. There was another disappointment. Though they were still short of their destination, the train began to slow dramatically. Hubbleday was jerked out of his daydream.

'What's going on?' he demanded.

'I don't know,' said Drake.

'This line was supposed to be clear for us.'

'Perhaps there's a reduced speed limit for some reason.'

'Something's happened,' said Hubbleday, getting to his feet. 'Look – we're slowing by the second.'

'I'm sure there's a reasonable explanation,' said Drake.

'Then I want to know what it is.'

'All will soon become clear, Cyril.'

'We have a strict timetable. We must stick to it, or everything is thrown out of kilter. During previous excursions, the trains always ran like clockwork. Why is this one letting us down?'

'It hasn't let us down yet.'

'Can't you feel what's happening, man? We're grinding to a halt.'

'I think you're right.'

Drake knew how dangerous it was to argue with the works manager. If his opinion were challenged, Hubbleday could be fiery and vengeful. It was safer to agree with him. Besides, it was now obvious that the train did intend to stop. It began to rock, hiss, squeal deafeningly and shudder, spreading alarm throughout the carriages. Then, without warning, it came to a jarring halt, throwing Hubbleday forwards. He thudded against the wall panel opposite and cursed aloud.

Regaining his balance, he was quivering with fury. After putting on his hat, he flung open the door and, with considerable effort, jumped down beside the line, finding that they had stopped in a deep cutting. He stormed to the front of the locomotive where the driver and fireman were standing.

'What the devil is going on?' yelled Hubbleday.

'There's an obstruction, sir,' explained the driver, indicating with his finger. 'Someone put sleepers across the track.'

'We're expected to arrive on time.'

'We can't move until those sleepers are shifted, sir.'

'Then go and move them at once.'

'We have to wait for the guard first,' said the driver. 'Here he comes.'

He pointed towards the rear of the train where a figure had jumped out of the brake van and was hurrying towards them. Hubbleday's only interest was in the obstruction thirty yards ahead of them. The sleepers were flanked by two large red flags, signalling danger. Prompt action by the driver had saved the excursion train from almost certain derailment. Instead of praising the man, however, Hubbleday started to blame him for the delay. His howls of rage were short-lived. A shot suddenly rang out and the works manager fell instantly to the ground with blood streaming down his face and with a gaping hole in his top hat.

CHAPTER TWO

Robert Colbeck was seated behind the desk in his office, reading a newspaper report of their latest success in bringing a killer to justice. Victor Leeming, meanwhile, was crouched in front of the grate, warming his hands on the little fire crackling bravely away. The sergeant gave an involuntary shiver.

'I'm still freezing,' he complained.

'Run around the block a few times,' suggested Colbeck. 'That will make you feel as warm as toast.'

'It's chilly out there.'

'I hadn't noticed.'

'Don't you ever feel the cold?'

'Yes, of course, but I try to ignore it.'

'You're not human, Inspector.'

'Fortunately,' said Colbeck with a smile, 'I have a dear wife who assures me on a regular basis that I am extremely human. The truth is that I'm too busy to notice the weather.'

'Well, I notice it,' said Leeming, ruefully. 'My teeth are chattering.'

Before he could launch into a recitation of his woes, he was interrupted by the arrival of Edward Tallis. Without bothering to knock, the superintendent opened the door and walked into the room, bringing a draught of cold air with him. Leeming crouched even closer to the fire.

'Ah, good,' said Tallis. 'I've caught you together. I have an important new assignment for the pair of you. You must go to the Worcestershire at once.'

'Christmas is just over a week away, sir,' protested Leeming, standing up. 'We need to celebrate it at home. Think of our families.'

'I'm thinking of the family of the murder victim. They need the reassurance that someone will find and arrest the man responsible for his death.'

'How much detail do you have, Superintendent?' asked Colbeck.

'Very little beyond what is written here,' said Tallis, waving a telegraph in the air. 'A man was shot dead beside a railway track. We must respond at once. It's unfortunate that it comes during the festive season but there is good news to lessen the disappointment.'

'We'll be pleased to hear it, sir.'

'I will be coming with you, Inspector.'

Leeming goggled. 'You call that good news?'

'Indeed, I do,' said Tallis. 'I am killing two birds with one stone, so to speak. I'll not only be able to lead the investigation, I'll have the pleasure of visiting Great Malvern to see if it really is such an ideal place for retirement.'

Colbeck was astonished. 'You are considering retirement?'

'None of us can go on indefinitely, Inspector.'

'But we've always regarded you as a permanent fixture here.'

'Fresh blood is needed from time to time in any organisation,' said Tallis, briskly. 'I would have thought you'd welcome my departure. It creates a vacancy, and nobody is more suited to fill it than you.'

Colbeck exchanged a glance with Leeming. Both had been shaken by the news. While they resented the stern military discipline that Tallis imposed, they recognised that he was a conscientious and efficient leader. Leeming was particularly alarmed. The decision meant that Colbeck would almost certainly be promoted, depriving the sergeant of his best friend. Their record of success as a team was unmatched in the Metropolitan Police Force. Leeming did not relish the idea of working with an inspector of less ability and, perhaps, with a more hostile attitude towards those ranked beneath him. There could be trouble ahead.

Colbeck took a more realistic view. When he studied the superintendent, he could see that Tallis's long years in the army and his subsequent dedication to law enforcement in the capital had taken their toll. The man looked old, weary and lacking the sense of duty he had always exuded. There had also been a period when Tallis had been forced to take time off to recover from a worrying illness that was as much mental as physical. On his return, he seemed to have renewed energy and purpose, but neither was visible now. He was a shadow of his former self.

'Are you unwell, sir?' asked Colbeck, solicitously.

Tallis stiffened. 'Do I look unwell?'

'No, no, sir, but this talk of retirement is worrying. Has it been prompted by medical advice?'

'It's been prompted by the relentless passage of time.'

'Then you should stay here and rest,' suggested Leeming. 'The last thing you should do is to put yourself through the rigours of a murder investigation. Leave it to younger men like us.'

'Are you daring to give me advice?' asked Tallis, eyelids narrowing.

'All that the sergeant meant,' said Colbeck, coming to the latter's rescue, 'is that this is the wrong time of year to visit somewhere like the Malverns. You should see the area at its best in the summer, not when its inhabitants are about to hibernate throughout winter.'

'The decision has been taken, Inspector. We will go there together.'

'As you wish, sir.'

'I know that you prefer to work alone but, with my help,

you'll be able to solve the crime in half the usual time.'

'Wouldn't you be better off staying here, sir?' asked Leeming. 'London is seething with crime. This is where you're really needed, not charging off to the countryside in answer to a hopeful summons.'

'It was not a summons,' said Tallis. 'It was a demand.'

'Whoever sent the telegraph had no right to demand anything of us. What sort of a man is he?'

'The telegraph did not come from a man. It was sent by a woman – Lady Emily Foley, to be exact. And, judging by her tone, she expects her orders to be obeyed at once. Let us go and find out why, shall we?'

Lady Emily Foley was a tall, stately woman in a fur coat and fur hat. Now approaching her sixtieth birthday, she was the daughter of the 3rd Duke of Montrose and had inherited his aristocratic mien. Having married into the Foley family in her late twenties, she had lost her husband after a mere fourteen years and, as a result, taken control of extensive estates in Staffordshire, Herefordshire and Worcestershire. She also became Lady of the Manor of Great Malvern and she never, for a moment, let anyone forget it.

When the railway station was built there, it was done under her direction. That was why a waiting room was constructed solely for her use so that she did not have to rub shoulders with the lower orders. She was now seated beside the fireplace, warming herself while deliberately keeping her back to the window. Harold Unwin, the stationmaster, needed almost a minute to gather enough courage to enter the room. He was a tubby man of middle years and medium height. After scratching his beard and adjusting his uniform, he tapped on the door and opened it tentatively.

'Excuse the interruption, Lady Foley.'

'Close that door. I do not want cold air in here.'

'Of course not,' he said, stepping into the room and shutting the door behind him. When she turned to face him, he gave a respectful nod then held up a letter. 'I've brought a message from Mr Appleby.'

'I've no wish to read it.'

'Would you rather hear it?'

'No, Mr Unwin, I would rather tear it up and put it on the fire. As you well know, Mr Appleby and I are not on speaking terms. We ceased communication of any kind several months ago. Besides,' she added, 'I know exactly what his letter says.'

He was startled. 'You do?'

'He is complaining that I had the sense to send a telegraph to Scotland Yard instead of letting him respond to the emergency. Appleby is a ditherer. He is also a newcomer and therefore unable to speak for this wonderful part of the country. I, of course, do have the requisite status to act as its spokesperson. That is why I took prompt action.' Voice rising imperiously, she got to her feet. 'If he had not brought another of those appalling excursion trains here,

22

the murder would never have occurred.'

'The messenger who delivered this letter is waiting outside.'

'Send him away without a reply.'

'Yes, Lady Foley.'

'And, if any reporters arrive, be sure to stress that I was the person with the initiative to summon the finest detectives in the kingdom. I settle for nothing but the best,' she said, thrusting out her chin. 'Mr Appleby, by contrast, will be dealing with those well-meaning buffoons from the Worcestershire Constabulary.'

'Now, that's unfair . . .'

'Did I ask for your opinion, Mr Unwin?'

'No, but . . . well, I think our police do a good job.'

'To some extent, I agree. When it is within their limited competence, they are reasonably efficient. But we are not talking about arresting drunken revellers or chasing naughty boys out of people's orchards. This is a case of cruel murder. It will spread fear throughout the area and far beyond it. That,' she concluded, 'is why I will stay here until the detectives from Scotland Yard arrive at this station.'

After nodding obediently, Unwin let himself out.

Jerome Appleby was a silver-haired man in his sixties. He was anything but a typical Midland industrialist. Those who met him for the first time thought that he had the air of a country parson – gentle, caring, dedicated to his calling. In fact, he was a hard-headed businessman, who, having made a great deal of money, was moved to share it with those less fortunate than he had been. Appleby was also a man of action. When news of the murder reached him, he was waiting at Malvern Link railway station with a fleet of carts and carriages to transport the excursionists to his home. He instantly commandeered a trap and drove the horse at speed the four or more miles needed. Arriving at the scene of the crime, he was shocked to see the body of his works manager beside the track, albeit covered by a tarpaulin.

The one redeeming factor of the crisis was the response of Ernest Drake. Taking charge of the situation, the chief clerk had apologised to the passengers for the delay and insisted that everyone remain in their carriages. The gunshot, he told them, had been fired by a farmer whose cow had wandered onto the line. It therefore had had to be put down. When they left the train at Malvern Link, the passengers were bound to notice that Cyril Hubbleday was no longer leading the outing, but they would soon be diverted by the various treats laid on for them.

Hearing how his chief clerk had behaved, Appleby was full of praise. Now that the flags and sleepers had been moved from the line, he insisted that the train continue to its original destination. They were unable to stop the children peering through the window with ghoulish fascination at what they thought was a dead farm animal. The passengers, however, were relieved to be on their way again. Among the many mouth-watering promises made to them was that they would see live reindeer at Appleby Court. That thought had excited the children more than anything else. A slaughtered cow could not compete with such an attraction.

By the time that Appleby had driven back to Malvern Link, the families were waiting patiently in their respective vehicles. They gave him a spontaneous round of applause. He basked in their approval then led them off on their parade through the hills, his broad smile concealing his inner turmoil.

One question tormented him – who had killed his works manager?

CHAPTER THREE

Victor Leeming had always hated travelling by train. It was therefore ironic that he worked exclusively with a man whose expertise in solving crimes committed on the rail network had earned him the title of The Railway Detective. Ordinarily, Colbeck would make any journeys by train more palatable for the sergeant by discussing the crime they had been sent to solve. Because they were not alone, that was now impossible. The presence of Edward Tallis, seated opposite them in an otherwise empty compartment, turned an unpleasant trip into an extended ordeal for the sergeant. He began to feel sick.

'To be quite honest,' said the superintendent, 'I didn't

know that we could reach Great Malvern by train.'

'The station was opened four years ago,' explained Colbeck, 'and is, by all accounts, quite remarkable.'

'In what way, Inspector?'

'It was designed by a celebrated architect, who also designed the Imperial Hotel nearby. First-class passengers staying at the hotel can reach it by means of the Worm, a subterranean passage that runs from the station for their exclusive use.'

'How ever do you find out these things?' asked Tallis, tetchily. 'You seem to be a walking encyclopaedia of railway development.'

'The new station caught the interest of one or two London newspapers, sir. They were impressed by what they saw as unique features. Such news items always arouse my curiosity.'

'What are these unique features?' asked Tallis.

'The most striking,' replied Colbeck, 'are to be found on the platforms. The canopies are supported by iron columns. The capitals on them are works of art, apparently, and were designed by a local sculptor. I hope to meet the gentleman at some point.'

'May I remind you that this is not a social visit? We are there to catch a cold-blooded killer.'

'In my experience, sir, killers are often hot-blooded. I think we should reserve judgement on this particular individual until we apprehend him.'

'And the sooner, the better,' said Leeming. 'My children want me home for Christmas.'

'When you are engaged in a murder investigation,' Tallis reminded him, 'you do not possess a family. It must disappear from your mind.'

'Nothing disturbs the sergeant's concentration,' said Colbeck. 'I can vouch for that. Like me, he will do everything in his power to bring this case to a swift and satisfactory conclusion. But let me return to the reason you are here with us,' he went on. 'Are you seriously contemplating retirement?'

'I am, indeed.'

'Have you discussed the matter with the commissioner?'

'Yes, I have. He urged me to remain.'

'I would do the same in his position, sir,' said Leeming. 'Scotland Yard will seem empty without you cracking the whip over the rest of us.'

Tallis sniffed. 'I can do without your advice, Sergeant.'

'You've been an inspiration to us.'

'And without your barefaced lies.'

'Great Malvern is a spa town,' observed Colbeck. 'Are you intending to seek the Water Cure, sir?'

'The only water that interests me is the small amount I add to my whisky.'

'Having lived a full life, I fancy that you might find the place rather dull.'

'That is its attraction, Inspector,' said Tallis. 'I will shed the multiple cares of office and escape from the inane comments that people like the sergeant feel obliged to make. Dullness is what I seek. I'll embrace it gladly.'

'What will you do all day?' asked Leeming.

'I will awake each morning with a smile of contentment.'

'I do that when I see my wife and children.'

'In time, I daresay, I will start work on my memoirs.'

'You may find that difficult in a town like Great Malvern,' warned Colbeck. 'Your military exploits in India and your career in the Metropolitan Police Force define you as a man who thrives on excitement.'

'I've always liked a challenge, it's true.'

'You'd have dozens every day if you remain at Scotland Yard, sir.'

'That's why I have to leave,' insisted Tallis, 'so please stop trying to talk me out of it. The time has come to move to pastures new.'

'Then we must respect your decision.'

'If you do write your memoirs,' said Leeming, hopefully, 'will there be any mention of me?' He collected a withering stare from the superintendent. 'I was just wondering, sir . . .'

The journey to Appleby Court exceeded all expectations. They were taken on a winding route through the Malvern Hills and shown wonders of nature that simply did not exist in the Black Country. Their lungs were filled with clean air for once. When they first caught sight of their host's country house, they were astounded. Set in an estate of a hundred acres, it was a veritable palace. Waiting for them on the lawn in front of the main entrance were four skittish reindeer, harnessed to a small, brightly painted cart. When the children were told that they could take it in turns to be driven around the lawn, they laughed with joy. All memory of the dead cow under the tarpaulin was instantly wiped away.

Peter Churt queued patiently for his turn in the cart, squealing with delight as the reindeer took him and his companions in a wide circle. When he got back to his parents, he was ecstatic.

'Can we have one as a pet?' he pleaded.

'No, son,' said his father.

'I'd feed it and look after it.'

'We can't afford it.'

'Besides,' said Agnes, 'we have nowhere to keep it.'

'We'll find somewhere,' argued the boy.

'It's out of the question, Peter.'

'You heard,' said Churt. 'Reindeer don't belong in Oldbury.'

Head falling to his chest, the boy sighed. Almost instantly, he recovered when he saw that Appleby was handing out a little parcel to each of the children, warning them not to open it until Christmas Day. Peter rushed to stand in line to claim his gift. He then rushed back to his parents to show them the parcel.

The meal was served in the sumptuous dining room, an ornate space easily able to accommodate the numbers involved. Tables had been set out and laden with the kind of food that children only ever saw on their birthdays. Ernest Drake was on hand to direct everyone to their appointed seats. From its position, the Churt family had a good view of the top table. While everyone else was eating their food,

Churt's attention was focussed on the empty chair beside their benefactor. His wife looked down at his plate.

'Eat your cake,' she suggested.

'I will in a minute, Aggie.'

'What are you staring at?'

'It's that empty chair. Mr Hubbleday should be sitting there.'

'Maybe he's not hungry,' she said, 'or maybe he's been took ill.'

'He'd never miss a chance like this to show off.'

'Then where is he, Derek?'

A smile spread slowly across her husband's face. He picked up his cake and ate it with relish. For the first time since they had left home, he started to enjoy the outing. He even applauded Appleby's speech with a degree of enthusiasm.

By the time that the train had reached Malvern Link, Colbeck had persuaded Tallis that it was best if they divided their resources. While the superintendent went on to Great Malvern, a mile or so away, Colbeck and Leeming would alight at the earlier station and find a way to visit the scene of the crime before the afternoon light faded too much. It meant that Tallis would have the pleasure of meeting Lady Emily Foley, a person of evident standing in the very town he was considering for his retirement. When the train chugged out of Malvern Link station, Leeming heaved a sigh of relief.

'You got rid of him at last,' he said.

'It's only a temporary freedom, Victor. The superintendent

will be with us for the whole of the investigation. This case might be his farewell to Scotland Yard.'

'I'd much rather he stayed there and let us work on our own.'

'Yes, having him breathing down our necks will be a problem. Whenever he's taken part in our investigations before he's always made things more difficult for us. In fact—'

Colbeck broke off as he saw a sturdy uniformed railway policeman approaching them. When he explained who they were, the man's face lit up with pleasure as he saw the opportunity to be involved.

'I'm Constable Berry,' he said, deferentially, 'and I heard about the murder when the excursion train stopped here. I made a point of going to the site.'

'You'd know the exact spot, then.'

'Yes, Inspector.'

'Is the body of the victim still there?'

'No, sir,' said Berry. 'Policemen from the Worcester Constabulary moved it to the hospital there.'

'That's a pity. It would have been helpful to know precisely where the man was shot dead.'

'I can show you that, Inspector. I stood near the spot with the driver and fireman. They were in a terrible state – and still are.' He indicated the excursion train standing nearby in a siding. 'Perhaps you should take statements from them first.'

'I'll insist on doing so,' said Colbeck. 'Lead the way.'

Berry took them along the track and into the siding.

The empty excursion train looked rather forlorn without its passengers. When he had introduced himself and Leeming to the two men on the footplate, Colbeck heaved himself up beside them. The sergeant followed him and took notes.

The railwaymen were still patently in a state of shock. Callum Paterson, the fireman, a craggy Scotsman with a fringe beard, could hardly bring himself to speak. Letting the driver, Stanley Lomas, do all the talking, Paterson confined himself to a series of nods and grunts. Lomas was a moon-faced man in his forties with a high voice that was reduced to a squeak when he became emotional.

'It could have been either Callum or me,' he said. 'We were standing so close to Mr Hubbleday. One of us might have been shot dead.'

'In your own words,' said Colbeck, 'please describe what happened.'

'We knew Mr Hubbleday, you see. We've driven excursion trains for him a number of times and never had a whisper of trouble, did we, Cal?' The fireman signalled agreement with a grunt. 'Think of his poor wife and children. A man goes on a journey he's made lots of times and he comes home in a wooden box.' Tears welled up in his eyes. 'It's a tragedy, Inspector.'

Colbeck agreed. It took time and patience to get a coherent account out of Lomas, leaving Colbeck to wonder if the man was in a fit state to drive the train back to the Black Country. When he'd extracted all he felt he would get from the driver, he thanked him and jumped down beside Leeming.

'Did you hear all that, Sergeant?'

'Yes,' moaned Leeming, 'I heard it, but I didn't write it all down. It's so cold that my hands were shaking. I kept dropping my pencil.'

'Constable Berry can confirm the details on our way to the scene of the crime.'

'It's an honour to work with you, Inspector,' said Berry, as they moved away. 'We're not entirely cut off from the world here, you know. I've read newspaper reports about your successes.'

'We've had our share of failures as well,' admitted Colbeck. 'Now then, we need to find some transport.'

'Ted Bridger will get us there in no time at all. He drove me earlier on, so he knows exactly where to go.'

'Excellent.'

Berry took them out of the small, rather nondescript station. Bridger turned out to be old, slight and in poor health. When they approached his carriage, he was talking quietly to his horse.

'Ted is almost deaf,' warned Berry. 'Let me handle him. Oh,' he went on as a thought struck him, 'and welcome to the Malverns!'

Before he met Lady Emily Foley, the superintendent had the sense to ask the stationmaster about her. Unwin explained that she exerted great power in the area, owning large tracts of it and insisting, whenever new houses were built, that they were well spaced, had large gardens and maintained many trees. Tallis realised that he was about to meet a woman with exacting standards.

After knocking on the door of her private waiting room, he entered quickly, closed the door behind him and whisked off his top hat.

'Good day to you, Lady Foley,' he said. 'I am Superintendent Tallis from Scotland Yard.'

'I hoped for a quicker response,' she complained.

Turning to look at him, she was impressed by his bearing and air of authority. For his part, he was struck by her grandeur. Sitting bolt upright, she was an arresting sight, features finely chiselled and eyes sparkling brightly. Tallis was a lifelong bachelor and had always preferred male company but there was something about her that stirred an interest in him that he had never felt before.

'I expected you to arrive with minions,' she said, tartly.

'Inspector Colbeck and Sergeant Leeming are far from being minions,' he told her. 'They are highly experienced detectives.'

'Then where are they?'

'I told them to get off the train at Malvern Link so that they could collect details about the murder before being taken to the spot where it occurred. Incidentally,' he added, 'the railway station there is vastly inferior to this one. I couldn't fail to notice that yours has considerable charm.'

'That was largely my doing.'

'I applaud your taste, Lady Foley.'

'You're here to solve a heinous crime, not to admire local

architecture. How soon do you expect to make an arrest?'

'It's impossible to put a timescale on detective work,' he said, cautiously. 'It is slow and methodical so that no detail – however minor – is missed. We have caught killers before in a matter of days, but it sometimes takes weeks, if not months.'

She was aghast. 'You're here for months?'

'Not necessarily.'

'Our Christmas celebrations will be ruined.'

'My minions, as you call them, would also suffer. Both are married men with a family. They would much rather spend Christmas at home with their loved ones. That will act as a spur to them to make as early an arrest as possible. Now,' he said, 'if I may, I would like to hear the full details of this distressing event.'

'I don't have the full details, Superintendent.'

He gaped. 'Then why did you contact us for help?'

'Nothing happens here that escapes my notice,' she boasted. 'The moment I heard that a murder had been committed, I sent that telegraph to Scotland Yard. Mr Appleby, I knew, would be certain to contact the Worcestershire Constabulary, but I wanted someone with far greater abilities.'

'Who is Mr Appleby?'

'You may well ask!' she sneered.

'That's exactly what I am doing.'

She wrinkled her nose. 'He owns some grubby little works in the Midlands,' she said, deprecatingly, 'and organises the occasional excursion here for his employees. One of those employees was shot dead the other side of Malvern Link. That is all I can tell you.' She wagged a gloved finger at him. 'An ugly red stain has appeared on our little paradise, Superintendent. Please remove it.'

'We will not disappoint you, Lady Foley.'

'I should hope not.'

'Our full resources are at your command.'

'I just want a quick resolution to this crisis.'

'You will have it.'

He held her gaze for a long time, marvelling at her poise and decisiveness. As a rule, he felt embarrassed at being alone with a woman but this one was different. He felt almost comfortable. It was she who terminated the conversation.

'You may leave now,' she said, crisply. 'Get on with your work. This is my private domain. Given your position, you will be familiar with the laws of trespass.'

While they were driven along, Colbeck and Leeming were given a slightly fuller version of events than they had heard from the engine driver. Berry had mastered the salient details and gave a clear account. Having dealt with railway policemen many times, they found that the majority resented Scotland Yard detectives taking charge of cases they felt belonged to them. A much smaller group, however, welcomed Colbeck's arrival and put themselves willingly at his beck and call. Raymond Berry belonged to the latter camp, an over-enthusiastic admirer of Colbeck who felt blessed to meet and work alongside him. He never stopped trying to impress the detectives.

'By the way,' he told them, 'it will be safe to go onto the track. I know the timetable by heart. There won't be a train in either direction for at least thirty-five minutes.'

'That's reassuring to hear,' said Colbeck.

In due course, Berry tapped the driver on the shoulder and the carriage slowed to a halt. The passengers got out. Berry signalled to Bridger that he should wait for them. He then led the detectives across the grass towards the cutting. When they reached the edge, Berry pointed to the sleepers and red flags that lay beside the track.

'That's what brought the train to a halt,' he said.

'Where was the victim standing when he was shot?' asked Colbeck.

'About thirty yards away, Inspector.'

'And the killer was waiting up here on this side, was he?'

'Yes, sir.'

'The driver told us he saw nothing when he looked up. He and the fireman were not even sure from which direction the shot came.'

'That's true.'

'Show me.'

'What do you mean?'

'Take the sergeant down there and stand beside him close to where you believe Mr Hubbleday was standing at the time.'

'Do I really need to go?' asked Leeming, eyeing the steep gradient. 'I'm not really dressed for it, sir.'

'You'll manage,' Colbeck assured him. 'Have you forgotten that cutting near the Sapperton Tunnel in Gloucestershire? You scrambled up and down it like a mountain goat. There was hardly a mark on your clothing.'

'I'll help you if you like, Sergeant,' volunteered Berry, offering a hand.

'I can manage,' said Leeming, waving him away. 'You watch.'

He went bravely down the incline, gathering speed as he did so and sliding more than once. But he somehow maintained his balance and reached the bottom without a blemish on his clothing. Berry was more reckless. Desperate to earn praise from the detectives, he descended at a faster pace, tripping halfway down, and finishing the rest of the journey on his backside. Clambering to his feet, he burst out laughing. He then took Leeming along the track to the point where he knew the driver, fireman and works manager had been standing when the shot rang out.

Colbeck, meanwhile, walked along the top of the cutting in search of a vantage point. The killer had chosen an isolated spot and deliberately brought the excursion train to a halt somewhere below him. Having fired the murderous shot, he had been able to escape without the slightest fear of being seen.

Prowling along the grass, Colbeck looked for any clues as to the exact position taken by the man. There was no sign of a spent cartridge or of any footprints. What he did find, however, was a shallow depression in the grass that suggested someone had laid there, full length. It was a start.

CHAPTER FOUR

Madeleine Colbeck was delighted when her best friend called on her that afternoon. After giving her a welcoming kiss, she took Lydia Quayle into the drawing room. The latter was able to take a good look at her. She saw the concern in Madeleine's eyes.

'Something's happened, hasn't it?' she said.

'Yes, Lydia.'

'Have you had a message from Robert?'

Madeleine nodded. 'He's been put in charge of a murder investigation in somewhere called Great Malvern. It's in the Midlands, apparently,' she said. 'With Christmas so close, I've been praying that he would be dealing with crimes here in London.'

'He's bound to be here on Christmas Day, surely.'

'Not necessarily. If the superintendent feels that Robert must put his job before his family, then that is what might well happen.'

'How did you learn about this latest assignment?'

'Robert sent me a brief letter by hand. You can guess who delivered it.'

Lydia smiled. 'Alan Hinton?'

'He asked me to pass on his best wishes to you.'

'That was nice of him.'

'Detective Constable Hinton is far more than nice to you. He is devoted. One of these fine days, you might actually notice.'

Lydia laughed. 'Stop teasing and tell me what Robert's letter said.'

'He warned me that he might be away from London indefinitely.'

'The Midlands are not that far away, are they?' asked Lydia. 'If he'd been sent somewhere like Scotland, I'd understand the position he'd be in. But he's bound to be able to sneak home at some point to see his wife and daughter.'

'I very much doubt it.'

'But he's done so many times before.'

'That was different.'

'The superintendent didn't even know that he'd popped back home to be with you and Helena for a night. What's to stop Robert doing the same thing again?'

'He hasn't gone alone.'

'Of course, not – I daresay he's taken Victor Leeming with him.'

'There's someone else he's taken.'

'Who is that?'

'Superintendent Tallis.'

'Oh, no!' cried Lydia. 'That changes everything.'

'Exactly. He'll not only keep a close watch on them, Robert feels that he'll hamper the investigation so that it takes much longer than it should.' Madeleine sighed. 'Can you see now why I'm so worried?'

Edward Tallis was not a man to sit idle. After leaving Lady Foley, he asked the stationmaster to unlock the door to the Worm so that he could walk up to the Imperial Hotel and take stock of it. Having booked a room there for himself, he went back to the railway station to be met by Harold Unwin.

'Lady Foley has gone,' he said. 'She left a message for you, Superintendent.'

Tallis extended his hand. 'Where is it?'

'It was a verbal message, sir. To be honest, it was more of a command. Lady Foley expects to be kept abreast of every stage of your investigation.'

'Why didn't she ask me that herself?'

Unwin rolled his eyes. 'I wouldn't dare to put that question to her.'

'Where does she live?'

'In a grand house in Stoke Edith.'

'Is that far away?'

Unwin pointed. 'It's on the other side of the hills, sir.'

'Is it possible to get there by train?'

'Yes, it is but I should warn you that a long, dark tunnel is involved.'

'Why should I worry about that?'

'Lady Foley refuses to travel through it,' said Unwin. 'If she needs to catch a train taking her eastwards, she is always driven here in her carriage and stays in her private waiting room until the train arrives. She is a lady of eccentricities,' he went on, taking a slip of paper from his pocket. 'I've written her address down for you and I humbly suggest that you abide by her request.'

'Strictly speaking, I should be dealing with Mr Appleby himself. The crime is linked to that excursion train of his which brought the murder victim here.'

'Everything that happens in the Malverns gets back to Lady Foley.'

'I'm afraid that she must wait her turn for any information.'

'Don't upset her,' advised Unwin. 'She is easily offended.'

'I'll run this investigation my way,' said Tallis, firmly. 'If I tread on a few toes, so be it. The priority is to identify, chase, and catch the killer as soon as possible. The man is probably still at large in the area. He could strike again.'

Robert Colbeck was known as the dandy of Scotland Yard, always immaculate and not without a touch of vanity about his appearance. As he descended the grassy bank, therefore, he did so with extreme caution, one hand holding his top hat in place. When he reached Leeming and Berry, he looked up towards the place where he believed the killer had been lying.

'He picked the perfect spot,' he observed.

'Yes,' said Leeming, pointing down the line. 'The track in that direction is dead straight for well over a quarter of a mile. When the train came round that bend, the driver and fireman would have been able to see those red flags in time to slow down and come to a halt.'

'How do we know he killed the right man?' asked Berry. 'I mean, there were three people standing here together. What if he was really aiming at the driver or the fireman?'

'He hit his target, I can assure you,' said Colbeck. 'I found the marks of a small tripod that would have supported a telescope. He watched the train from the moment it came into sight, then he picked out the man he was after. What puzzles me is how he knew that Mr Hubbleday would oblige him by leaving the train. According to you, no other passenger did so. Was it a lucky guess or could he guarantee that the works manager would almost certainly jump down from his compartment to see why the train had been stopped?'

'If that was the case,' said Leeming, 'the killer must have known Mr Hubbleday.'

'That was my feeling.'

'There's something I haven't mentioned,' Berry put in. 'Excursion trains are very unpopular because they bring hordes of people here. Most of them get off at Malvern Link and explore the hills. Wealthy visitors travel by ordinary trains and go on to Great Malvern for the Water Cure.'

'What are you trying to tell us, Constable Berry?' asked Colbeck.

'People are always writing letters of complaint to the local paper about the regular invasions. In summer,' he said, 'we get as many as five thousand flooding into the area on a single day. Think of the noise they make and the mess they leave behind. It's disgusting,' he groaned. 'Go into any pub and you'll hear folk grumbling. Most of them want to damage the trains seriously, but I've heard more than one – when they were drunk enough, that is – threatening to kill someone if it's the only way to make the hoi polloi from the Midlands understand that they're not wanted here.'

'There's nothing wrong with people from the Midlands,' said Leeming, defensively. 'I've got an uncle and aunt living in Birmingham – lovely people.'

'Constable Berry raises a good point,' said Colbeck, thoughtfully. 'I could be wrong in my assumption. The sniper may never have met or seen the works manager before. He was there simply to kill someone who was involved in the excursion. In short,' he concluded, 'Mr Hubbleday could have been shot as a warning to others.'

Having told his detectives to meet him at the railway station in Great Malvern, the superintendent found himself recalling what Colbeck had said about the capitals on the columns supporting the canopy. He studied them closely and saw that they were superb examples of ironwork. What the sculptor had created was a series of bunches of flowers, fashioned so exquisitely and painted so brightly that they looked almost real. Tallis was entranced. He was still peering at the floral decorations when he heard footsteps approaching. Turning around, he saw a tall, slim, middle-aged man in the uniform of the Worcester Constabulary. The newcomer's thick eyebrows formed a chevron of disapproval.

'I am Inspector Vellacott,' he said, sharply, 'and Mr Appleby has asked me to take charge of the murder investigation.'

'Lady Foley asked me to do the same thing,' said Tallis with emphasis. 'I am Superintendent Tallis from Scotland Yard. As you will appreciate, I and my detectives have the authority to relieve you of this case.'

'I'll contest that authority.'

'Save yourself the embarrassment, Inspector.'

'We know this area intimately whereas you and your men are complete strangers. You'll be groping around in the dark.'

'We'll be following our usual procedures,' said Tallis, curtly. 'They always produce results. May I ask how many murder cases you have handled?'

Vellacott was caught off balance. 'There was one in Worcester some years ago,' he replied, uneasily.

'Were you in charge of it?'

'No, Superintendent. I was only a constable at the time.'

'It was probably a long time ago, then.'

'Serious crimes like murder are rare events in this part of the country. That's because the Worcestershire Constabulary maintains law and order here.'

'I'm pleased to hear it,' said Tallis. 'You obviously reap the benefit of dealing with small rural communities like the one in this town. We, on the other hand, operate in the largest and most dangerous city in Europe. The Metropolitan Police Force has dealt with untold numbers of murders and brought almost every single case to a satisfactory conclusion. Put yourself in Mr Appleby's position,' he went on. 'On whom would you place more trust? A man like you, who played only a supporting role in a distant murder investigation, or those with vastly greater experience and who — in the case of Inspector Colbeck — has a name that is synonymous with fighting crime on the railway system?'

'Mr Appleby turned to us first,' said Vellacott, shifting his feet. 'I resent your attempt to steal the case from under our noses.'

'Nothing could be further from the truth, Inspector. We are eager to involve you. As you pointed out, you have priceless local knowledge. We need to harness it. However,' stressed Tallis, looking him in the eye, 'you will work under our supervision. Is that understood?'

There was a long pause. Vellacott's pride was wounded. When the murder had occurred, he had been invigorated by the summons to lead the investigation because it could be a way to advance his career. At a stroke, Tallis had demoted him. It was unfair. His eyebrows bristled with defiance.

'Mr Appleby has faith in us,' he argued. 'Let him be the judge.'

While Madeleine Colbeck knew exactly how her father would react, it was impossible to keep the news from him. When the doorbell rang, she was still in the drawing room with Lydia Quayle. She warned her friend that a minor explosion was on the way. Caleb Andrews was soon shown into the room. Madeleine got up to give her father a kiss then the old man beamed at Lydia. While there was an exchange of pleasantries, Madeleine gave him time to sit down before she told him where her husband had gone. Andrews was back on his feet at once.

'Not the wilds of Worcestershire!' he wailed.

'Orders are orders, Father,' said Madeleine.

'He should refuse to obey them. Robert simply must be here for Christmas. If he is not, his daughter will never forgive him. More to the point, I'll never forgive him. Christmas means everything to a child. Don't you agree, Lydia?'

'Yes,' she replied. 'It's a time of the year when families ought to be together.'

She tried to conceal the profound sadness she felt. Lydia was estranged from her family and only one member of it was in contact with her, albeit fitfully. Because she had become so close to Madeleine, however, she shared Christmas celebrations with the Colbeck family.

'It's Robert's responsibility to be here,' said Andrews, jabbing at her with an irate finger.

'He's aware of that, Father,' said Madeleine, 'and will make every effort to be here. We just have to hope that he solves the murder in time.'

'It's the superintendent who ought to be murdered, Maddy. He shouldn't have singled out Robert. There are lots of unmarried detectives at Scotland Yard. Why didn't he pick on some of them? They won't be missed by a wife and daughter.' He tapped his chest. 'Or by a father-in-law.'

Andrews waved his arms like the sails of a windmill. Waiting patiently, Madeleine let him rant on. She was careful not to remind him that, during her childhood, he had driven a train on Christmas Day on more than one occasion, justifying his absence by the fact that he would be given a bonus. Inevitably, the railway company involved in the murder came in for criticism.

'Why can't they protect their passengers?' he demanded. 'That's what the LNWR did when I worked for them. Passenger safety came first. We didn't let anyone get shot in broad daylight.'

'You don't know all the facts,' warned Madeleine.

'That's true,' added Lydia. 'It's wrong to jump to conclusions.'

'I blame the Old Worse and Worse,' said Andrews, bitterly.

'That's the Oxford, Worcester and Wolverhampton Railway,' explained Madeleine for Lydia's benefit.

Andrews nodded. 'They teamed up with two other

companies to build a line between Hereford and Worcester. It went through the Malvern Hills. Whatever the Old Worse and Worse did has a curse on it. That's why this man was shot dead,' he claimed, raising a fist in the air. 'He was a victim of the spell the OWWR casts over everything it does.'

'Don't be ridiculous, Father,' said Madeleine, stifling a laugh.

'It's true, Maddy.' He turned to Lydia. 'You believe me, don't you?'

'I know little about railways, Mr Andrews,' she said, tactfully, 'except for the fact that they've transformed our lives for the better. I'm grateful for that.'

'So you should be,' said Andrews before turning to his daughter. 'And what's all this about an excursion train?' he demanded. 'Nobody goes on an excursion at this time of year. The weather in late December can be atrocious. I know that to my cost. In the week before Christmas, I've driven engines through torrential rain, gale-force winds, and thick snow. Whoever organised this excursion must be out of his mind.'

Given the circumstances, Jerome Appleby was able to console himself with the thought that everything had gone well. His employees and their children had enjoyed a wonderful outing and were brimming with happiness. During his speech at the end of the celebratory meal, he had blamed the absence of Cyril Hubbleday on some chest pains from which the works manager suffered. While everyone else had been taken to Appleby Court, the man in charge of the excursion train, they were told, had gone to Worcester Hospital for examination. Hubbleday would not be returning to Oldbury with them. In his absence, Ernest Drake would take control on the journey home.

When the carts and carriages had been filled up in order, Appleby bestowed a benevolent smile on his guests before getting into a trap at the head of the cavalcade. Drake sat beside him. The company accountant was worried.

'They'll have to know the truth sooner or later, sir,' he said.

'Then it will be later,' insisted Appleby. 'Nothing must spoil this day.'

'What about Mr Hubbleday's family?'

'I'd like you to break the news to them, Ernest.'

Drake was alarmed. 'Wouldn't it be better if it came from you, sir?'

'I'll be too busy assisting the police with their enquiries. Besides,' said Appleby, 'you travelled on the train with Cyril. You are therefore well placed to give them details that I simply don't possess. Pass on my deepest sympathy and assure the family that I will be in touch very soon.'

'Yes, Mr Appleby . . .'

'You sound unhappy.'

'I'm not sure that I'll be equal to the task.'

'Of course, you will,' said the other, patting him on the knee. 'You're a man who is at his best in an emergency. Look at the way you handled the situation when the train was forced to stop.'

'Somebody had to step into the breach, sir.'

'And that's what you did. I won't forget it, Ernest.'

'Thank you, Mr Appleby.'

'First of all, take the passengers back home. When you have done that, get in touch with Cyril's family and warn them that the police will call on them in due course. Assure them that I will take care of all the funeral expenses. Right,' said Appleby, snapping the reins, 'let's get everyone back on that train, shall we?'

Light was now fading badly at the scene of the crime, and the track was covered with shadows. After examining the area carefully, Colbeck went off into a long silence. Berry tried to ask the inspector a question, but Leeming semaphored a message to him, and the railway policeman held his peace. It was minutes before Colbeck emerged from his meditation. He turned to Berry.

'How do you know exactly when trains are due around here?' he asked.

'I've memorised the timetable,' said Berry, proudly. 'I know what comes and goes on every day of the week.'

'But excursion trains aren't in the timetable.'

'That's right, Inspector. They're fitted in between regular services.'

'Then how did the killer know at what time today his target would be coming in this direction?'

'He couldn't possibly know, sir,' said Leeming.

'And yet he obviously did.'

'I suppose,' said Berry, removing his hat to scratch his head, 'that he could have asked the stationmaster when the excursion train was due this morning.'

'I doubt it,' said Colbeck. 'He'd be giving himself away. If he was planning to shoot someone aboard a particular train, he would be very stupid if he showed such interest in it.'

'That's a good point,' said Leeming. 'Careful planning went into the crime.'

'What do you deduce from that fact?'

'He found out the precise time when the train would reach this point, sir.'

'In other words, he knew when it would be setting out. I regret my earlier suggestion that Mr Hubbleday was a random victim sacrificed as a warning to others. He was the target all along. Evidently,' said Colbeck, 'the killer could rely on Hubbleday getting out of the train to see what had caused the delay.'

'I thought the killer was a local man,' admitted Berry.

'I was lured into making that assumption, Constable. When I thought it through, I scolded myself for reaching such a hasty judgement. The search for the killer,' decided Colbeck, 'must not begin here because we'd never find him.'

'Why not?' asked Leeming.

'It's because he lives somewhere in the Black Country.'

At a time when he should have been concentrating on how to solve a major crime, Edward Tallis was instead thinking about Lady Emily Foley. When told that she had to be informed about the progress of the investigation at every stage, he had dismissed her as an impediment. He now regretted his response. She had, after all, been the person who made them aware of the murder in the first place. Without her intervention, Scotland Yard would never have heard about the tragedy. Tallis recalled his brief meeting with Lady Foley, a woman with a kind of brittle beauty and an aura of unchallengeable authority. The stationmaster had told him that she had been a generous benefactor of churches and schools in Great Malvern. Her devotion to the area was clearly impressive. It deserved to be acknowledged by according her preferential treatment.

Having made his decision, he tried to focus his mind on his duty. Instead of using the waiting room, Tallis was seated alone in the stationmaster's office, huddled over the fire, and wishing that the wind would stop whistling incessantly under the door. Checking his watch, he clicked his tongue in irritation then looked up at the clock on the wall.

'Where, in God's name, are you, Colbeck?' he grumbled.

As if in answer to his question, Harold Unwin opened the door and motioned the detectives into his office before retreating into the gloom. Tallis got to his feet.

'What kept you?' he demanded. 'I expected you ages ago.'

'Thoroughness takes time, sir,' said Colbeck.

'While you've been away, I have not been twiddling my thumbs. I met Lady Foley, visited the splendid Imperial Hotel and tussled with Inspector Vellacott of the Worcestershire Constabulary.'

'Did you find time to look at those capitals I mentioned?'

'They are an irrelevance.'

'Not to me, sir,' said Colbeck. 'I can't wait to study them in daylight.'

'You'll be too busy solving a heinous crime.'

'Where will we be staying, sir?' said Leeming.

'I have booked a room for myself at the Imperial Hotel, but our budget does not allow all three of us to stay there. You and the inspector will have to settle for more modest accommodation. The stationmaster has recommended a few places.'

'Can we go to one of them now? I'm exhausted.'

'All in good time,' said Tallis. 'You have an errand to run first.'

'Where do you want us to go, sir?' asked Colbeck.

'You'll stay with me, Inspector. Leeming is going to the home of Lady Foley with a message from me.' He shot the sergeant a warning glance. 'Show her the respect due to her, Sergeant. She is like minor royalty in these parts. I know that because I had the pleasure of a conversation with her.'

'What's the message?' asked Leeming.

'Tell her that I've crossed swords with Inspector Vellacott and put him firmly in his place.'

The sergeant was bemused. 'Why on earth should she want to know that?'

'Lady Foley wishes to know everything.'

'What will we be doing, sir?' asked Colbeck.

'We will be paying a visit to Appleby Court,' said Tallis. 'It's high time that Mr Appleby is acquainted with the fact that the investigation is now in safe hands and that we are confident of making an arrest before the new year.'

'The new year?' croaked Leeming. 'What about Christmas?'

'You may have to forego that particular date in the calendar.'

Panic set in. 'But that's cruel, sir!'

Tallis's eyelids narrowed. 'You heard me, Sergeant.'

CHAPTER FIVE

Because the passengers were so enchanted by their experience, they lost all track of time. Their train seemed to get them home in a matter of minutes. The children talked endlessly about the bewildering succession of treats they had enjoyed, and looked forward to boasting about them to friends forced to spend their day at school or at work. Peter Churt could not stop grinning. Still holding his gift in both hands, he turned to his mother.

'Can I open it?' he pleaded.

'No, Peter,' she said. 'It's a Christmas present.'

'I'm dying to see what it is.'

'You won't have long to wait.'

'I want it now.' Subdued by a glance from his father, the

boy explored another avenue. 'Can we go back one day and see those reindeer?'

'No, we can't,' said his mother. 'They were only hired for this outing.'

Peter was disappointed. 'Oh, I see.'

'You've had a grand day, lad,' said his father. 'Be grateful.'

'I am, I am . . .'

'So am I, Derek,' said his wife, squeezing her husband's arm in gratitude. 'I'm very lucky to be married to someone who works for Mr Appleby. Our neighbours are so jealous.'

'It was a good day,' agreed Churt.

He caught the eye of a friend who sat opposite him with his family. The man gave him a knowing smile. Evidently, he had made the same assumption about the unscheduled stop that they had been forced to make on their way to Malvern Link. It was the best possible gift that they could have wanted.

'It was a very special day,' murmured Churt.

Alone in the compartment next to the locomotive, Ernest Drake took a very different view. In his eyes, the excursion had been disastrous. The works manager had been shot dead, careful planning for the event had been thrown into disarray and – he shuddered every time he thought of it – he was responsible for informing the Hubbleday family of its terrible loss. He felt hopelessly unequal to the task. He lived in a world of numbers. There was safety and certainty there. Though he shared a house with his sister, he felt ill at ease in the company of women. To pass on the appalling news to Cyril Hubbleday's wife and two daughters would be a sustained ordeal for him.

And yet it had to be done. The family deserved to be told before it became common knowledge. The murder victim had been a key figure in one of the most successful enterprises in the Black Country. Every newspaper would carry details of his doomed visit to the Malverns. The police would be heavily involved. Drake trembled at the thought that, having shared a compartment alone with Hubbleday, he was bound to be questioned about the man. How would he be viewed? Would they treat him as a friend of the deceased or as a suspect? How deep would they pry into his life? Biting his lip, he quailed. The prospect of a police interrogation was almost as daunting to him as the thought of his forthcoming visit to the Hubbleday family. His predicament was agonising.

Ernest Drake closed his eyes and began to pray.

After a journey by train and then cab, Victor Leeming arrived at the house and stared at it in wonder. It was more than imposing, and yet only one person lived there with her servants. He rang the bell. The massive front door was soon opened by the butler, a tall middle-aged man who was less than impressed by the sight of Leeming.

'Yes?' he asked.

'I wish to speak to Lady Foley.'

'That will not be possible, I'm afraid. May I give her a message?'

'No,' said Leeming. 'I have to deliver it in person.'

'Lady Foley is about to have dinner and cannot be disturbed.'

'All I need is a moment with her, and I'm not leaving without it.'

'I'm afraid that you'll have to,' said the butler, loftily.

Leeming was irked. 'Who do you think you're talking to?'

'If you won't leave your message, I'll bid you good evening.'

'You'll do nothing of the kind,' said Leeming, stung by the butler's attitude and raising his voice in protest. 'Now summon your mistress before I get very angry.'

When he was still refused admission to the house, a real argument began, and voices were raised. The unseemly noise brought Lady Foley into the hall.

'What's going on?' she demanded.

Leeming was momentarily stunned by her appearance. Dressed for dinner, she looked quite stunning.

'I'm sorry to disturb you, Lady Foley,' said the butler with a bow, 'but this gentleman insists on speaking to you in person.'

'Really?' Her steely gaze shifted to the visitor. 'Who, may I ask, are you?'

'I am Detective Sergeant Leeming,' he replied, 'and I am working with Superintendent Tallis to solve the murder that took place earlier today. I've been sent to deliver a message.'

'He refused to tell me what it was,' complained the butler.

'It's meant for your ears only, Lady Foley. The

60

superintendent sends his regards and wishes you to know that he has – in his own words – crossed swords with Inspector Vellacott and put him firmly in his place.'

'Excellent!' said Lady Foley.

'That's it,' said Leeming. 'I'm not sure that it was worth the effort of coming all the way here on a miserably cold evening to pass on that information, but I obeyed my orders.'

'Then I'll give you some more orders to obey, Sergeant.'

'More orders?'

'Yes,' she said in a voice like the crack of a whip. 'First, you must thank the superintendent for sending you.'

'I will.'

'Second, when you deliver other messages here, be sure to use the tradesman's entrance. We observe strict standards in this house.'

Turning on her heel, she walked away with great dignity. The butler grinned at Leeming and grasped the door handle meaningfully.

'Good day to you, Sergeant,' he said.

During the drive to Appleby Court, Colbeck and Tallis saw nothing of the rolling countryside around them. A blanket of darkness deprived them of that pleasure. Having travelled most of the way in silence, the superintendent suddenly spoke.

'You were right,' he admitted. 'Great Malvern does have a very pretty station. There's none of the grime, ugliness and deafening clamour of the railway stations in London.'

'They have to cope with much heavier traffic, sir.'

'Those capitals you mentioned are quite extraordinary.'

'I only had the merest glimpse of them.'

'The stationmaster told me that he is so proud of the floral decorations that he dusts each one every morning. It's a chore that lifts his spirit.'

'What is your first impression of the town, sir?'

'I've seen too little of it to reach a judgement,' said Tallis, 'but there have been moments when I felt strangely at home. It's almost as if I've been guided here.'

'You'll miss the advantages of city life.'

Tallis smiled complacently. 'I'll be celebrating that fact every day.'

Colbeck was dismayed. He believed that the superintendent was most at home when seated behind a desk at Scotland Yard, issuing orders and smoking his pungent cigars. That was his true milieu. But it was not Colbeck's place to challenge his companion's unexpected decision to retire. He could simply hope that the notion might, in time, lose its appeal.

When they saw Appleby Court, silhouetted against the sky, they realised how wealthy its owner must be. Impressive from a short distance away, the house was quite overwhelming at close quarters. Colbeck wondered how the excursionists had responded to it earlier in the day. They lived in mean, dingy accommodation in an area blighted by industry and grinding poverty. To the wide-eyed children who saw it, Appleby Court must have looked like something out of a fairy tale.

Admitted to the house by a butler, they were escorted to the drawing room, a large room with expensive furniture and walls covered in gilt-framed oil paintings. Jerome Appleby leapt to his feet to welcome them, shaking hands with each in turn. He gestured to the other person in the room. Looking wounded, Inspector Vellacott was seated near the fireplace. When Colbeck was introduced to him, he made a point of shaking the man's hand.

'I hear good things about the Worcestershire Constabulary,' he said, affably. 'I am glad that we will be working side by side on this case.'

'I wish that I could share your enthusiasm,' said Vellacott, stiffly.

Appleby waved the newcomers to chairs then resumed his own seat.

'The inspector and I have a difference of opinion,' he explained. 'While he objects to your arrival, I am delighted. It's a privilege to have you both here.'

'That's reassuring,' said Tallis, 'though, in fact, there are three of us in total. When I met him earlier, Inspector Vellacott insisted that you should decide whether our presence here was welcome or intrusive. I am glad that your response is so positive.'

'Relegating us to a minor role is unjust,' argued Vellacott. 'You will be claiming credit for intelligence that my officers gathered.'

'What intelligence is that?' asked Colbeck, politely.

'We have already identified two possible suspects.'

'Are they in custody?'

'No, Inspector, neither of them was at home when my officers called.'

'Were they working in concert or acting independently?'

'Each was acting of his own volition.'

'You sound very sure of yourself,' said Colbeck.

'We know these men – you don't.'

'What motives do you ascribe to these individuals?'

'In the first case,' said Vellacott, 'the man views excursionists as anathema. He thinks that the only way to stop them pouring in here during the summer like molten lava is to deter them. I don't believe that Mr Hubbleday was the chosen target,' he added, slapping the arm of his chair for emphasis. 'The assassin was ready to kill the first person on that train who came within his sight. That would be enough to make holidaymakers think twice before daring to come here again.'

'Does this assassin, as you call him, have a criminal record?' asked Tallis.

'Let us say that he is well known to us, Superintendent.'

'What about the second suspect?'

'His motive would be slightly different,' said Vellacott. 'He was not striking against excursionists in general. His target – albeit indirectly – was Mr Appleby.'

'Dear me!' exclaimed Appleby.

'He resents the fact that a wealthy industrialist has bought one of the finest estates in the Malverns. I have no quarrel with your presence here, sir,' he went on, turning to

Appleby. 'You are entitled to live wherever you wish, and I welcome you with open arms. But passions run high among country folk,' he warned. 'They believe that their way of life is under threat from the spread of industry with all of its attendant noise, filth and sheer ugliness. Through no fault of your own, Mr Appleby, you represent all that they hate. That was the message the killer wanted to send to you.'

'I can understand his dislike of me, but did he have to go to such extremes?' Appleby turned to the superintendent. 'Do you have any comment to make?'

'Yes,' said Tallis, coolly. 'What we've just heard is idle guesswork without a shred of evidence to support it.'

'These two men have a history,' retorted Vellacott. 'We know how their minds work.'

'I am more interested in how your mind works,' said Colbeck, levelly. 'May I ask what type of weapon was used in the murder?'

'I believe that it was a rifle of sorts.'

'Could you be more specific?'

'Of course, not – we haven't seen it.'

'You have the bullet that it fired,' Colbeck pointed out. 'That will tell you what weapon was used. If you know that either of the two men you've identified possesses such a weapon, you have grounds for an arrest.' He raised an eyebrow. 'The bullet has been extracted, has it?' Vellacott fell silent. 'I thought not. You have been less than thorough, Inspector. First thing in the morning, I will pay a visit to the hospital and view both the body and the bullet. Do you have any objection to that?'

'No, no . . .'

'It's something you should have done yourself,' said Tallis.

'I had . . . other priorities.'

'Mr Hubbleday was shot by someone high above him, I believe.'

'That's right, Superintendent. The bullet pierced his hat and lodged in his head. Death would have been instantaneous.'

'The killer was a marksman,' said Colbeck. 'I located the exact spot from which he fired his weapon.' He turned to Vellacott. 'Would you describe either of your suspects as a real marksman, Inspector?'

'Well . . .'

'You seem unsure.'

'One of them certainly has a gun,' said the other, 'because he's been caught poaching more than once.'

'Shooting deer, pheasant or rabbit is rather different to killing a human being.'

'That's true . . . but I stick to my judgement of these two men.'

'Your reasoning is unsound, Inspector,' said Colbeck.

'I disagree,' snapped Vellacott.

'According to you, one of the suspects set out to kill someone on that train as a warning to those who organise excursions here.'

'That is undoubtedly true.'

'Then why didn't the man shoot the engine driver or the

fireman? Both were clearly in view. Why did he pick out Mr Hubbleday?'

'Well,' said the other, groping for words, 'I suppose that it . . . it was because the gentleman was . . . in charge of the excursion.'

'How did the killer know that?'

'I can't say at this stage.'

'And how could he be sure that anyone involved in the excursion would take the trouble to get out of the train when it stopped? It's quite dangerous to jump down to the ground from that height. Anybody else would have let the guard investigate the problem. That's what he's paid to do, after all,' said Colbeck. 'If he had waited, the killer could have shot driver, fireman or guard. The murder of a railway employee would have acted as a powerful deterrent to anyone about to organise an excursion.'

'Inspector Colbeck makes a valid point,' agreed Tallis. 'A local hothead from the Malverns would have no idea who Mr Hubbleday was. Why single him out?'

'When we arrest the man,' said Vellacott, 'we'll ask him.'

'Humour us for a moment,' said Colbeck. 'Consider our theory that Mr Hubbleday was shot by someone who knew and despised him. It means that the killer is not from this part of the country at all.'

Vellacott was on his feet. 'I'd stake my reputation on it!'

'The murder may have taken place in the Malverns but it was planned somewhere in the Black Country.'

'That's absurd!'

'We shall see, Inspector. But have no fear,' added Colbeck. 'We are by no means dispensing with your services. There is important work for you and your men.'

'I refuse to venture into that industrial hellhole.'

'That is where we will search but you will be needed here. Two men were involved in the murder. On his own, the killer could not have lifted those sleepers across the line. And where could he acquire two red flags? The answer is simple. He must have had an accomplice who knows this area well and who was able to source both the sleepers and the flags. Find this man, Inspector,' urged Colbeck. 'In doing so, you will be making a significant contribution to the investigation.'

'I refuse to rule out our suspects yet,' said Vellacott, gritting his teeth.

'That's your business.'

'Inspector Colbeck's explanation is very convincing,' said Appleby. 'Cyril Hubbleday was a very efficient works manager, but he was far too strict to be popular. By nature, he was always forthright. I can well imagine him jumping off a stationary train to see what had caused it to stop.'

'Someone knew that he would be certain to do just that,' concluded Tallis. 'We need to track this man down immediately.'

'And his accomplice,' said Colbeck. 'Both men deserve to hang.'

* * *

When the train reached its destination, the first thing that Ernest Drake had to do was to control the departure of its passengers. Deputising for the works manager, he stood at the exit with an unconvincing smile and collected gabbled thanks from adults and children alike. Everyone went off happily. The few enquiries he had about Cyril Hubbleday were waved away. Drake was eventually left alone on a cold, deserted platform, feeling sick and trying to find the words he would use when he delivered the momentous news to the family. Taking a deep breath, he set off.

Madeleine Colbeck had been looking forward to dining with Lydia Quayle and her father but the news that her husband had been sent away on a new case had taken some of the pleasure out of the occasion. As they began to eat their meal, her father kept raising the possibility that his son-in-law would miss the Christmas festivities with his family.

'Stop fearing the worst,' said Madeleine.

'We have to face facts, Maddy,' he replied. 'He could be trapped in the Malverns with that dreadful superintendent of his. It's shameful.'

'Robert has to do as he is told,' Lydia reminded him.

'Let's talk about something else,' suggested Madeleine.

'But we haven't discussed the case itself,' protested her father. 'A passenger has been shot dead on a railway line in broad daylight. That's an outrage, Maddy. The safety of rail travel is a downright necessity.'

Andrews was soon in full flow on the subject, and it

was impossible to stop him. Madeleine gave her friend an apologetic smile. Lydia gave her an understanding nod. When Andrews changed tack, the two women pricked up their ears.

'It could be worse, I suppose,' he said. 'Robert is in a beautiful part of the country. Thank goodness he hasn't been sent to somewhere like the Black Country. That would be a threat to his health. Every time I drove a train through it, I felt sorry for the poor devils trapped there. It's like twilight during the day and lit up at night by a fiery glow. The stink is terrible. I'm used to smoke and coal dust but what they breathe there is far worse. Their lungs must be clogged up with soot from the mines and fumes from the chemical works.' He pronged a potato with his fork. 'Robert is far better off in the countryside . . .'

'Oldbury?' protested Leeming. 'Where the devil is that?'

'It's in the Black Country,' said Colbeck. 'You must contact the local police to introduce yourself then go to the Railway Carriage and Wagon Company.'

'Where will you be in the meantime?'

'I'll be at Worcester Hospital, examining the body of the deceased and the bullet that killed him. I daresay that Inspector Vellacott will be there to watch me like a hawk. Once I've done that, I'll catch the next available train and meet you at Appleby's Works.'

'I was hoping we'd be gathering evidence here in the country.'

'Vellacott can do that – with the superintendent bellowing in his ear.'

'That's one thing, I suppose,' said Leeming. 'We'll have more of a free hand in Oldbury. Also, it may save me having to take messages to Lady Foley. She looked down her nose at me as if I was a nasty stain on her carpet.'

'If we solve this crime,' said Colbeck, 'she'll probably embrace you.'

Leeming shivered. 'No thank you! That woman is made of solid ice.'

'Yet she obviously impressed the superintendent.'

'Then he can deliver his blooming messages to her in person.'

Having enjoyed a warm and satisfying meal, they were seated in the dining room in a small hotel in Great Malvern. It had the advantages of being snug, homely and a comfortable distance away from the Imperial Hotel where Tallis was staying. It also had an owner who treated them more like friends than stray visitors who had descended on her out of the blue. They had been given a cordial welcome, a cosy room apiece and an exceptionally good meal.

Ruby Renshaw came into the dining room with a broad smile. They were struck by her demeanour and colourful attire. Now in her sixties, she made light of her age and substantial weight by tripping along on her toes with the grace of a dancer. She spoke in an educated voice couched in a pleasing local accent.

'Did you enjoy your meal?' she asked.

'Yes, we did,' said Leeming with enthusiasm. 'It was just what we needed on a cold evening like this.'

'Please pass on our thanks to your cook,' added Colbeck, standing up. 'When we arrived, Mrs Renshaw, we had no time to explain what we were doing in this part of the country. Given the circumstances, it's only fair that you should know.'

'But I already do,' she replied with a smile.

'How could you?'

'Well, it wasn't because I was eavesdropping,' she assured them. 'I would never stoop to spying on my guests. The moment I saw you, I guessed that you must be detectives who had come to investigate the murder.'

'Who told you about the murder?' asked Leeming.

'Nobody did,' she replied, sweetly. 'I just knew. I have a sixth sense, you see. It allows me a peep into the future. I had a vision that something terrible would happen on the railway line. It had to be a murder. Your arrival confirmed it.' The detectives traded a worried glance. 'Oh, don't worry,' she went on, cheerfully. 'I know you don't believe me. Nobody does. They think I'm soft in the head. I've learnt to live with their sniggers. But I'm neither mad nor deluded,' she went on. 'I really do have a gift. I give you my word of honour.'

* * *

Before he could bring himself to deliver the fateful news, Ernest Drake walked up and down the road for a long time. Large, detached and well-built, the Hubbleday residence was in the more affluent part of Oldbury. Drake had been there often and always enjoyed his visits. This time it was different. He was carrying a message that would shatter the lives of an entire family. Nevertheless, it had to be delivered. Steeling himself, he went up to the front door and used the knocker, stepping back guiltily at once. He licked his lips and rehearsed once again what he was going to say to the Hubbleday family.

Expecting the door to be opened by a servant, he was taken aback to see a uniformed policeman answering his knock. The man glared suspiciously.

'Who might you be, sir?' he asked.

'My name is Ernest Drake,' said the other. 'I'm the accountant at the Appleby Works and a friend of the Hubbleday family.'

'What are you doing here?'

'I have some sad news to pass on.'

The policeman sighed. 'They've had enough of that already, sir.'

'What do you mean?'

'Earlier today, Mr Hubbleday was shot dead in the Malverns.'

'But that's the message I came to deliver,' said Drake, reeling. 'Who could possibly have told them?'

'A note was put through their letter box,' said the

policeman. 'That's why we were called in. Nobody is allowed into the house. Good day to you, sir.'

'Oh, I see . . .'

Mind racing, Drake staggered off in a state of utter confusion.

CHAPTER SIX

Great Malvern was only eight miles south-west of Worcester so the journey to the county town was relatively short. Arriving early that morning, Robert Colbeck was driven from the railway station to the Royal Infirmary. Mercifully, there was no sign there of Inspector Vellacott and he was duly grateful. He met the director, Hugo Lipton, a pallid individual in his forties with the kind of cultured beard that required constant attention. The man was also excessively smart, even more so than his elegant visitor. Colbeck noticed the full-length mirror on one wall and surmised that Lipton spent a lot of time in front of it. Impressed that someone from Scotland Yard would come all the way to the area, the director began to tell his visitor about the history of the building.

'Excuse me,' said Colbeck, interrupting, 'but I came here to view the body of a murder victim, not to listen to a commentary on the growth of this hospital.'

Lipton was offended. 'It's a place of great interest,' he claimed, 'and we are proud of the way that it has developed. For instance, the Jenny Lind Chapel was built here some years ago. The Swedish Nightingale, as she is called, was kind enough to allow us to use her name. She is a remarkable lady.'

'You don't need to tell me that, Mr Lipton. I once had the privilege of acting as Miss Lind's bodyguard. As a result, I and my sergeant enjoyed hearing her sing in front of an adoring audience. I cherish the concert programme that she was kind enough to sign for me.'

'Oh, I see.'

Visibly deflated, the director led the way to an office next to the mortuary. He introduced Colbeck to the pathologist who had come from Birmingham to perform the post-mortem. Dr Montgomery Peck had none of the irritating self-importance of Lipton. He was a short, stocky, middle-aged man who looked more like a gardener than a senior member of the medical profession. He was glad when the director left them alone. His brow crinkled.

'Colbeck?' he said, ransacking his memories. 'Now that's a name I've heard before. You are something to do with railways, are you not?'

'They are my principal concern, as it happens.'

'I seem to recall seeing your name in a Birmingham newspaper.'

'My work has taken me there on more than one occasion. It's a place for which I have the greatest affection.'

Peck laughed. 'Not many people would say that. It's a busy, brash, horribly loud manufacturing city. Why do you have such affection for it?'

'It's where I proposed to the dear lady who is now my wife.'

'Ah, well, that's different, Inspector. I proposed in a summerhouse in Ottery St Mary. I experience a thrill whenever my wife and I visit the place. However,' he added, 'it's rather indecent of us to be talking about a significant moment in our respective lives when we are here to discuss someone who lost his so dramatically.'

'I agree, Dr Peck. How far have you got?'

'As it happens,' said the other, 'I should be finished before too long. I came here yesterday and worked well into the evening. Cause of death was easy to establish but I wanted to take a closer look at the cadaver.'

'What did you find?'

'Well, it's a gruesome thought but the killer may have done him a favour.'

'A favour?' repeated Colbeck in surprise.

'If he hadn't died instantly from a bullet wound, he might have had a much more painful death. Mr Hubbleday had a serious heart condition, a cancerous growth in the throat and a peptic ulcer. There were additional health problems as well.' He pursed his lips. 'I'd have given him no more than six months to live.'

'May I view the body?'

'Be my guest, Inspector.'

Peck led him into the mortuary and Colbeck felt the sudden drop in temperature. Covered in shrouds, a few dead bodies rested on individual tables. The two men went through a door into a room with an abiding smell of disinfectant and a grim sense of finality. Lying on a table beneath a shroud was the body of Cyril Hubbleday.

'Do you have a strong stomach, Inspector?' asked Peck.

'I won't disgrace myself, if that's what you mean.'

'Good man.'

Peck drew back the shroud to expose the head and shoulders of the murder victim. Colbeck was startled. When it pierced the skull, the bullet had left a grotesque depression in the middle of the bald head. Yet, with the blood washed off it, the face looked as if its owner were simply asleep.

'The killer not only ended his life prematurely,' said Peck, 'he ruined Mr Hubbleday's highly expensive hat.'

He indicated the top hat that stood on a windowsill. Colbeck picked it up and examined the hole in it.

'You've just answered a question I've been asking myself,' he said, replacing it on the windowsill. 'How did the killer know that he was shooting the right person?'

'I don't follow, Inspector.'

'Well, he couldn't see his victim's face from the top of the cutting. I know that because I found the exact spot from which he fired the fatal shot. As he gazed down at the figures below him, all that he would have seen was what they were wearing on their heads. That distinctive top hat told him that his quarry was directly below him.'

'I see what you mean.'

'Did you extract the bullet?' asked Colbeck.

'I have it here,' said the other, reaching for a glass tray. 'Do you know much about firearms, Inspector?'

'I know how lethal they can be.'

'Over the years, I've extracted many bullets from cadavers. This one was fired out of a Pattern Enfield rifle musket. It's the weapon that replaced the smoothbore musket towards the end of the Crimean War and is far more effective.' Taking the bullet out of the tray, he put it into the inspector's hand. 'Can you hear what I'm telling you?'

'Yes,' said Colbeck, examining the bullet. 'A military weapon was used. The killer may well have served in the army.'

Taking careful aim with his rifle, the man pulled the trigger and the bird fell out of the air amid a small blizzard of feathers. The dog raced off to retrieve it.

The visit to Oldbury seemed to Victor Leeming like a descent into hell. Behind him lay the delightful town of Great Malvern, nestling in verdant hills and enjoying all the advantages of country life. In front of him now was a bustling community of over ten thousand people, most of them employed in the steel works, the chemical works, the furnace iron works, the barge yards, the brick and tile fields, the corn mills, the malting or brewing concerns and all the other industrial units that polluted the air, darkened the sky, and bombarded the eardrums. There was a doom-laden feel to the town. Leeming hoped that their time there would be very short. As soon as he arrived, he covered his mouth and nose with a hand to block out the stench. London had its own noxious stink, but it was not as penetrating as the one he now experienced.

Because the town was in Worcestershire, it was policed by the constabulary responsible for Great Malvern. Given the choice, he knew which of the two places he would prefer to work in. When he got to the police station, he was given a much warmer welcome than Inspector Vellacott had accorded them. Leeming was promised complete cooperation from the local force. There was an immediate shock. He had assumed that news of the murder would have reached the police in Oldbury by means of a telegraph, but that the task of informing the family would have fallen to someone in the employ of Jerome Appleby. When he heard that Hubbleday's wife and children were made aware of his death by means of a crude note pushed through the letter box, Leeming was horrified. It was an act of sheer cruelty.

* * *

'Where were you yesterday morning?' demanded Tallis.

'Why d'you want to know?' asked Hamer, gruffly.

'Just answer the question.'

'What's going on?'

'I think you know full well.'

'So don't you dare to lie to us,' added Vellacott.

In response to a message from the inspector, Tallis had joined him on a visit to the home of one of the suspects. Alec Hamer was a farm labourer, a swarthy man in his thirties with broad shoulders and bulging muscles. In his ragged attire, he looked like a tramp who had slept under a hedge. Vellacott knew him of old and had good reason to distrust him. Tallis found the man sly and uncouth. The three of them were in a tied cottage that was depressingly small and cluttered.

'If you must know,' said Hamer, resentfully, 'I was in the top field yesterday morning, repairing a fence. You ask Mr Gurney.'

'We've already done that,' Vellacott told him. 'The farmer says you were told to mend fences for most of the day – but he didn't actually see you at work. You could easily have slipped away or got someone to take your place while you went off to do something more important.'

'What's more important than my job?' wailed Hamer. 'I need somewhere to live and money to buy food. I always obey Mr Gurney's orders because he's been good to me.'

'More fool him! Most farmers wouldn't touch you with a barge pole.'

'Quite rightly,' said Tallis. 'When someone has been in

trouble with the police, they need to be watched carefully.'

'It was years ago!' protested Hamer.

'Once a villain, always a villain.'

'That's unfair!'

'Where were you yesterday evening?' asked Vellacott. 'When my officers called here to speak to you, the cottage was empty.'

'I went to see my mother in Drugger's End.'

'We'll check.'

'It's the truth, Inspector. She sent for me because she was sick.'

'You don't look like a dutiful son to me,' said Tallis, watching him carefully.

Hamer was surly. 'How would you know?'

'Show some respect,' warned Vellacott.

'Then don't let him insult me. I love my mother. I always have.'

'When did you get back?'

'Some time after midnight.'

'Why was it so late?'

'It's a long walk, Inspector.'

Vellacott continued to ply him with questions, but Tallis had heard enough. In his view, the suspect was patently innocent. Shabby and disreputable Hamer might be, but he lacked the intelligence to plan and execute the murder. What possible connection could he have had with a works manager from Oldbury? He could also be discounted as an accomplice. Nobody with any sense would recruit someone as stupid and unreliable as Hamer. It was a point that Tallis made to Vellacott when the two of them eventually left the cottage.

'It was a waste of time even talking to him,' he complained.

'I disagree. Hamer would do anything for money.'

'He'd draw the line at killing someone.'

'If paid enough,' said Vellacott, 'he'd be tempted.'

Tallis was blunt. 'Is your other suspect as unconvincing as this one?'

'I still think that Hamer was worth speaking to.'

'But not in such a confined area as that cottage,' said Tallis, grimacing. 'Does the man never wash? The stink was intolerable.' They climbed into the trap and set off towards Upton upon Severn. 'What's the name of your second suspect?'

'James Carmody.'

'I hope he's more coherent than Hamer.'

'Oh, Carmody is much sharper in every way.'

'What made you pick the man out?'

'We've had to lock him up once too often,' said Vellacott. 'Also, he used to work on the railway. If someone needed sleepers and two red flags, Carmody would know exactly where to find them.'

When he got to the Railway Carriage and Wagon Company, Leeming discovered that the person now in charge was Oliver Innes, the former deputy works manager. Short and stooping, he was a complete contrast to his predecessor. He had none of Hubbleday's bluster and sheer physical presence. Innes was subdued and watchful. Leeming took an instant liking to the man. He was polite, alert and helpful.

For his part, Innes was pleased that Scotland Yard detectives were handling the investigation.

'Don't you trust the local police?' asked Leeming.

'Of course, but they have no experience of a case like this.'

'I'm glad that you appreciate our record of success.'

Leeming glanced around the office. It was large, nondescript and utilitarian. Every wall was covered by charts. There were two desks, one much bigger than the other. Innes pointed to it.

'That belonged to Mr Hubbleday,' he said.

'It's almost twice the size of yours.'

'He was senior to me, Sergeant.'

'Not any more. You can move into his chair now.'

'That would be too presumptuous.'

Opening a drawer in his own desk, Innes took out a sheet of paper.

'I know what you're going to ask me,' he said. 'Did Mr Hubbleday make any enemies here? Unhappily, he did – but only because he acted in the best interests of this company.' He offered the paper to Leeming. 'This is a list of employees he was forced to sack. They did not go quietly.'

'I see,' said Leeming, taking the list and glancing at the names. 'There must be a dozen or more here. What reason were they given for their dismissal?'

'In most cases, they were lazy or bad timekeepers. We expect people to earn their money here and punctuality is our watchword. One man – his name is at the bottom of the list – resorted to violence. When he was dismissed, he made the mistake of throwing a punch at Mr Hubbleday.'

'Why was it a mistake?'

'He picked the wrong man, Sergeant. Cyril Hubbleday was big and strong. He knocked Waycroft out with a single punch. What upset him was not so much the fact that the man was late yet again, but that there was a strong smell of beer on his breath. We don't stand for that. Men are entitled to have a drink at the end of the shift, but they are not allowed to stagger in here after swilling down beer in the morning.'

'What sort of man was Samuel Waycroft?'

'He was a very stupid one,' said Innes. 'He lost his job, the house he rented from us and his chances of working in Oldbury again. It was a pity, really. Waycroft was a first-rate carpenter. I reminded Mr Hubbleday of that. It was the reason he didn't report the assault on him to the police.'

'Where is Waycroft now?'

'There was a rumour that he was living with his sister in Tipton.'

'Would you describe this man as vengeful?'

Innes spoke firmly. 'Yes, I would.'

Work in his paint shop continued as usual but the conversation was far more animated. As the one person there who had been on the excursion, Derek Churt became the centre of attention. His fellow painters were fascinated.

'When did you suspect he'd been shot, Derek?' asked one of them.

'It was when Mr Drake came to our compartment and told us that a cow had strayed onto the line. I didn't believe him,' boasted Churt, tapping his chest. 'I mean, what farmer keeps a herd in the fields at this time of year? There's no grass to eat. The cows were indoors, being fed with hay.'

'I never thought of that.'

'I did. Also, it was the way Mr Drake spoke to us. It was . . . well, a bit odd. It made me think. I seem to have been the only one.'

'You always were a clever sod.'

'Everyone else on the train was fooled by that nonsense about a dead cow. Later, when we had this sort of banquet at Mr Appleby's house, there was an empty chair at the top table. It was Hubbleday's. When I saw it,' said Churt, 'I knew for certain he was dead. Someone did us all a favour and shot the bastard.'

'I'd like to shake the killer's hand,' said the other.

Churt grinned. 'Wait your turn in the queue.'

The laughter was loud and harsh.

Victor Leeming was still in the office of the new works manager when Colbeck arrived. From the moment they met, the inspector was impressed by Oliver Innes. Like the sergeant, he found him calm, well organised and eager to help. Since Leeming had already taken extensive notes, Colbeck did not detain Innes for long. The person he really wanted to meet was the man who had taken charge on the excursion train when Cyril Hubbleday was shot dead. Innes gave them directions to the office belonging to Ernest Drake.

When they first met him, the detectives were amazed that he had come to work that morning. He looked weary, ill at ease and desperately ill. The colour had drained from his face and his voice was no more than a croak. Seated behind his desk, he had to make a conscious effort to rise to his feet when they went into his office. On hearing that they were Scotland Yard detectives, he was shaken.

'I've already spoken to the police,' he explained.

'We've taken charge of the case now,' said Colbeck.

'Oh, I see. It's a tragedy, Inspector. Mr Hubbleday was the heart and soul of this place. I don't know how we'll manage without him.'

'That's a problem for Mr Appleby to solve. Our concern is to find the killer.'

'Before Christmas, if possible,' interjected Leeming.

'First of all, please explain why you were on that excursion train.'

'Well,' said Drake, 'it's like this . . .'

While Leeming took notes, Colbeck studied the man in front of them. In his judgement, Drake was modest, capable, and devoted to his job. It soon became clear that he was rather more than an accountant. He was effectively in charge of the financial affairs of the whole company yet carried his responsibility lightly. He reported on revenue, controlled budgeting, disbursed funds to all departments and trained accounting staff. Huge sums of money were involved. Only someone as trustworthy as Drake would be employed to look after it.

'Mr Appleby is a genius,' he told them. 'Moving to this site was his idea. It means that we're adjacent to the railway and have a pit shaft nearby drawing coal. There are at least thirty iron rolling mills within a two-mile radius and – a deciding factor – we're close to a canal that links us to London and Liverpool. It's a connection that helps shipments abroad.'

'Why does Mr Appleby offer these excursions?' asked Colbeck. 'I can't imagine that many would do that.'

'The answer is that he's a true Christian. Everyone thinks that industrialists are all cruel taskmasters, driven by the urge to increase profits, but not Mr Appleby. He cares for his employees and wants to show his appreciation. He's not the only one with a religious impulse,' said Drake. 'Those tall towers you saw on your way here belong to Albright and Wilson's chemical factory. They produce potassium chloride, and white phosphorous for the heads of matches.'

'So that's where the stink comes from,' said Leeming.

'Mr Albright and Mr Wilson are Quakers.'

'I'd quake if I had that smell in my nostrils all day!'

'We can do without your comments, Sergeant,' said Colbeck. He looked at Drake with concern. 'Are you sure that you're well enough to come to work today?'

'I can't let Mr Appleby down,' said the other. 'Besides,

I'm not ill in the accepted sense. I'm just horrified by what's happened. What really upset me was that I was asked to break the dreadful news to the Hubbleday family. You can imagine how I felt when I learnt it had already been delivered – and in the most heartless way. I know Mrs Hubbleday well. She's a dear lady and her daughters are both delightful. One of them is due to be married next Easter,' he went on, tears forming. 'Who is to take her down the aisle now?'

Having been given the use of the stationmaster's office as a base from which to operate, Edward Tallis was well placed to see anyone who came to and from the railway station in Great Malvern. When he spotted Jerome Appleby arriving, he went quickly out onto the platform.

'When you get to Oldbury,' he said, 'you'll find Inspector Colbeck and Sergeant Leeming there.'

'Good,' said Appleby. 'Have you made any headway here?'

'That remains to be seen. Inspector Vellacott and I grilled a man he regarded as a suspect, but Hamer was nothing of the kind. When we went to the home of a more likely culprit, we were told that he was away for a few days. We'll find out if that's true when we run him to earth.'

'And you think he's a more promising suspect?'

'Oh, yes. He worked on the railway and is familiar with the track around here. He knows exactly where the deepest cuttings are.'

After discussing the investigation for a few minutes, Tallis saw an opportunity to gather information about the area for his own benefit. He lowered his voice.

'Do you like living here, Mr Appleby?'

'My wife and I love the area.'

'Why is that?'

'It's beautiful, it's welcoming and it's safe. Well,' said Appleby, 'until yesterday, it had no serious crime. Murder is almost unknown. Vellacott will assure you of that.'

'He's done so a number of times,' said Tallis, ruefully.

'If you like a gentle pace of life, there's no better place to live. Because of the fame of its spa, celebrated people have visited. I'm told that no less a person than Charles Dickens came here so that his wife could enjoy the Water Cure. No,' affirmed Appleby, 'I couldn't speak more highly of the place. The only disagreeable aspect of life in the Malverns is that we've been spurned by Lady Foley, who is our nearest neighbour.'

'Yes, the stationmaster told me that. It's very unfortunate.'

'She has a lot of influence here.'

'Deservedly so, I gather,' said Tallis. 'Lady Foley is a philanthropist, I'm told. She's given money towards the building of churches and schools.'

'I know nothing about the schools,' admitted Appleby, 'but there may be another reason why the churches came into being.'

'Oh? What is it, I pray?'

'The Priory church is one of the most beautiful I've ever had the pleasure of visiting,' said Appleby, 'but there have been mutterings about some of those in the congregation.

Lady Foley would call them riff-raff, I daresay, unworthy of joining the privileged elite there. Those local churches she supported could simply be a means of luring the lower classes away from a place of worship she considers above them.'

'Could she harbour such an unkind motive?' asked Tallis, shocked.

'I speak as I find, Superintendent.'

'Then we must agree to differ, Mr Appleby.'

'Why is that?'

'When I met Lady Foley, I had a very different impression of her. She struck me as a God-fearing woman, who believes in upholding high standards of behaviour.'

'Try living close to her,' said the other, bitterly. He glanced down the line at the approaching train. 'It looks as if my transport is here.' He touched the brim of his hat. 'I bid you good day.'

Madeleine Colbeck was working in her studio when she heard her father arrive at the house. Putting down her paintbrush, she wiped her hands on a rag and went downstairs to greet him. A maidservant was hanging up his coat and hat. Andrews gave his daughter a kiss.

'How are you today, Maddy?' he asked.

'To be honest,' she said, 'I'm glad that you've come to cheer me up because I'm feeling down in the dumps.'

'Why?'

'I've had a letter from Robert this morning. He says that the case is more complex than he thought. Worse still, he'll be spending most of his time in Oldbury.'

'That's in the Black Country!' howled her father.

'Yes, he told me that. Only yesterday, you were saying we should be grateful that he was out in the fresh air instead of working in one of those grim little towns.'

'It's worse than grim, Maddy. It's a danger to his health.'

'Robert will survive somehow. He always does.'

'Has he given you details of the case?'

'Not really,' said Madeleine.'

'When he does, let me see them. I may spot something that Robert doesn't.'

She laughed. 'That will be the day!'

'I've got the instincts of a detective. My son-in-law should use me.'

'He does, Father. Robert uses you as the best child-minder that Helena could possibly have. She's upstairs in the nursery, by the way, dying for you to come. We're grateful that you can spend so much time with her.'

'She's the loveliest granddaughter in the world.'

'You wouldn't say that if you saw her when she's in one of her moods.'

'Helena is always as good as gold with me.'

'That's because you have a magic touch,' said Madeleine, fondly. 'Now take it upstairs and give Nanny Perkins a rest.'

Ernest Drake was a mine of information about the company and its key figures. Colbeck and Leeming were fascinated by the details they gleaned from him. People like Hubbleday, Appleby and Innes came vividly fully to life. With Drake's help, they had kept the works operating at full throttle and producing sizeable profits.

'The other thing about Cyril,' said Drake, 'was his amazing memory. He knew the names of almost everyone employed here. It was uncanny. He could walk through any of the shops and name all the men working there. It used to shake them. They couldn't believe it.'

'How many of their names do you remember?' asked Leeming.

'Very few. I have little direct contact with our employees.'

'The name of Samuel Waycroft would mean nothing to you, then?'

'Ah,' said the other, 'now that's one I do remember.'

'Oh?'

'Cyril told me about him. When he sacked the man on the spot, Waycroft punched him. Cyril knocked him out.'

'That means he had two grudges to hold against Mr Hubbleday,' said Colbeck. 'The first was because he was dismissed and the second because he was beaten in a fight. Mr Innes told the sergeant that Waycroft was vengeful.'

'I heard the same thing from Cyril himself.'

'Why did the company employ the man in the first place?'

'He was an excellent carpenter, I'm told. Also, he was a brave man. When he was in the army, Waycroft fought in the Crimean War and won a medal. Cyril liked him at first. That was before he started drinking heavily and turning up late.'

'We must find this man as a matter of urgency,' decided Colbeck.

'The search must start in Tipton, sir,' said Leeming.

'Then that's where we'll go right away.'

'Don't we need to report to the superintendent first?'

'We'll do so,' said Colbeck. 'We can contact him directly to explain the situation. Fortunately, Great Malvern has its own telegraph station.'

The two of them got to their feet, thanked Drake for his help and left the room. Once outside, Colbeck reached a decision.

'We need assistance,' he said.

Leeming smiled. 'Detective Constable Hinton, perhaps?'

'The very man I had in mind. While we're busy exploring the Black Country, Hinton can stay right here in the works.'

'Why?'

'Unless I'm mistaken, someone from here was involved in the plot to kill Mr Hubbleday, if only by supplying crucial details about that excursion train. We need someone inside the building with a knack of talking to people. Hinton will be perfect. Also,' said Colbeck with a grin, 'it's something of which my wife would certainly approve – not to mention Lydia, of course. Follow me, Victor,' he said, moving off. 'When I send that telegraph to the superintendent, I'll insist that we need Hinton as soon as possible.'

CHAPTER SEVEN

Harold Unwin loved his job. He had an obedient staff, the respect of the passengers and a place of work that was uniquely decorative among railway stations. When visitors of distinction came to Great Malvern, he was always the first to greet them. People as famous as Charles Darwin, Florence Nightingale and Alfred, Lord Tennyson, the Poet Laureate, had all been welcomed by him. Perhaps the most satisfying aspect of his job, however, was the fact that he was seen by everyone as a vital part of the community. Unwin wallowed in his popularity.

When he saw a familiar figure walking towards him, he smiled broadly. Ruby Renshaw was striding along with a basket over her arm. It was always a good sign. After exchanging greetings with him, she took something out of her basket. 'There you are, Mr Unwin,' she said. 'One good turn deserves another. You very kindly recommended my hotel to those detectives from Scotland Yard.'

'I thought it would be ideal for their purposes, Mrs Renshaw.'

'These cakes should be ideal for *your* purposes. When my cook made them earlier on, your name popped straight into my mind.' She handed the package to him. 'Thank you.'

'You're very kind,' he said.

'It's not the first time you've done me a favour.'

'And it won't be the last.'

They shared a laugh then turned to local gossip. Watching them through the window of the stationmaster's office, Tallis was intrigued. He could see the affection between the two of them and was struck by the slightly exotic appearance of the woman, with her brightly coloured clothing and wide-brimmed hat. She was as unlike Lady Foley as he could imagine yet she aroused his interest in a way that the former had done so. Tallis stepped out onto the platform.

Unwin was quick to introduce him to Ruby, pointing out that she owned the hotel where his detectives were staying. It gave Tallis a reason to speak to her.

'I hope that they are behaving themselves, Mrs Renshaw,' he said.

'They have been, Superintendent. I wish that all my

guests were as pleasant as they are. They can stay as long as they wish.'

'We're here on urgent business. Once that's completed, we'll be off.'

'Yes, I know.'

'Mrs Renshaw has the best hotel in the town,' said Unwin, loyally. 'The Imperial is much bigger, but visitors get a warmer welcome from her.'

'So Inspector Colbeck tells me,' said Tallis. 'He was very complimentary about the accommodation.'

'Thank you,' she said. 'The inspector is a true gentleman – and so is the sergeant, in his own way. Neither of them laughed at me.'

'Why on earth should they do that?'

'Some of my other guests have done so.'

'It's only because they don't know you as well as I do,' said Unwin. 'Ignore them.' He turned to Tallis. 'Mrs Renshaw has a gift.'

'What kind of gift?' asked the other.

'She can see into the future.'

Ruby chortled. 'You make me sound like that fortune-teller at the annual fair,' she said. 'I don't ask people to step into my tent and cross my palm with silver.' She turned to Tallis. 'What happens, Superintendent, is that I have occasional warnings of danger. They usually catch me unawares. Take yesterday, for instance,' she went on. 'The moment I got up, I sensed that something dreadful would happen on the railway line not far away. My fear was that a murder would take place.'

'Could it not have equally well have been a train crash?' asked Tallis.

'Oh, no, that would have involved a lot of serious injuries. I got the feeling that only one person was at risk – and I was right.'

'You usually are, Mrs Renshaw,' said Unwin.

Tallis was sceptical. 'How often do you get these . . . visions?'

'Well, they're not really visions,' she explained. 'They're sort of . . . uneasy sensations. I just know something bad is about to happen.'

'Do you never get intimations of something good?'

'I wish I did, Superintendent. Mr Unwin described it as a gift, but it seems more of a curse. I've sometimes been woken up in the middle of the night by this sense of approaching doom. It used to frighten the life out of my husband – God rest his soul! He thought I was mad.' She studied his face. 'I can see that you share his opinion.'

'That's not true at all,' said Tallis, apologetically. 'I accept that what you tell me is true. You look to be a person of radiant honesty.'

'Mrs Renshaw could not tell a lie if she tried,' insisted Unwin.

'It's just that . . .'

'You don't believe me,' she said.

'I'm dubious, that's all. But if you had such a strong sensation yesterday morning, why didn't you report it to the police?'

'They'd only have ridiculed me, Superintendent. They always do.'

'Oh, I see.'

'They don't appreciate Mrs Renshaw,' said Unwin.

'Sadly,' she agreed, 'that's right. All they see is a deranged old woman giving them dire warnings and wasting their precious time. You'd do the same in their position, I daresay. Don't feel guilty about it,' she added. 'I never bear grudges.'

'I'm a detective,' said Tallis, seriously. 'My only interest is in solid evidence.'

She shrugged. 'Then I'm afraid that I'm no use to you at all.'

Madeleine Colbeck was in the drawing room at her home. The Christmas tree had finally arrived and been given pride of place beside the fire. Taking time off from her studio, she was starting to decorate it and thinking about the look of joy on her daughter's face when the child first saw it. Before that happened, Madeleine would have put the presents – bought for Helena during the previous weeks – under the tree. She was sad that Colbeck would not be there to share his daughter's pleasure.

When she heard a knock on the front door, she hoped that Lydia might have come to help her, but it was a man's voice that drifted into her ear. She went out in the hall and was thrilled to see Constable Hinton on her doorstep. Madeleine dismissed the servant who had opened the door and invited her visitor in, daring to hope that he had brought good news about her husband's latest investigation.

'Do you have a message from Robert?' she asked.

'Not exactly,' he replied, 'but it's all his doing, I'm sure.'

'What is?'

'I've been ordered to join the inspector at once.'

'How wonderful!' she exclaimed.

'Superintendent Tallis sent for me by means of telegraph so I'm on my way to somewhere called Oldbury.'

'It's in the Midlands,' she told him. 'My father described that area as an industrial nightmare, but he always exaggerates.'

'I don't care what it's like, said Hinton, happily, 'because it means that I'll be working on a murder investigation again. Besides, it's always an honour to help Inspector Colbeck.'

'He knows how reliable you are, Alan.'

'I hope so.'

Constable Hinton was a tall, lithe, handsome young man who had been promoted to the Detective Department because of the significant arrests he had made while in the uniform branch. Madeleine had got to know him because he had come to Lydia Quayle's assistance when she was being stalked. Hinton had eventually arrested the man and, during the time spent with Lydia, had grown close to her. Madeleine was delighted to have good news about him to pass on to Lydia. It was, she knew, the reason he had called at the house.

'Do you have any message for your husband?' he asked.

'Tell him that we're praying for his early return,' said Madeleine, 'and, if you will, take the letter from me that I was going to post to him. In your hands, it will reach Robert a day earlier.'

'I'll be glad to act as your courier.'

'Is there anything I can do for you?'

'Well,' he said, trying to sound nonchalant, 'if you happen to see Miss Quayle, you might pass on my good news to her.'

'Pass it on?' she said with a laugh. 'I'll trumpet it. If I didn't do so, Lydia would never forgive me. I'll send a message to her by hand this very day.'

He smiled. 'Thank you. I was hoping you'd say that.'

A crowd of reporters was waiting for Jerome Appleby when he arrived at the works in Oldbury. Demanding some comments on the murder, they surged around him. They had to be content with a prepared statement, which he read out before going into the building. All that they could do was to stand outside and fume. Appleby, meanwhile, went straight to Ernest Drake's office.

'I had to fight my way through a gang of reporters to get here,' he said. 'I daresay that they've been badgering you as well.'

'Mr Innes has been keeping them at bay, sir.'

Appleby peered at him. 'Are you unwell, Ernest?'

'No, sir,' replied Drake, 'I just feel so guilty at having let the family down. You asked me to break the sad news to them but, when I got there, someone had already done so in the most callous way.'

'Yes, I heard about that. It must have added to the family's distress.'

'Their whole world is suddenly in ruins.'

'I'll call at the house myself,' said Appleby. 'Hopefully, the news about the help from Scotland Yard may bring some comfort. I gather that the detectives have already been here.'

'They spent time with Mr Innes before coming here to me. I must say that I admire their thoroughness. They wanted to know everything that had happened in that excursion train before the murder.'

'Where are they now?'

'They've gone to question a suspect.'

Appleby was impressed. 'They've identified someone already?'

'It's a man who used to work here. They're searching for him in Tipton.'

Tipton was one of a cluster of Staffordshire towns transformed out of all recognition by the march of industry. Open fields had given way to coal mines, iron works, chemical factories, and many other enterprises, while rippling streams had been supplanted by a network of canals. Having reached the place by rail, the detectives took a cab to the police station. While Colbeck was buoyant, Leeming was uneasy.

'This could be a wild goose chase, sir,' he said. 'I was only told that Waycroft might be living here with his sister. We've no means of knowing if that's true. Even if it is, we have no idea where this woman is or if she uses a married name.'

'We'll soon find out,' said Colbeck.

'How?'

'When he's inebriated, Waycroft is spoiling for a fight. Look at the way he tackled the works manager, even though the man was big and strong. It suggests that he was far too drunk to consider the consequences.'

'Ah, I see what you mean.'

'If he is here in Tipton, the chances are that he might well have been involved in a drunken brawl in some pub or other. The police will have a record of it – and of his current address.'

'Why didn't I think of that?'

'You're too busy worrying about being stuck here on Christmas Day.'

'I am!' said the other with feeling. 'It's preying on me.'

'We must hope for the best, Victor. Meanwhile, let's enjoy the sights.'

'What sights? This place is as dark and dreary as Oldbury.'

'Tipton is known as the Venice of the Midlands.'

'Is it?' cried Leeming in disbelief. 'All that I can see, hear and smell is heavy industry. My lungs feel as if they're silting up already.'

Jerome Appleby was in a solemn mood. When he went to the Hubbleday house, he took Ernest Drake with him because the accountant was anxious to pay his respects as well. There was no uniformed policeman on duty now. The front door was opened by Hubbleday's brother, Reuben, who looked like a younger, much slimmer version of the works manager. He was in mourning attire. Recognising them, he invited the visitors in, and they stepped into the hall.

'It's good of you to come, Mr Appleby,' he said, shutting the door, 'and that goes for you as well, Mr Drake.'

'We came to offer our condolences,' explained Appleby, 'and, I hope, to offer a shred of comfort. I'm pleased to tell you that the case is in the hands of Scotland Yard detectives who rushed up here from London.'

'That is heartening,' agreed Reuben.

'We want the killer caught and hanged as soon as possible.'

'I share those sentiments.'

Reuben Hubbleday was softly spoken and lacked his brother's underlying truculence. He held a senior position in management at the Chance glassworks.

Appleby lowered his voice. 'How is Dorcas?'

'My sister-in-law is distraught and so are my nieces. If you were hoping to speak to any of them, I'll have to disappoint you. They can't see anyone.'

'I understand. Pass on our condolences.'

'Yes,' said Drake, 'and tell Mrs Hubbleday that, when she is able, she can call on me to give her any details of the excursion that she wishes to hear.'

'I'm sure that Dorcas will take advantage of that offer in due course,' said Reuben. 'At the moment, we're all consumed with grief. My brother was not in the best of health, but I did think he'd survive for some years yet.' He bit his lip. 'It was not to be. His life was snuffed out prematurely.'

Drake had to fight back tears. Appleby put a consoling hand on his arm.

'Unable to come here myself yesterday,' he said, 'I asked Ernest to pass on the dreadful tidings. For reasons we all know, he arrived here too late. What I had also instructed him to say was that I will be responsible for all expenses relating to the funeral.'

'That's very kind of you, Mr Appleby,' said Reuben, 'but that burden should rightly fall on the family.'

'I insist. Your brother was a tower of strength to me. He routinely took care of any vexing problems I had. I intend to show my gratitude to him in this and in other ways. Please make his wife – his widow, I should say – aware of that.'

'I will.'

Appleby noticed that Drake was clearly in discomfort, if not in actual pain. Being in Hubbleday's house had, apparently, brought back vivid memories of what had happened on the excursion. He was feeling oppressed. Opening the front door, Appleby had a few parting words with Reuben Hubbleday, then ushered his companion out. Drake almost stumbled into the fresh air.

'Are you all right, Ernest?' asked Appleby.

'I'm sorry,' said the other. 'It was too much for me.'

'You were fond of Cyril, weren't you?'

'Yes, I was, sir. We were friends.'

* * *

Not for the first time, Colbeck's guess had borne fruit. Samuel Waycroft was not only known to the police, they had given him a stern warning. On each of the two occasions when he had started a fight in a public house, he had spent a night in a cell. Banned by the licensees in both places, he was told by the police that a third lapse would bring serious punishment. Since then, it appeared, he had behaved himself. As they left the police station, the detectives had an address for Waycroft and directions as to how they might get there.

Tipton had almost twice the population of Oldbury, most people working long hours for modest wages. The detectives had to walk through streets where squalor and deprivation were all too apparent. Terraced houses, haphazardly constructed, were on both sides of them. Ragged children were playing in the road and dogs were roaming at will. In one street, a hurdy-gurdy man was grinding out some music at elderly people who watched from their doorways. Much of the sound, however, was crushed beneath the insistent boom of industry. It was an area unused to the sight of two men wearing frock coats and top hats. The detectives collected open-mouthed stares and resentful sneers on all sides.

Leeming was angry. 'Why can't they build decent housing?' he demanded.

'They prefer to maximise profit, Victor.'

'It shouldn't be allowed.'

'I agree, but we've no means of stopping it. Like Oldbury, this place would have been open farmland at the start of the last century. They'd have had a relatively small population.'

'And the people who lived here would have been happy.'

'I wouldn't go that far,' said Colbeck. 'Farm labourers have bleak lives and are out working in all weathers.'

'But they wouldn't have had this continual din in their ears. Anyone close to those steam hammers will be bound to go deaf. It's cruel.'

'Manufacturers would argue that it's a small price to pay for progress.'

'They aren't the ones who lose their hearing.'

Colbeck brought them to a halt with a raised hand. They had reached the street where Samuel Waycroft had been living. Short and narrow, it had refuse piled up in the gutters and the occasional pool of liquid sewage. The house where the Kinchen family lived was halfway down the street. When Leeming knocked on the door, it was opened by a woman so haggard that it was impossible to tell her age. She had a baby in her arms. Two other children, clutching her skirt, stared at the visitors.

'Mrs Kinchen?' asked Colbeck.

'Yes,' she grunted.

'The sergeant and I are detectives from London.'

Her face fell. 'Sam's not in trouble again, is he?'

'We're not certain. We just need to speak to him.'

'He swore it wouldn't happen again and I believed him. Something happens to him when he's had a drink, you see. Miriam couldn't stand it no more.'

'Miriam?'

'That's Sam's wife. When they got thrown out of their

house, she went back with the kids to her parents in Wolverhampton. There's no room for them here, anyway.'

'Where is your brother?' asked Leeming.

'I don't know, sir.'

'It's a crime to conceal information from us.'

'It's the truth,' she said, desperately. 'He goes out looking for work every day. Sam is not a bad man, really. He fought for his country in the Crimean War. Doesn't that count for something?' She broke off as she was seized by a fit of coughing. They waited patiently until she had recovered. 'He means well,' she argued. 'If he's been fighting in a pub again, he knows he'll be locked up even longer.'

'It could be more serious than that, Mrs Kinchen,' said Colbeck.

'What do you mean?' she cried in alarm.

'It's important that we speak to him as soon as possible.'

'Where might he be?' said Leeming.

'I don't know. He didn't come back last night.'

'You must have some idea where he went.'

'Well,' she replied, 'he usually hangs about the canals. He can sometimes pick up work there. Sam is strong and willing. He'll take anything he can get.'

'We heard that he was a good carpenter.'

'Not any more.' Her face clouded. 'He was forced to sell his tools.'

Because of the possibility that he might one day retire there, Edward Tallis was tempted to take a closer look at the town.

A sense of duty, however, kept him at the railway station. He was therefore still sitting in the stationmaster's office when Unwin brought him the telegraph from Colbeck. Agreeing with the inspector, he had acted on his advice to summon Alan Hinton from London. Most of his time was spent sifting the evidence but he broke off occasionally to stretch his legs on the platform and admire the colourful ironwork on the capitals. Tallis was out there when Lady Foley suddenly appeared.

'Good day to you!' he said, doffing his hat slightly. 'I have news for you, Your Ladyship.'

She raised an eyebrow. 'Does it concern an arrest?'

'Not exactly – but it has moved us closer to making one.'

He told her how he had deployed his men and how he expected positive results from them in due course. She seemed mildly pleased.

'Well,' she said, 'I would much rather hear any tidings from you, instead of from that rather unsavoury person you sent to my home.'

'Sergeant Leeming is a brave and competent detective.'

'Does he have to look so scruffy?'

'I have taxed him on that subject,' said Tallis.

'Do so again.'

'Yes, Your Ladyship.'

'The news was welcome,' she conceded, 'even if the messenger was not. I was pleased to hear that you had brought Vellacott to heel. When I get to Worcester, I've a mind to visit the police station to see if the inspector is obeying your orders.'

'He is doing so, Lady Foley. Earlier on, he and I interrogated a suspect he had identified then went off in search of a second man who was of interest to us.'

'Was either of these individuals involved in the crime?'

'The first one most certainly was not. Unhappily, the second was not at home, so we will have to await his return in a couple of days.'

She gave a sniff of displeasure. 'I see.'

'Do you have business in Worcester, may I ask?'

'No, you may not, Superintendent,'

'Oh, I do beg your pardon.'

She regarded him with something vaguely akin to interest. 'Inspector Vellacott and you are chalk and cheese,' she said. 'He is exactly what one would expect of a provincial policeman, but you have more of a military bearing.'

'I am proud to have served Queen and country for many years.'

'And so you should be.'

'Before I moved to Scotland Yard, I was based in India.'

'In that case, you must talk to Colonel Yardley.'

'Why is that?'

'He spent some years in the subcontinent as well. The colonel is a most interesting man. He dines with me occasionally.'

Turning abruptly away, she went into her private waiting

room. Tallis was not offended by her rudeness. He was too busy digesting the news that there was a fellow army officer in the area. More to the point, the man was deemed fit to sit at Lady Foley's dining table. Great Malvern suddenly took on an increased appeal for him.

Alone in his gun room, Colonel Yardley polished the rifle with exquisite care, holding it up to the window from time to time to inspect it. When he was satisfied with his work, he replaced it carefully on the two vacant hooks in the cabinet. After standing back to admire his arsenal, he locked the door of the cabinet and went out.

Within its boundaries, Tipton had over thirteen miles of navigable waterways. As they walked through the streets, Leeming was mesmerised by the sight of so much water.

'I did tell you that it was the Venice of the Midlands,' Colbeck said.

'Do the canals in Italy look as filthy and smell as foul as these do?' asked Leeming. 'I'd hate to spend my day sailing up and down these dirty black strips of water. I'd keep waiting for a dead dog to surface.'

'The people of Tipton are justly proud of the system. It makes the movement of heavy goods so easy. Ah,' Colbeck went on as another canal came into view. 'Let's see if we have more luck here.'

'This will be the third one we've stopped at.'

'Try to enjoy the walk, Victor. It's healthy for us.'

'I felt ill the moment we arrived in the town.'

'You'll adjust in due course. You always do.'

Colbeck led the way to a narrowboat moored nearby. The bargee was a weather-beaten old man with a clay pipe in his mouth and a cap set back on his head to expose the endless array of wrinkles on his forehead. As they approached him, he put down the rope he was coiling and gave them a cautious nod.

'Good day to yow,' he said in his strong local accent.

'We're looking for a man named Samuel Waycroft,' explained Colbeck. 'I'm told he's in his late thirties and very sturdy.'

'Waycroft . . . ?'

'I daresay that everyone calls him Sam.'

'Oh, we got Sams galore round 'ere, sir. I've a brother called Sam.'

'We're not interested in him,' said Leeming, impatiently. 'We're policemen from London and we're very anxious to speak to this man.'

'Why?'

'That's our business.'

'Is yower Sam in trouble?'

'He could well be.'

'Can't help yow,' said the old man. 'Why're yow searchin' here?'

'We were told that he often sought work on the canals.'

'Doin' what?'

'Whatever he can get,' added Colbeck. 'He's a skilled

carpenter but his sister said that he can turn his hand to almost anything.'

'Yow 'ave to be like that if yow live on the cut. Tell yow what, sirs. Walk for five minutes in that direction,' he advised, using a skeletal finger to point, 'and yow'll come to a basin, loik. Lots of narrowboats are tied up there. It's the sort of place your Sam might have gone.'

'Thank you very much.' As they walked away, Colbeck turned to Leeming. 'There was no need to be so irritable with him.'

'I didn't mean to be, sir.'

'What's got into you, Victor?'

'Canals bring back awful memories.'

Colbeck laughed. 'Ah, I'm with you now,' he said. 'You're talking about the Cotswolds.'

'I hated having to leg that narrowboat through a long, dark tunnel.'

'What about me? I was the one who went into the water to retrieve the dead body. I still have nightmares about that.'

'But it's not the only reason I'm on edge, sir,' confessed Leeming. 'I keep asking the same question. Will I get to see Estelle and the boys on Christmas Day? If I'm not at home with them, it will be . . . unnatural.'

'I face the same problem, Victor. That's why we must redouble our efforts and hope that Hinton arrives soon to help us. Meanwhile, let's head for this canal basin. Sooner or later, someone is bound to have heard of Samuel Waycroft.'

Walking through a backstreet, he came to a pub named the Rose and Crown. The sound of laughter from within made him stop and listen. He felt the pull of temptation. He thrust his hand into his pocket and took out his remaining few coins. As he realised how little money he had, he remembered his promise to his sister. Samuel Waycroft thrust the coins back into his pocket and strode on.

'Oh!' cried Lydia. 'It's absolutely beautiful!'

'Do you think that it will do?' asked Madeleine.

'It's absolutely perfect.'

'I've spent ages working on it.'

'You've done a wonderful job,' said Lydia, gazing at the decorations on the Christmas tree. 'You have the touch of a true artist. Helena will be delighted.'

'We'll soon see. I was just about to bring her down when you arrived.'

'Then that's an extra bonus. I really came in response to the letter you sent me about Alan's news. I want to know absolutely everything he told you.'

'That will have to wait,' said Madeleine. 'Helena comes first – and my father, of course. He's in the nursery with her.' She headed for the door. 'I'll fetch the pair of them immediately.'

While she waited, Lydia took a closer look at the tree. Most of the decorations had been bought at Hamley's but there were several that had obviously been made by Madeleine herself. The best example was the fairy princess at the very top of the tree, carefully fashioned out of wire and silver painted paper. It positively dazzled. Hearing the child's squeals of delight, she went into the hall to welcome Helena, who ran into her arms to receive a warm hug. In her role as an auxiliary aunt, Lydia was always thrilled by the child's fondness for her. Caleb Andrews gave Lydia a welcoming smile then told his granddaughter to close her eyes before they took her into the drawing room.

'And no peeping,' warned Madeleine. 'Do you promise?'

'Yes,' said Helena, closing her eyes.

Holding her mother's hand, she was led into the room with Lydia and Andrews behind her. Helena was now approaching her fifth Christmas but it had retained every bit of its novelty for her. When she was told to open her eyes, she stared at the tree in amazement, transfixed by the lighted candles and by the fairy princess. She clapped her hands gleefully.

'I think that we can safely say that she approves,' observed Lydia.

'You did a grand job decorating the tree, Maddy,' said Andrews. 'It's even better than last year's.'

'Yes, it is,' added Helena.

'That's right, darling.' He lifted her up in his arms. 'Mummy is so clever.'

'Letting her see it for the first time is always such a treat,' said Madeleine. 'It's just such a pity that Robert had to miss this special moment. I've been praying that he'll be here for Christmas Day itself. And if my husband is here,' she added with a smile at Lydia, 'it may even be that Alan Hinton will pop in at some point.'

'Is that a promise?' asked Lydia.

'No,' said Andrews, gloomily. 'Face the truth, Maddy. We all know that Robert is going to be trapped in the Black Country for eternity.'

When they questioned the owner of a narrowboat in the canal basin, they finally made some progress. He told Colbeck and Leeming that he had employed Samuel Waycroft a fortnight earlier to make repairs to the vessel.

'Did he do a good job?' asked Colbeck.

'Yes, he did,' replied the other, a stringy man with a fringe beard. 'Best carpenter we ever had, though he had to borrow our tools, mind you. I liked him but my son didn't take to him, though.'

'Why not?'

'Sam was too surly.'

'What do you mean?'

'Well,' said the man, 'when Rob – that's my son – asked him to go to a pub for a drink, Waycroft refused. Matter of fact, he was downright nasty. If it hadn't been for the good work he did, I'd have tossed him into the cut.'

'Have you any idea where he is now?' asked Leeming.

'Searching for work elsewhere, I suppose. What he'd really like is full-time work on a narrowboat like this, but them jobs go to people as is born to it. We don't teck just anyone.'

'When did you last see him?'

'It was yesterday, Sergeant. He walked past me in the street with a big grin on his ugly face.'

'I thought you said he was surly.'

'That was earlier – when he worked here. There was nothing surly about him yesterday. He was almost jaunty – as if he had something good to celebrate.'

The detectives made the same deduction.

CHAPTER EIGHT

While he was enjoying the change of scene, Edward Tallis was also missing his office in Scotland Yard. Seated behind his desk, he coped each day with a never-ending stream of crimes, assigning detectives, giving them orders, studying their interim reports, berating those who made slow progress. The sense of power was almost dizzying and there was always a buzz of excitement in the air. Single-handed, he liked to think, Tallis was helping to cleanse the capital of its villains.

There was no such feeling in Great Malvern. He was leading a murder investigation from the stationmaster's office yet felt strangely detached from it. Back in London, he would be working without a break throughout an entire day. Dozens of people would come and go. Masses of information would pour in. All that happened in the pleasant county of Worcester was that he had an occasional chat with Harold Unwin to break up the long, leaden periods alone.

On the other hand, he reminded himself, he was there for a secondary purpose. He might well be sitting close to his future home. Tallis felt a sudden urge to inspect it more closely. Granting himself some unprecedented freedom, he began the walk uphill to the town. As he did so, he recalled Unwin telling him that, when the idea of railway access was first mooted, Lady Foley insisted that the station was built well away from the town itself so that Great Malvern's rural feel was not compromised. Tallis now began to relish that feel. It was oddly seductive. When his long strides got him within sight of the Priory, he stopped to marvel at its sheer beauty. Attending worship in such a place every Sunday would be a source of pleasure as well as inspiration.

He hurried on towards it, hoping to see it at close quarters and immerse himself in its charm. Sundays in London were often spent working at Scotland Yard. Here, they would be occasions of peace and devotion. The town's pull on him strengthened. Before he reached the entrance to the Priory, however, he saw Ruby Renshaw coming out, wearing the same idiosyncratic attire as earlier. When she beamed at him, he touched the brim of his top hat by way of welcome.

'We meet again, Mrs Renshaw,' he said.

'That's what happens in a small place like this.'

'I thought it was invaded by excursionists from the Midlands.'

'Only in the warmer months,' she explained. 'People do come for the Water Cure at this time of year, but they don't get under our feet.'

'How would you describe life here?'

'Most of the time, it's wonderful.'

'You'd recommend it, then?'

'I can only speak as a hotelier and a long-time resident. I'm not sure if it would suit a man with your interests.'

'My interests have been focussed on fighting crime,' he said, 'and it has made my life seem important to me. But it has also been exhausting.'

'Nothing really happens here,' she said.

'How can you say that when a murder was committed only a mile away?'

'That was a freakish event. It won't happen again for a long time. When I told you about my visions, I didn't mention that they were few and far between. Until yesterday, I hadn't experienced one for almost a year.'

'I see.'

'You believe it was a coincidence, don't you?'

'I'm afraid that I do.'

'What if it happens again?'

'We'll be long gone before that happens.'

Ruby looked at him shrewdly. 'Will you?' she asked. 'At the moment, you might live in a big city, but I have a strange feeling that you might learn to like Great Malvern – and it would certainly like you.'

Tallis was taken aback.

On the train journey there, Alan Hinton was in a state of suppressed excitement. When he reached the industrial Midlands, however, that excitement began to wane. All that he could see through the window was an unbroken succession of towers and chimneys, belching out smoke that hung in the sky like a thick, dark pall. On the previous occasion when he'd worked on a murder investigation with Colbeck, he had been based in Cambridge, a university town with clean air, pleasant views, and a sense of history. His latest assignment, he feared, would have none of those benefits.

Arriving in Oldbury, his spirits rose when he saw that Colbeck was there to welcome him. After an exchange of greetings, they hired a cab to take them to the Railway Carriage and Wagon Works.

'I was hoping I'd be in time to meet you,' said Colbeck. 'Sergeant Leeming is in Tipton. I've just come from there.'

'I see.'

'Let me bring you up to date with events here.'

'Before you do that, sir,' said Hinton, taking a letter from his pocket, 'I was asked to deliver this from your wife.'

'I was hoping you would act as a postman,' said Colbeck, slipping the missive into his pocket. 'Reading that is a treat that will have to wait.'

He gave his companion a brief account of developments

in the case before handing him a sheet of paper. Hinton stared at thirteen names.

'Who are these men?' he asked.

'They are former employees at the Works. All of them were summarily dismissed by Mr Hubbleday, so they left with a grudge against him. One of them may have wanted revenge and been party to a plan to kill him. Ignore the last name on that list,' advised Colbeck. 'The sergeant is currently searching for him in Tipton.'

'What am I supposed to do, sir?'

'Go through these names one by one. As you can see, Mr Innes, who provided the list, was kind enough to specify which trade each of these men followed. Talk to their workmates and find out all you can about the twelve individuals.'

'I see.'

'Waycroft stands out because he tried to assault Mr Hubbleday, but it's by no means certain that he was involved in the murder. There was bad blood between the works manager and all twelve of the men listed.'

Hinton grinned. 'I'm glad it's not thirteen, sir.'

'Why – are you superstitious?'

'No, but I feel safer dealing with a round dozen.'

'They'll be more than enough to keep you occupied.'

'How many are employed at the Works?'

'Eight hundred or more.'

Hinton gasped. 'As many as that?'

'It's a thriving concern,' said Colbeck. 'They work hard

to meet the demand at home and abroad. Appleby carriages and wagons have an excellent name in the trade.'

'What about the murder victim?'

'Cyril Hubbleday was an efficient works manager, by all accounts. However, he does seem to have enjoyed throwing his weight about.'

'In other words,' said Hinton, 'he made lots of enemies.'

Colbeck turned to him. 'Let me put it another way – he made few friends.'

On receipt of the terrible news about her husband, Dorcas Hubbleday had collapsed. She was so grief-stricken that a doctor had to be summoned to give her a sedative. Her daughters were equally horrified but strong enough to bear the shock and devote themselves to supporting their mother. The elder of them, Marion, came downstairs and went into the drawing room where her uncle was seated.

'How is your mother?' asked Reuben.

'She's still unable to believe what happened.'

'The same could be said of all of us, Marion. It was a bolt from the blue.'

'He was such a wonderful father,' she said, holding back tears. 'I can't understand why anyone would want to murder him.'

'The killer will be caught and punished.'

'We might take satisfaction from that, Uncle Reuben, but it won't bring Father back, will it? He's gone for good.'

'Don't distress yourself by brooding on it.'

'I can't help it.'

Marion was an attractive woman in her early twenties with an elfin face now pockmarked with sadness. Having provided support and comfort to her mother and to her younger sister, Marion was now in need of them herself. She sat on the sofa beside her uncle and dabbed at her eyes with a handkerchief.

'Is it true that Mr Appleby will take care of all the arrangements?' she said.

'He's insisting on it.'

'He's always been so generous to us.'

'It's no more than you deserve. Your father effectively ran the Works.'

'He so loved doing it,' she recalled. 'The only problem was that he devoted himself so much to his job that we saw precious little of him.'

'You and your sister were always in his thoughts, Marion – along with your mother, of course. My brother lived for his family.' He squeezed her hands gently. 'Listen,' he warned. 'There are going to be problems ahead. Please remember that you can call on us at any time. Your aunt and I will help in any way. Pass on that message to your mother and sister. Let us take some of the burden off your shoulders.'

'Thank you, Uncle Reuben.'

'There'll be help from another source as well,' he went on, releasing her hands. 'When Mr Drake called here earlier with Mr Appleby, he was visibly shaken. After all, he was there when . . . when it happened.'

'Yes, I know.'

'He seems to have recovered now. I had a letter from him, delivered by courier half an hour ago. He offered to assist me in sorting out your father's financial affairs. To be frank, it's something I was dreading. I'll be happy to let him help me.'

'Mr Drake is such an odd man, isn't he?'

'Why do you say that?'

'Well, he was always so shy when he came here.'

'I don't know him well,' said Reuben, 'but I get the impression that he's not at ease in female company.'

'He came to spend time with Father, not with us.'

'What did they talk about together?'

'I don't know,' she said. 'They went off to the study and played chess all evening. It used to annoy Mother. She wanted Father to be with us instead.'

Reuben was pensive. 'I didn't realise my brother was that close to Mr Drake.'

For the benefit of his visitors, Ernest Drake recounted the events that led up to the murder. Colbeck and Hinton were attentive listeners. The inspector had wanted his companion to hear exactly what had happened on the excursion. For his part, he collected significant details not mentioned before. When Drake's recitation was over, he looked at Hinton.

'Welcome to Oldbury,' he said. 'What do you know

about the construction of carriages and wagons?'

'Next to nothing,' confessed Hinton.

'Then you are in for an education.'

'Most of the men in that list are either carpenters or smithies,' noted Drake. 'Then there's one from the saw mill and another from the paint shop. Oh, a warning to you – be prepared to shout if the steam hammer gets going.'

'Thanks for the warning,' said Hinton.

'I think you should talk to Mr Innes. He'll be able to tell you something about each man on that list.'

'You'll be speaking to their friends,' warned Colbeck. 'They'll be defensive.'

'I'll remember that, sir,' said Hinton. 'But thank you, Mr Drake. Having heard what happened on the excursion, I feel a little more prepared than I had been. What you told us about Mr Hubbleday has made things a lot clearer.'

'I just want you to catch the devil responsible for Cyril's death,' said Drake with a surge of passion. 'It will be the best possible Christmas present for me.'

Victor Leeming was slowly learning to like Tipton. Left alone to continue the search, he adjusted to the local dialect and began to hear exactly what was being said. While he still aroused a few jeers as he walked around the town, he was either tolerated or ignored by most people. Along the way, his keen ear picked up snatches of conversation. He heard two men discussing the races in which their whippets would compete and a bevy of women complaining yet again about the dirt that soiled their washing when it was put out on the line. Another general topic was the poor quality of the beer.

'They don't brew it proper,' said one voice. 'They sell the bloody stuff before it's ready.'

''Tis why us gets them belly-aches,' agreed another.

By keeping to the bank of one canal, Leeming picked up two mentions of Samuel Waycroft. One related to a day he'd spent loading cargo onto a narrowboat but the other was more interesting. He learnt from a man sitting on an upturned bucket beside the canal that someone called Sam had sailed off for the whole day to somewhere beyond Birmingham.

'Him'll be back 'ere termorrer,' said the man.

'At what time?' asked Leeming.

'Who knows?'

'Will they moor somewhere near this spot?'

'Daresay they will, sir.'

'But this man didn't give his full name, you say?'

'He's called Sam and he sounds just like the fella as you told me about.'

'And he said he was a carpenter, did he?'

'Aye, he did.'

It was enough for Leeming. He resolved to be back there the next day.

Returning to the railway station, Tallis found a clutch of telegraphs awaiting him. All related to other cases for which he was responsible. After drafting replies to each one, he went to the telegraph station and had his orders dispatched. It gave him the feeling that he was still in touch with Scotland Yard and not stranded in a rural backwater. He was back in the stationmaster's office when a train came in. As he glanced through the window, he saw passengers alighting and picked out one of them immediately. It was an elderly, straight-backed man of medium height. Alert and well-dressed, he carried a cane that he rapped on the platform as he walked. Seizing the opportunity to introduce himself, Tallis went swiftly out of the office.

'Colonel Yardley?' he asked, intercepting the man.

'Yes,' replied the other, coming to a halt. 'Who might you be, sir?'

'I'm Detective Superintendent Tallis from Scotland Yard and I'm leading the investigation into a murder that occurred not far from here.'

'Then more power to your elbow, dear fellow. I saw mention of the crime in the morning paper. It's outrageous that someone dared to tarnish our reputation for safety. Hunt the villain down.'

'We are endeavouring to do so, Colonel.'

'How did you know my name?'

'Lady Foley happened to mention you.'

'Ah,' said Yardley with a ripe chuckle, 'you've met Emily, have you?'

'It was she who summoned us here.'

'That's typical of her. She has the habit of command. I

acquired it in the army, but Emily was born with it. How do you find her?'

'Lady Foley is . . . rather forthright.'

'Your description of her is too kind,' said Yardley. 'Most people view her as a harridan and many of them have felt the sting of her tongue. In essence, however, she is a kind-hearted soul, robbed of her husband far too early and maintaining the standards of behaviour here that he helped to set.' He narrowed an eye. 'What prompted her to mention my name?'

'I told her that I had once served in India.'

'What a coincidence! Simply by looking at you, I guessed that you'd been in the army but had no idea that it had taken you to the subcontinent. Emily will have told you that I, too, spent many years in India.'

'That's correct, Colonel.'

'We must get together and compare our experiences.'

'I'd appreciate the opportunity,' said Tallis, warmly. 'First, however, there's the small matter of solving a murder. That must always remain my priority.'

Before he sent Hinton off on his search for information, Colbeck explained to him how carriages and wagons were built, and what sort of craftsmen he was likely to meet in the course of his work. The detective constable listened intently.

'A typical carriage,' said the inspector, 'comprises an almost entirely wooden body. It's mounted on a wooden subframe with iron or steel running and drawgear.'

'You've lost me already, sir,' confessed Hinton.

'The body framework is usually oak or teak.'

'They're expensive woods, aren't they?'

'Yes, they are – especially as they will probably be imported. Mr Appleby insists on the best materials. Oak and teak are also used for the exterior body panelling.'

'What about the roof?'

'That will be made of oak or deal boards, covered in canvas.'

'How do you know all this, Inspector?'

'I've got a fascination with detail.'

'You told me to start off among the painters.'

'That's right,' said Colbeck. 'Only one person of interest to us worked there – a man named Will Ashton. Brace yourself for the pervasive smell of varnish. They apply several coats to protect the paintwork.' He laughed at the expression on Hinton's face. 'Don't look so surprised, Alan. My father-in-law worked on the railway all his life, remember. He loves to talk to me about it.'

'I'll make a start at once, sir,' said Hinton, looking at a name on the list. 'Why was Will Ashton sacked?'

'The records say it was because he was a poor timekeeper, but he may have upset Mr Hubbleday in another way. Find out what it was.'

'I will.'

'Try to win the men's confidence before you press them. If you're too heavy-handed, you'll get a poor response. You need to coax information out of them. Right,' said Colbeck. 'Off you go to the first of the paint shops.'

Hinton was surprised. 'There's more than one of them?'

'Oh, yes. There are lots of carriages to paint.'

Though it would involve a long walk, Leeming decided to pay a second visit to Waycroft's sister in the hope of squeezing more information out of her. At their first encounter, she had been stunned by the news that her brother was being sought by the police as a matter of urgency. Having had time to let the implications sink in, she would realise how serious a position Waycroft was now in.

When he reached the house, Leeming did not need to knock on the door because Mrs Kinchen had spotted him through the window. Leaving the children inside the house, she came out in a slightly more aggressive mood.

'What's going on?' she demanded, arms folded across her chest.

'We're still hunting your brother, Mrs Kinchen.'

'But you won't tell me why.'

'He could be involved in a serious crime,' said Leeming.

'Never!' she exclaimed. 'Sam's got his faults – don't I know it – but he's not a criminal. He'd never break the law on purpose.'

'He might if he was desperate.'

'Only if he'd been drinking. That's what changes him, see. When Sam is sober, he wouldn't hurt a fly. He's wonderful with my children. They love him to bits. I can't believe that he'd do . . . well, anything serious.'

'Does he own a weapon of any kind?'

The question startled her. 'No, no, he doesn't . . .'

Leeming saw the look in her eyes. 'I think you're lying to me, Mrs Kinchen.'

'It's the truth. Sam's got no money – that's why he had to sell his tools.'

'What else did he sell?'

'Nothing.'

'Tell the truth.'

'That's what I'm doing,' she insisted.

'Your brother was in the army, wasn't he? When soldiers are discharged, they usually try to keep souvenirs. Sailors like tattoos but soldiers prefer weapons. Is that what your brother did, Mrs Kinchen?' He saw her quail and take a step backwards. 'It was a rifle, wasn't it?'

'He made me promise to tell nobody about it.'

'Did he sell it?'

'No, he didn't.'

'Then it's somewhere in the house.'

'It isn't, I swear it. My husband wouldn't let him keep it there.'

'So where has he hidden it?'

'Sam didn't tell us.'

'Are you quite sure of that?' he asked, intensifying his tone.

'Yes, I am,' she bleated. 'We only took him in if he agreed to behave himself. Next thing we know, the police have locked him up for fighting – twice in a row. My husband warned him that he could only stay if he got rid of that gun. It frightened us, having it here. What if the children started playing with it?'

'I understand, Mrs Kinchen,' said Leeming, taking pity on her. 'I've got children of my own. I know what scamps they can be sometimes. As for your brother,' he added, confidently, 'we'll find him. Nobody escapes us.'

It was late in the afternoon when Colbeck finally had the opportunity of a conversation alone with Jerome Appleby. The latter was full of apologies.

'I'm sorry to have kept you waiting, Inspector,' he said, 'but I had a long list of things to do when I finally got here. Not least among them was a visit to Cyril Hubbleday's family and a tour of the whole Works.'

Colbeck was puzzled. 'A tour?'

'The entire workforce is devastated by the murder. Wild theories are already flying about. I felt that I ought to make an appearance to assure everyone that the case was in good hands, and that there was no point in idle speculation.'

'That was very considerate of you, sir.'

'I value a personal connection with my employees.'

'That makes you rather . . . individual.'

Appleby smiled. 'Business rivals use much coarser words than that.'

They were in his office, a large, well-appointed room with a window that looked out on to the saw mill. The office was purely functional. Shelves were stacked with ledgers on three walls, leaving no room for pictures of any kind. There was a pile of correspondence on the desk. Seated behind it, Appleby looked very much at home. He took a moment to weigh up his visitor.

'Does the name of Robert Owen mean anything to you, Inspector?'

'Yes, of course,' said Colbeck. 'I remember him well. He was given a share of his father-in-law's mills in New Lanark and made himself the dominant partner. Owen believed that, if you treat employees well, you get the best results out of them.'

'Exactly!'

'He not only gave them a decent wage, he built a model factory, a model village and a model school for them.'

'His example inspired me,' said Appleby. 'It's not necessary to exploit employees or to impose punitive hours on them. That's what he said. He took a paternal attitude towards them. I've tried to do the same with my workers.'

'Hence the excursions you arrange for them.'

'Yes – other industrialists think I'm mad.'

'I applaud what you've done, sir,' said Colbeck. 'Mind you, Owen had great success at first, but he went too far when he began to establish farming villages based on common ownership. Some were successful but many failed miserably. I think he was ahead of his time. The world is not yet ready for his advanced ideas.'

'I agree, Inspector. I'd never try to create the utopia that he envisaged. But I do follow his example when it comes to treating my employees well. They're human beings, after all, not worker ants.'

'The results speak for themselves, Mr Appleby. You've built up one of the most successful enterprises in the Black Country.' He leant forward slightly. 'What I'd dearly like to know is if Mr Hubbleday shared your paternal attitude.'

Appleby sighed. 'Only to a very limited extent.'

'Then why did you employ such a man?'

'He was remarkably good at his job, Inspector.'

'Even though he created enemies as he did so?' asked Colbeck. 'You see, I believe that someone who worked for you is involved in the murder. He might not have fired the fatal shot, but he somehow assisted the person who did.'

'That's a chilling thought,' admitted Appleby.

'It's the reason I needed the help of another officer, someone who can make his way through the Works and get closer to your employees.'

'You have a free hand to do whatever you wish, Inspector.'

'Thank you, sir.'

'But I'll be very upset to discover that I once paid the wages of a killer.'

'There will be a consolation.'

'Will there?'

'Yes,' said Colbeck. 'You'll have the satisfaction of knowing that we managed to root him out.'

'You actually went on that excursion?' asked Alan Hinton.

'Yes, I did,' said Derek Churt. 'I took my wife and son.'

'Then you must have heard the gunshot that was fired.'

'We all heard it. Then Mr Drake went to each compartment in turn to explain that a cow had wandered onto the line and had to be put down.'

'Derek didn't believe him,' said another man.

'I knew something serious had occurred,' added Churt.

'Why was that?' said Hinton.

He listened carefully to the painter, noting the air of confidence with which he recounted the details. Evidently, he had already shared them with his workmates because they made comments as he went along. They were obviously proud that Churt, a natural leader among them, was not fooled by the excuse that a cow had been shot dead on the track.

'Derek knew that something nasty had happened,' said one of them.

'Yes,' added another. 'When he saw the empty chair at the top table in Mr Appleby's house, he began to suspect that a human being was under that tarpaulin.'

'It had to be Mr Hubbleday,' said Churt.

'How did you feel about that?' asked Hinton.

'What do you mean?'

'The works manager was leading the excursion, wasn't he? It must have been a terrible shock to realise that he'd been killed. How did you react?'

'I felt numb,' said Churt.

'That's not what you told us, Derek,' said one of the others.

'Yes, it is,' snapped Churt, shooting him a glare. 'I

couldn't believe it at first. It seemed impossible. Why would anyone pick out Mr Hubbleday? He'd led excursions lots of times and there was never any trouble. Then, out of the blue, someone shoots him dead. I was completely confused.'

'When did your mind clear?' said Hinton.

'It took ages.'

'And how did you feel then – shocked, saddened, frightened it might have happened to you?' He heard a muffled laugh from one of the other painters. 'How did you get on with Mr Hubbleday?'

'He was our boss. We did whatever he told us.'

'Was he easy-going or a bit of a martinet?'

'He was strict – but, then, he had to be in his job.'

'How do you feel now?'

'I'm still getting used to the idea that we've lost him for good.'

'So am I,' said someone with quiet relish.

'Why do you say that?' asked Hinton, turning on the man. 'Didn't you like Mr Hubbleday?'

'Nobody likes bosses,' replied the other.

'Mr Appleby is your real boss. Do you dislike him as well?'

'No, no . . .'

'What he means,' said Churt, speaking up, 'is that we all appreciate what Mr Appleby's done for us. No other craftsmen in this town get treated so well. He makes us feel as if we're part of a huge family.'

'Was the works manager part of that family?' asked Hinton.

'Well . . . yes, he was.'

'You don't sound very sure about that.'

'We respected Mr Hubbleday.'

'That's not the same as admiring him, the way that you clearly admire Mr Appleby. How will you feel on the day when Mr Hubbleday's funeral is held?'

'I'll feel sorry for his family,' said Churt.

'No tears left for the works manager himself?'

'None at all,' muttered someone.

'I was asking Mr Churt,' said Hinton.

'I'd rather not say,' confessed Churt.

'Why not?'

'It's because you're here to spy on us. If any of us criticise Mr Hubbleday in any way, you'll report us and we'd lose our jobs. I've said all I'm going to about our late boss except this.' He took a deep breath. 'He earned his wages. Mr Hubbleday worked harder than anyone I know. That's how I'll remember him.'

'Then that's how I'll remember you, Mr Churt,' said Hinton, taking out his notebook and writing something into it. He looked around the faces. 'Yes, I know what you're thinking. How can an outsider like me understand how difficult it is to work under the thumb of a tyrannical boss.'

'That's exactly what he was,' said a voice.

'Then you have my sympathy. Ever since I joined the Metropolitan Police Force, I've had to work under someone who also loves to impose discipline on those beneath him.' Hinton smiled. 'And I fancy that my boss would have put your Mr Hubbleday in the shade.'

After going to the telegraph station to see if there were any messages for him, Tallis left empty-handed. Feeling more isolated than ever, he went back to the office he was using and flopped into a chair. To stave off boredom, he sifted through some out-of-date periodicals belonging to the stationmaster. None held his attention. When he picked up an old local newspaper, however, his interest was immediately sparked. It contained a photograph of the man who had recently won a shooting competition.

His name was Colonel Yardley.

CHAPTER NINE

Victor Leeming left Tipton with a measure of optimism. He felt that he was slowly getting closer to his quarry. As soon as he arrived back in Oldbury, he reported to Colbeck at the Works. The detectives had been given the use of an office that was small and rather bare but nevertheless serviceable. While Leeming delivered his report, Colbeck listened with approval.

'You've done well, Victor,' he said at the conclusion. 'Go back to that canal tomorrow and wait until Waycroft returns.'

'It could be a long wait, sir.'

'However long, you have to be there when he steps off that barge.'

'They call them narrowboats around here.'

'I stand corrected,' said Colbeck. 'While you were watching narrowboats going up and down the canal, I've made some interesting discoveries. I've also set Alan Hinton to work on the people on that list we were given.'

'He's not touching Samuel Waycroft,' said Leeming, possessively. 'He's all mine. Make that clear.'

'Hinton wouldn't dream of poaching him from you.'

'Good – now what's your news, sir?'

Colbeck told him about Hinton's arrival and what instructions the newcomer had been given. He then talked at length about Appleby's philosophy and how it led to a fatherly attitude towards his employees.

'However,' he added, 'his concern for his workforce has not prevented him from making a vast amount of money and living in a magnificent house. He mixes paternalism with profit.'

'I wish we had someone like him at Scotland Yard,' said Leeming. 'We're never going to get that sort of kind treatment from the superintendent. He enjoys having the whip hand over us.'

'We've learnt to live with it.'

'Yes, we grit our teeth and endure the pain.'

'It doesn't hurt any more.'

'I've just thought – where is Alan going to stay? There's room for him at our hotel in Great Malvern.'

'He needs to be closer to here,' said Colbeck. 'Mr Drake has given me the addresses of a few places. Once we've got him settled into one of them, we'll return to Mrs Renshaw on our own.'

'That's a relief. Fresh air once again!'

'I'm thinking of the wonderful food we get there. First,' he went on, 'we'll have to report to the superintendent.'

'Couldn't you do that for both of us, sir?'

'No, Victor, he'll want to hear what you've been up to in your own words.'

'If he's not at the railway station, we might have a chance to peep inside the Imperial Hotel.'

'That's where wealthy people stay when they come for the Water Cure.'

'Talking of which,' said Leeming, 'what exactly is it?'

Light had faded almost completely, and the temperature had fallen even lower. Tallis felt that it was time to abandon his vigil. He first went to the telegraph station, but no messages awaited him. Before he headed for his hotel, he had a last word with Unwin.

'What do you make of Colonel Yardley?' he asked.

The stationmaster measured his words. 'I don't really know him, sir.'

'He seems to have settled in well here.'

'That's true. He's very sociable and has built up a circle of friends. They love to hear his stories about army life.'

'I noticed in your newspaper that he won a shooting competition.'

'It happens every time one is held,' said Unwin,

chuckling. 'Some people refuse to enter any competition because they know they'll be beaten by him.'

'Is he married?'

'Oh, yes, but his wife is an invalid. We rarely see her.'

'Why did they come to this part of the world?'

'The colonel had heard about the properties of Malvern water and thought that it might help to improve his wife's health. When she spent six weeks here, having the Water Cure, they decided they would move to the area permanently. Colonel Yardley bought an estate famed for its game birds.'

'I thought that you didn't really know him.'

'You pick up things in my job, sir.'

'Then you can pick up something for me,' said Tallis with heavy-handed humour. 'I need the key to that secret passage. Unlock the door for me, please, and I will retire to my hotel.'

'Very good, Superintendent.'

'Oh, and if my officers turn up here . . .'

'Yes, sir?'

'Tell them where they can find me.'

Before they left the town, Colbeck and Leeming accompanied Alan Hinton to his hotel. It was small and dowdy, but it had the virtue of being within walking distance of the Works. As they strolled along, Hinton was able to tell them about his experiences with the firm's painters.

'You were right about the varnish, Inspector,' he said.

'Every shop reeked of it. I'd hate to inhale that stink throughout my working day.'

'It's better than smelling the superintendent's cigars,' said Leeming, pulling a face.

'Let Alan finish his report,' suggested Colbeck.

'Sorry, sir.'

'There's not much to tell you,' Hinton apologised. 'I took your advice and tried to win them over, but I never really succeeded. They were too wary. They don't like policemen in uniform or out of it.'

'Did anyone arouse your interest?' asked Colbeck.

'Oddly enough, one man did.'

'What was his name?'

'Derek Churt. He seemed to be the spokesman for the first group I questioned. There was a good reason for that. Unlike the others, he'd been on the excursion. He told me several things about it that were new to me.'

'Did any of them feel sorry for what happened to Mr Hubbleday?'

'They pretended to be,' said Hinton, 'but I could see that they viewed it as a bonus. The works manager was detested.'

'Why?'

'He strutted about as if he owned the place.'

'Just like Superintendent Tallis,' complained Leeming.

'Yes, but he doesn't sack people at short notice. Hubbleday did that all the time, it seems. They had to be on their best behaviour when he was around.'

'Tell me more about this fellow, Churt,' said Colbeck.

'He's very good at his job,' said Hinton. 'I can tell you that. He was painting the side of a carriage when I went in there. It was so ornate. He left it gleaming.'

'You told us that he was a sort of spokesman.'

'Yes, the others looked up to him.'

'Who went on the excursion with him?'

'His wife and young son.'

'Did they enjoy the outing?'

'Mrs Churt and their son did,' said Hinton, 'because they had no idea what had happened when they heard the gunshot. Churt was different. He soon guessed that the works manager must have been shot.'

'Guessed?' echoed Colbeck. 'Did it eventually dawn on him, or did he know in advance what would happen?'

Derek Churt arrived back home to a welcome from his wife. After washing his hands at the sink in the scullery, he sat down in the living room with her.

'What kind of day have you had?' asked Agnes.

'It was much the same as usual until a detective from London turned up.'

She was worried. 'What was he doing there?'

'Asking us lots of questions,' he replied.

'Was it about Mr Hubbleday?'

He was surprised. 'You've heard, then?'

'Mrs Higgins told me. It's all over the town.'

Churt grinned. 'Mrs Higgins can spread gossip faster than anyone I know.'

'She was shocked,' said Agnes. 'And so was I. It's frightening, really. I mean, we spoke to Mr Hubbleday on the station platform but, before we even got to where we were going, he was shot dead. Things like that just don't happen.'

'More's the pity,' murmured Churt.

'What did you say?'

'Nothing.'

'What did your friends in the paint shop think?'

'They were amazed, Aggie. Because I was the one who went on the excursion, they wanted to know everything that happened. They were jealous that they had to work as usual, while I had a hearty breakfast followed by that meal in Mr Appleby's house. They wanted to know why I was picked and not them.'

'Your name came out of a hat. That's what you said.'

'It's what I thought might have happened,' he admitted, 'but Mr Drake told me today that I went on that outing because I run our paint shop. See what I mean? It was a reward. Everyone chosen did something special at the Works.'

'Oh,' she said, hand on his shoulder. 'I'm so proud of you, Derek.'

'It's no more than I deserved.'

'When did you first realise . . . what had happened . . . ?'

'It was at Mr Appleby's home. There was an empty chair at the top table. I knew it was set for Mr Hubbleday. So where was he?' asked Churt. 'There was only one answer.

He'd been shot dead. That nonsense about a dead cow was a big lie. The animal killed was a mad, old bull named Cyril Hubbleday.'

She was shaken. 'Why do you speak like that about him?' she cried. 'He was murdered in cold blood. Don't you have any sympathy for his family?'

'I'm sorry for them, Aggie, but not for him.'

'Why not?'

He shrugged. 'It doesn't matter.'

'You speak of him so harshly.'

'Hubbleday deserves it.'

Agnes needed a few moments to take in what she had heard.

'When you worked out what had happened,' she asked him at length, 'why didn't you tell me?'

'I wasn't absolutely sure. Besides, it would have spoilt the excursion for you and Peter. I wanted the two of you to enjoy every second of it.'

'We did at the time – not any more.'

'Where is he?'

'Upstairs in his room, playing with that toy train you made him.'

'Is he still talking about those reindeer?'

'He never stops.'

Churt smiled. 'It's not what I'll remember about that excursion.'

* * *

Until they saw it, neither Colbeck nor Leeming had any idea that the Imperial Hotel was such a substantial structure. The superintendent had returned there by means of the subterranean passage, but the detectives had to walk up the hill. The hotel loomed above them. Even in the gloom, they could see that it was an imposing edifice, built in the Gothic style. It had four storeys and dormers, and a big, sloping roof that reminded Colbeck of the French style.

'It puts our little hotel to shame,' said Leeming.

'No, it doesn't, Victor. We have personal service from the proprietor. I don't think that the Imperial will have anyone as kind and caring as Mrs Renshaw.'

'That's true.'

'And why stay in a monstrosity like this when we have a comfortable Regency house that answers all our needs?'

'Will you say that to the superintendent?'

Colbeck grinned. 'I value my neck.'

Entering the hotel, they found Tallis in the lounge, enjoying a drink before dinner. He beckoned them over and they sat either side of him.

'What sort of beer do they serve here?' asked Leeming.

Tallis sniffed. 'This is not a social occasion, Sergeant.'

'It's been a long day, sir. Throats get dry.'

'You'll have to wait until you get back to Mrs Renshaw. I had the pleasure of meeting her, by the way. She came to the station with cakes for Mr Unwin.'

'What did you make of her?' asked Colbeck.

'I think that's she's an extraordinary woman, though I didn't believe a word of that nonsense about foreseeing a disaster.'

'I believed her implicitly.'

'Really? That's most unlike you, Inspector. You're usually a hard-headed, down-to-earth realist. You can't possibly believe in her so-called "sensations". Before you know it, Mrs Renshaw will be telling you that she talks to fairies. No,' he went on, 'I must apologise. It's unfair to denigrate her. She struck me as being kind, intelligent, hard-working, and devoted to this lovely part of the world.'

'Did Mrs Renshaw make you feel at home here?' enquired Colbeck.

'That's my business.'

Tallis went on to describe his encounters with Lady Foley and Colonel Yardley. The latter's prowess with a rifle made the others sit up. The superintendent then recalled another person who'd come to the station.

'Inspector Vellacott deigned to pay me another visit.'

'Did he have anything of value to say?' asked Colbeck.

'He started with a complaint about you, Inspector.'

'Oh?'

'Apparently, you upset a Mr Lipton, who runs the hospital in Worcester.'

'I went there to talk to the pathologist, not to listen to some drivel about the development of the hospital. Was there a complaint from Dr Peck as well?'

'No' said Tallis. 'The pathologist spoke well of you, as it happens.'

'Why was Inspector Vellacott here, sir?' asked Leeming.

'He came to find out what you two were doing, and to boast about the efficiency of his officers. Vellacott identified two suspects. We questioned the first of them and soon realised he was completely innocent. The second man – James Carmody – worked in a pub in Upton upon Severn. He'd once been employed here on the railway,' said Tallis. 'I thought that significant.'

'Did you question the man, sir?'

'No, Sergeant. We were told he'd gone away for a few days.'

'Where?'

'To Hereford. He has a sister there, apparently. Vellacott finally had the sense to send someone to Hereford to track the woman down. She laughed at the idea that her brother would come to see her. They haven't spoken for years.'

'So where did he go?'

'For some reason,' said Tallis, 'he'd bought a train ticket to London. In discovering that, Vellacott's men showed some initiative, I suppose. He had the gall to suggest that I return there to search for him. I sent him off with a flea in his ear.'

'I know how he must have felt,' mumbled Leeming.

'What did you say?' snapped the superintendent.

'Nothing, sir.'

'I distinctly heard something.'

'One piece of good news, sir,' said Colbeck, jumping in to rescue the sergeant yet again. 'Detective Constable Hinton has arrived and started work immediately. He's going to be a valuable addition to our investigation . . .'

Alan Hinton was pleased with his hotel. Seen from outside, it looked down-at-heel, but his spirits lifted when he entered the place. It was clean and comfortable. His room was bigger than expected and there was a fire to welcome him. Breakfast would be served in the morning, but other meals needed to be bought off the premises. Hinton knew from experience that it was wise to take a second set of clothes whenever he joined an investigation outside London. In a place like Oldbury, his frock coat and top hat would make him stand out. He therefore changed into less distinctive apparel that would allow him to mix more easily with the local population. After examining his appearance in the mirror, he left the hotel and went in search of a place where he could buy an evening meal.

Sipping his drink, Edward Tallis listened to the details of what his officers had been doing in Oldbury. Colbeck took care to stress that, because of his tenacity, Leeming had found out where he could confront Samuel Waycroft. The information drew a rare compliment from the superintendent. Leeming savoured it.

'It was clever of you to establish that the man owns a rifle,' said Tallis.

'We don't know exactly what sort of weapon it is, sir,' warned Leeming, 'but we can assume that Waycroft had a strong motive to shoot Mr Hubbleday.'

'Also,' Colbeck pointed out, 'he had many friends at the Works. It would have been easy for him to find out precise details of the excursion.'

'He could be the man we are after,' said Leeming.

'Let's not get ahead of ourselves,' warned Tallis. 'We need far more evidence of this man's involvement. Tackle him tomorrow.'

'I will, sir.'

'I'm hungry,' said the other, emptying his glass. 'Is there anything else to report before I have my dinner?'

'Yes,' said Colbeck. 'I had a most illuminating conversation with Mr Appleby about the way he deals with his employees. He argued that, if they are treated well, they tend to work harder. They also feel as if they're part of a family.'

'I'm not sure that I agree with his premise.'

'Mr Appleby's workers are the envy of the Black Country. Their productivity is remarkable, apparently.'

'That was because Mr Hubbleday got the best out of them.'

'Might it not be that they are happy in their work?'

'Mr Appleby is considerate towards them,' said Leeming, pointedly.

Tallis rounded on him. 'Is that a barbed insult aimed at me?'

'No, no, sir.'

'Am I supposed to take some of my officers on an excursion from time to time, and let the criminals they should be arresting walk freely around London?'

'It's not a fair comparison, sir,' insisted Colbeck.

'Yes, it is. Mr Appleby has his way of doing things. I have mine, and it does not involve befriending those beneath me. Discipline is paramount and one can't impose that without an element of fear. If Mr Appleby wishes to be liked by his employees,' said Tallis, 'that's his business. My priority is to make my men respect me for my unrelenting commitment to law enforcement.' He stood up. 'Appleby has a need for affection. It's a sign of weakness. My preference is for wielding power. That is a sign of strength.'

Without another word, he walked off briskly to the restaurant.

Because his son-in-law was away from home on police business, Caleb Andrews insisted on dining with his daughter so that she was not left alone. After the meal, they adjourned to the drawing room and admired the Christmas tree once more.

'It's the best you've ever had, Maddy,' he said.

'I thought last year's was better,' she said. 'Robert was responsible for decorating that.'

'Yes, he was actually here when he needed to be.'

'Don't start criticising him again, Father.'

'It's not Robert I'm complaining about. It's that

thoughtless superintendent. Because he has no family himself, he doesn't understand a father's obligations. The man is heartless.'

'He's simply wedded to his work. Be fair to him. He hasn't simply dispatched Robert and Victor to the Malverns. He's gone there himself because he knows the impact that a murder will have on such a small community.'

'He'll only slow down the investigation.'

'Robert won't let him.'

'When do you expect to hear from him?'

'Tomorrow – with luck.'

He sat back in his chair and studied her with a mixture of pride and affection.

'Who would have thought we'd ever be doing this?' he said.

'Doing what?'

'Sitting in a fine house like this while a servant clears the table in the dining room. I still can't believe it, Maddy. How could it possibly happen?'

'I suppose that you were to blame for it, Father.'

He was startled. 'Me?'

'Yes,' she recalled. 'If you hadn't been badly wounded by the men who robbed the train you were driving, I'd never have met Robert. He was put in charge of the case. That's how our paths crossed.'

'You don't need to remind me of that.'

'It never occurred to me for a second that he and I would be . . . well, drawn together. I'd been brought up to believe that someone in my position could only have limited expectations.'

He laughed. 'And look at you now!' he said. 'You're a wife and mother and you've turned yourself into a real artist. You've bettered yourself, Maddy.' He pursed his lips. 'I just wish that your mother had been here to enjoy your success.'

'So do I . . .'

For a few moments their eyes moistened. He reached out to touch her.

'However,' he went on, taking a deep breath, 'it's no good trying to change the past. What happened is behind us now. All we can do is to live in the present and count our blessings.'

'How many have you got?' she teased.

'There's you, for a start, Maddy, and there's that angel of a granddaughter asleep upstairs. Then there's Robert, of course, for making it all possible and for having such an interest in railways.' He beamed complacently. 'We've had long talks together. He's learnt so much from me.'

'When he was a boy, he wanted to be an engine driver.'

'Thank goodness he never did! He's far more use keeping the rail network free of crime. Besides,' he said, 'he's far too fussy about his clothing to be a driver. I used to come home with my uniform caked in filth.'

'I know, Father – I washed it for you.'

'I'll never forget it, Maddy. You were a Trojan.' He lowered his voice. 'What have you bought Robert for Christmas?'

'It's a secret.'

He was hurt. 'You don't have secrets from me.'

'Oh, yes, I do,' she said.

'I promise not to tell Robert.'

'You won't get a chance.'

'Then let me ask you a much more important question.'

'What is it?'

He cackled. 'What have you bought for ME?'

There was no shortage of public houses in Oldbury. After peeping into two of them, Alan Hinton decided he wanted somewhere less rowdy. His third choice was The Waggon and Horses, a survivor of the time when farming was virtually the only form of employment in the area. Most of the customers were clustered around the fire.

He bought a glass of beer and a meat pie, taking them to the one vacant table in the bar. The place was half-full but there was none of the drunken laughter he'd heard in the other pubs. Hinton was able to sit quietly on his own and enjoy his meal. He was unaware that two people who had just come into the pub were watching him. As he came to the end of his meal, the men slipped out of the bar and into the street. Bidding farewell to the landlord, Hinton got up and went out. As he stepped into the street, he was in relative darkness and did not even see the two men who jostled him.

'We know who yow are,' snarled one of them. 'Dress up in any clothes yow like. We can always smell a policeman.'

Hinton was shoved hard against a wall. Before he could fight back, his attackers had fled into the darkness. He had been warned.

* * *

Colbeck was up at the crack of dawn. When he was joined by Leeming, they took their places at the table and ordered their breakfast. The sergeant was pale, drawn and kept yawning.

'How did you sleep?' asked Colbeck.

'I didn't, sir.'

'Why not?'

'I had nightmares about what Mrs Renshaw told us.'

'Well, it was your own fault,' said Colbeck, laughing. 'You insisted on knowing what exactly the Water Cure was.'

'It's not a cure,' protested Leeming. 'It's a blooming torture.'

'Then how do patients survive it?'

'I wouldn't, sir. I know that.'

The sergeant regretted that he had ever broached the subject. But, over a meal the previous evening, he had asked Mrs Renshaw exactly what the Water Cure was. Since she had had guests staying at the hotel before going on for treatment, she knew only too well what happened in the hydropathy clinics.

'Do they really get the patients up at six in the morning?' said Leeming.

'Apparently.'

'I kept dreaming about those attendants who come in with a wet sheet in a large tub. They made me strip naked then wrapped me in the sheet before covering me with blankets and an eiderdown. I was helpless.'

'You're supposed to relax, Victor.'

'Relax!' yelled the other. 'How can I do that when I'm terrified?'

'Did they subject you to a douche in the nightmare?'

'Yes, they did. One minute I was wrapped up in that cold sheet; the next, I was hit by a stream of icy cold water poured from a great height. It was like a waterfall. Do any patients actually survive that treatment?'

'They must do, or they wouldn't come back for more. In any case,' said Colbeck, 'the douche is only occasionally used. As Mrs Renshaw told us, the main aim is to get the patients out on a long walk in the hills, inhaling the clean air and stopping at various springs to sample the water.'

'I did that in my dream – the water was forced down my throat.'

'That never happens, Victor. Compulsion would frighten clients away. Malvern water is known for its purity. That's why this place has become a renowned spa town, able to rival places like Bath and Cheltenham. It couldn't build such a reputation if it forced people to submit to the kinds of things that you experienced in your nightmare. I'm sorry you had such a bad night,' said Colbeck. 'What was it that really frightened you?'

'It was those attendants who set on me.'

'What about them?'

Leeming shuddered. 'They all looked like Superintendent Tallis.' Colbeck laughed. 'It's not funny, sir.'

'No, of course not. I do apologise. It must have been horrifying.'

'I kept waking up in a cold sweat.'

'You have my sympathy,' said Colbeck, seriously. 'Are you all right now? I need you fully awake, not yawning at me every few minutes.'

'I'll be fine when I've had my breakfast.'

'You have an important job to do today.'

'Yes, I know. I haven't forgotten Waycroft. In fact—'

Leeming broke off as Ruby Renshaw came into the room. Instead of exchanging a greeting with them, she was lost in a private world. She looked grim and preoccupied. Colbeck rose to his feet in concern.

'Are you all right, Mrs Renshaw?' he said.

'Oh!' she exclaimed, coming out of her reverie. 'I'm sorry. I didn't see either of you when I came in. It was very rude of me.'

'Not at all. Your mind was on other things, that's all.'

'It's true, Inspector. I'm confused. Only yesterday, I told the superintendent that my sensations come along very rarely. There's been a gap of years between some of them. Yet I think I had another sensation only minutes ago. That means it's happened twice in three days.' She brought her hands to her face. 'It's so perplexing.'

'What happened this time?'

'The same thing as before,' she replied. 'I had the feeling that something terrible had happened.' She gave an apologetic shrug. 'I've no idea what it is, I'm afraid. That's what troubles me.'

* * *

159

Biddy Leacock was a creature of routine. Even though bad weather was likely to deter anyone from climbing the Worcestershire Beacon, the highest point in the Malverns, she braved the cold wind and driving rain to walk to the base of the hill. Unlocking the door of the stables, she went in to be given a loud and affectionate welcome by her donkeys. She fed them in turn, stroking each one as she moved along. The animals were her major source of income. If atrocious weather came in the new year, they'd be taken back down to the smallholding where she and her sister lived. For the time being, however, visitors were still coming to the Malverns and there were always those who found the climb daunting. Biddy's donkeys came into their own on those occasions, carrying people of all weights up to the top of the Beacon so that they could enjoy the view.

During spring and summer, it was a profitable enterprise and, since the railway had opened, autumn also brought the crowds at weekends. Now in her sixties, Biddy was an unprepossessing woman who dressed in a way that made it impossible to determine her sex. Her considerable bulk, long stride and deep growl of a voice made her seem more like a man. Because of her truculence, other donkey owners kept well clear of her. Experience had taught them that arguments with Biddy were pointless. She could be fiery and foul-mouthed. Given her total lack of consideration for others, it was surprising how many customers preferred to hire her. They liked the quality of her donkeys and the way that she kept them under control.

She came out into the rain and ambled up the hill for a few minutes, relishing a sense of ownership. The Beacon, she felt, was hers. She paused and turned around to look down at her home in the distance. Her sister would be milking the cow or collecting eggs from the hen house, chores that she had done every morning since she was a child. After a while, Biddy felt the need to relieve herself. She walked on to a hollow completely hidden behind some thick bushes. As she lifted her skirt and crouched down, she saw something out of the corner of her eye that made her freeze instantly.

Sticking out of a patch of ferns, was a human leg.

CHAPTER TEN

When he reached the railway station, Robert Colbeck was greeted by a donkey. It was tied to one of the iron columns supporting the canopy. It brayed loudly when he approached it. Edward Tallis came out of the stationmaster's office.

'Thank goodness you've come,' he said. 'I was just about to send for you.'

'What's happened, sir?'

'There's been a development. Another body has been found.'

'I thought that might happen,' said Colbeck.

Tallis was nonplussed. 'What makes you say that?'

'Mrs Renshaw had another of her . . . presentiments.'

'Forget her. It's another woman who brought the news. According to the stationmaster, her name is Biddy Leacock. Believe it or not, she rode here on that donkey. She's not very coherent, I'm afraid. Unwin made her a cup of tea but she's still shivering with fright.'

'Where's the body?'

'It's near the foot of the Worcestershire Beacon.'

'That's not all that far away, sir.'

'It's what I was told. When she's recovered, we'll get her to show us the exact spot. Meanwhile, I sent a telegraph to Inspector Vellacott in Worcester. He'll probably catch the next train here.'

'Let me speak to the lady.'

'She's no lady, Inspector,' said Tallis, darkly. 'She's a donkey woman and smells like it. Be warned.'

He led the way into the stationmaster's office. Biddy was crouched over the blazing fire. Its heat was making steam rise from her sodden coat and hat. When Tallis introduced the inspector, she did no more than glance at Colbeck. He stepped closer, then recoiled from the stink.

'What exactly did you see, Mrs Leacock?' he asked.

'She's not married,' hissed Tallis.

'I do beg your pardon, Miss Leacock.' She remained silent. 'Where exactly is this body?' There was still no response. 'We'd like you to take us there. Will you do that, please?'

Biddy looked at him properly for the first time and nodded.

'Unwin has rustled up a cart for us,' said Tallis, 'and he was also able to loan us a tarpaulin. We'll need that to cover . . . whatever we find.'

'I'll ride behind,' grunted Biddy.

'You're welcome to sit on the cart with us.'

'I want my donkey.'

'Then let's be on our way, shall we?' suggested Colbeck. 'It's raining hard out there, sir,' he said to Tallis. 'We'll need my umbrella.'

'Then I'll hold it over the two of us because you'll have to drive the cart.'

'I'm happy to do that.'

'Where's Leeming?'

'He caught an early train to the Black Country,' said Colbeck. 'I daresay that he's already in Tipton, waiting for the suspect to return.'

With rain dripping off his umbrella, Leeming splashed his way through the puddles on the pavement. He eventually came to the point on the canal from which the man he hoped would be Samuel Waycroft had set off. Looking around for a dry place in which to wait, he spotted a bridge less than thirty yards away. It might offer him some measure of protection. When he reached it, he realised that he was completely sheltered. He therefore felt able to lower his umbrella and shake it out. If the suspect did return, Leeming would have a clear sight of him. All that he knew about Waycroft was that he would need to be handled with great care.

* * *

Colbeck drove the cart at a measured pace so that the donkey could keep up with it. Seated astride the animal, Biddy Leacock ignored the rain as it soaked her hat and coat. The detectives eventually saw the hill, rising majestically before them. When they reached the base, they were overtaken by Biddy, who kicked her donkey into a sudden spurt. The cart followed her the short distance to the stables.

'I'll lead the horse by the bridle,' volunteered Colbeck. 'It will be too steep for it to drag us up there. If we both get off, sir, it will make the cart lighter.'

'Oh, all right – if you say so.'

'You keep the umbrella.'

Jumping to the ground, Colbeck took hold of the bridle and watched as Tallis struggled to get off the cart. Biddy urged her donkey up the incline and Colbeck led the horse and cart after her. Tallis brought up the rear, trying to control the umbrella in the wind. They did not have to pick their way very far. Biddy reached a point where she jumped off the donkey and left it to stand on its own. After indicating where the others should go, she held the horse's bridle so that Colbeck and Tallis could walk on alone.

Both men wondered what it was that had upset the woman. She was clearly too frightened to venture behind the bushes. When they did so, they immediately caught sight of the leg protruding from the ferns. Colbeck went cautiously across to the dead body and stepped into the ferns beside it.

'Well,' said Tallis, 'what have you found?'

'I've discovered that Mrs Renshaw really does have a gift, sir.'

'What do you mean?'

'She sensed that something horrible had happened,' said Colbeck. 'I'm standing right next to it.'

Tallis moved forward. 'Let me see for myself.' He reached the ferns and looked down. 'Dear God!'

'Miss Leacock did tell you that'd she'd found a dead body, sir,' recalled Colbeck. 'What she was unable to say was that its head was missing.'

Alan Hinton walked briskly towards the Works. He was wearing the clothing that he'd had on the previous evening. It had proved a poor disguise. However, Hinton had not felt threatened when he was jostled. During his years in uniform, he had been toughened by a series of difficult arrests. What he had received was a warning to be more careful. During his interviews with the painters, he decided, he must have spoken to men with something to hide. Did that mean that they were accessories to the murder of the works manager? Or did they have other secrets to conceal? For some reason, the name of Derek Churt popped into his mind. He had stood out from the others. Hinton needed to speak to the man again.

When he got to the office set aside for the detectives, he was disappointed to find that Colbeck was not there. He knew that Leeming would be in Tipton, but the inspector had promised to meet him at the Works. Yet there was no sign of him. He was mystified. The inspector was always fastidious about keeping his appointments. Only something serious would prevent him from coming to Oldbury. Hinton wondered what it might be.

The corpse had been carefully wrapped in the tarpaulin. Biddy Leacock watched them load it gently onto the back of the cart. Still disturbed by the shock of discovery, she asked for permission to return home. Tallis allowed her to do so. Mercifully, the rain had now stopped, and the wind had eased. As they sat side by side, Colbeck drove the cart slowly back towards the town, wondering who their passenger could possibly be.

'It was pure coincidence,' said Tallis, airily. 'Mrs Renshaw couldn't possibly have known that a second person had been killed.'

'She was right about the first murder,' Colbeck reminded him. 'You may dismiss her claims as worthless, but I believe that she does have second sight.'

'It was a lucky guess on her part, that's all.'

'There's nothing lucky about finding a headless body, sir. Mrs Renshaw was very distressed when she told us that she'd had this strange feeling of doom. She'll be even more upset when she learns what we found.'

'Let's put her aside,' said the other, 'and simply deal with the practicalities. A second murder has taken place in the area in a matter of days. Do you think that it has any connection with the first one?'

'It's too early to say for certain, sir.'

'What does your instinct tell you?'

'The two are linked,' said Colbeck after a pause. 'The first was a rare event in a county largely free of serious crime. When a second murder occurs so soon after the other one, then it must be connected to it somehow. On the other hand,' he added, thoughtfully, 'one victim was shot and the other was beheaded. Killers tend to stick to a modus operandi. Perhaps we need to look at the possibility that there are two separate people working together.'

'We haven't picked up the scent of one of them yet,' said Tallis, worriedly. 'If there is a second killer at large, we may be here for months.'

'You're being unduly pessimistic, sir.'

'This morning's discovery complicates the investigation.'

'I'm rather hoping that it will bring clarity,' said Colbeck. 'Once the victim is identified, we'll have valuable new evidence to add to what we've already found.'

'Someone has made identification more difficult by decapitating the man.'

'Nevertheless, we'll find out who he is.'

'How?'

'Well, for a start, he may be reported missing.'

'Only if he hails from around here.'

'Oh, I have a feeling he has a local connection, sir,' said Colbeck, 'and that he was left near the base of the Worcestershire Beacon deliberately. Sooner or later, someone was bound to find him there.'

'Unfortunately, it fell to that strange woman to find him.'

'I fancy that she's strong-minded enough to recover from the shock.'

'What did you make of her?'

'She is an interesting character.'

'Not if you get too close to her,' said Tallis, grimacing. 'She stinks terribly and there's a brutish look to her.'

'You're being unkind, sir.'

'I'm being honest, Inspector.'

They drove on in silence for a while. It was Tallis who eventually spoke again.

'The commissioner is not entirely pleased about this,' he confessed.

'Is he unhappy about your absence, sir?'

'His telegraph did say that I was badly missed.'

'Then you must feel free to return to Scotland Yard,' urged Colbeck. 'Now that we have an additional pair of hands at our disposal, the sergeant and I feel that we can cope without you.'

'Don't be ridiculous, man!' exclaimed the other. 'A second murder has made this case even more complex. You need my guiding hand to solve it. Besides,' he went on, smiling, 'I have personal reasons for remaining in this part of the country. It is beginning to cast a spell over me . . .'

Victor Leeming had watched two different narrowboats stop at the wharf so that cargo could be unloaded onto waiting carts. They were then driven off. Neither of the vessels had someone aboard who fitted the description he'd been given of Samuel Waycroft. It was the third one that made the sergeant take more interest. As it was moored, he sensed that the man he wanted might be on board this time. He walked slowly towards the wharf. When he reached the narrowboat, cargo was being unloaded. He looked at the men handling the boxes, sacks, barrels and other items. They were soon stacked up to await collection.

Leeming was about to step aboard the narrowboat when he saw the bargee paying off a member of the crew. After studying the latter carefully, he believed that he might well be Samuel Waycroft. The man was the right age and had the stocky build described to him. It made sense that Waycroft would leave the vessel there so that he could walk to his sister's house. He seemed happy with the money paid to him. Thrusting it into his pocket, he climbed onto the wharf and set off. Leeming was quick to fall in beside him.

'Are you Sam Waycroft, by any chance?' he asked.

The man was wary. 'Who wants to know?'

'I daresay that your sister, Mrs Kinchen, would.'

'Was it Lil as sent yow?'

'Then I have got the right man,' said Leeming, stepping in front of him to bring him to a halt. 'I'm Detective Sergeant Leeming from Scotland Yard and I'm involved in the search for the man who killed Cyril Hubbleday.'

'What?' cried the other, laughing with joy. 'Hubb is dead?'

'I believe that you and he had an argument.'

'Of course – the bastard sacked me.'

'You punched him.'

'Yow'd have done the same in my place. I had mouths to feed. Losing my job means my wife and children went hungry. Hubb had no cause to get rid of me. I knew my trade.'

'But you drank too much.'

'Only now and then . . .' He laughed again. 'Someone murdered him, did they? Thass great news. How did he do it, like? I hope it was slow and painful. Thass wor Hubb deserved.'

'He was shot dead in the Malverns.'

'Give my thanks to the bloke as put the bullet in him.'

'What's his name?'

Waycroft was outraged. 'How should I know?'

'You might have helped him.'

'Don't be stupid. Hubb dying is news to me – good news, though.'

'Where have you been?'

'It's none of your bleedin' business.'

'Let's continue this discussion at the police station.'

Waycroft bridled. 'What's all this about?' he demanded. 'You can't think I had anything to do with it, can you?'

'You own a gun.'

'I did own one,' said the other, stunned for a moment. 'Who told you?'

'Where is it?'

'Look, it's gone. I pawned it.'

'Can you prove it?'

'Yes, I can, as a matter of fact,' said Waycroft, thrusting a hand into his pocket and taking out a wad of papers. 'It's here somewhere. I'm not as daft as I look. I always keeps receipts, see.' He picked out a tattered piece of paper and handed it over. 'There it is. Everything's legal and proper.'

The moment that Leeming took the receipt from him, he knew that he'd been tricked. He was hit with a sudden uppercut that sent him sprawling backwards before falling to the ground. By the time the sergeant came to his senses, Samuel Waycroft had disappeared. Getting to his feet, Leeming rubbed his chin ruefully and looked at the piece of paper in his hand. It was a receipt from a pawnbroker.

Derek Churt was annoyed to be summoned to the office used by the detectives. When he arrived, he was seething.

'I've got work to do,' he complained.

'So have I,' said Hinton. 'That's why I sent for you.'

'We spoke yesterday. I told you everything I knew.'

'It's that story about realising Mr Hubbleday had been shot . . .'

'What about it?'

'I'm not sure that I believe it.'

'It's the truth,' he affirmed.

'I wonder.'

Hinton gave him a long, hard stare. Churt met it without flinching.

'I ate at a pub last night,' said the detective. 'It was the Waggon and Horses. Do you know it?'

'I'm a family man. I always eat at home with my wife and son.'

'Is that what you did yesterday?'

Churt was offended. 'Why do you want to know?'

'Answer the question, please.'

'I've already done so. Every evening is spent with my family.'

'Do you live anywhere near that pub?'

'I do, as it happens.'

'Then it wouldn't have taken you long to stroll there, would it?'

'No – but I wouldn't have any reason to go there.'

'You might have had one last night.'

'What are you on about?' asked Churt.

'When I came out of the pub,' explained Hinton, 'I was accosted by two men who must work here. They warned me that I was being watched. Now, the only employees I spoke to yesterday were painters, so two of them must have followed me when I left the Works and seen where I was staying. I think they waited for me to come out in search of a meal then lurked outside the pub.' He looked deep into Churt's eyes again. 'Were you one of those men?'

'I haven't a clue what you're talking about,' said the other, vehemently.

'Can anyone confirm that you were at home around eight o'clock?'

'Yes, my wife can. Ask her – and ask my son, Peter, as well. Do you have children, Constable Hinton?'

'I'm not married.'

'Then you don't understand what it means to be a father.'

'No,' conceded Hinton, 'that's true.' He inhaled deeply.

'Perhaps I was wrong to suggest that you were involved in that incident last night – but that doesn't mean you were unaware that it happened.'

Sturt shook his head. 'I don't follow.'

'You could have given orders to those two men.'

'I've no idea who they were.'

'You're obviously a sort of leader in your shop.'

'Somebody has to be,' said the other, angrily. 'But why should these two men be workmates of mine? There are lots of other painters there. You must have spoken to them as well. Why pick on my shop? I know you've got your job to do, Constable, but so have I – and you're keeping me away from it. Can I go now, please?'

'No, you can't.'

'Why not?'

'Well,' said Hinton, quietly, 'I think that I owe you an apology . . .'

Inspector Vellacott alighted from the train at the railway station in Great Malvern. He had two uniformed constables in tow. Spotting the trio through the window of the stationmaster's office, Tallis and Colbeck came out to meet them.

'Where is it?' asked Vellacott.

'The body is in a shed Mr Unwin uses for storage,' said Tallis.

'Do you have any idea who the man is?'

'None at all, Inspector. His pockets had been emptied so

there is no means of identification.'

'How was he killed?'

'We're not entirely sure,' said Colbeck. 'Before you see the body, there's something you should know – it has no head.'

Vellacott gaped. 'Thank you for warning us.'

Colbeck led the way to the large shed that stood just outside the station. Producing a key, he opened the door and ushered the others inside. Draped in the tarpaulin, the body lay on a trestle table. Colbeck slowly peeled back the tarpaulin to reveal the corpse. When he saw the blood-soaked remains of the neck, one of the constables started to retch. Vellacott sent him outside. He turned back to Tallis.

'Where was the body discovered?' he asked.

'Near the base of Worcestershire Beacon.'

'Who reported it?'

'A woman named Biddy Leacock.'

'Oh,' said Vellacott with a hint of a sneer, 'we all know Biddy. She rules the roost on that hill. The other donkey owners are terrified of her.'

'Miss Leacock has a softer side,' Colbeck put in. 'She was in a dreadful state when she came here. She couldn't even bring herself to say that the man had been decapitated. We let her return home.'

'We'll get a statement from her later.'

'You must take charge of the body,' said Tallis.

'We'll take it back to Worcester on the next train,' said Vellacott. 'I'll have to wait until one of my men has finished emptying his stomach first,' he added, glancing over his shoulder. 'This is the second murder victim in a row,' he said through gritted death. 'Finding dead bodies is getting to be a habit.'

'You exaggerate, Inspector,' said Colbeck. 'We believe that this crime is related to the death of Mr Hubbleday. When we solve one murder, therefore, we will solve both.'

'It's too early to make that assumption, Inspector. I'd prefer to get more evidence before I accept that the two cases are in any way connected. I'm surprised that a cautious man like you made such a hasty judgement.'

'Inspector Colbeck's hasty judgements are invariably correct,' said Tallis.

'He may have slipped up this time.'

The second constable had been staring fixedly at the body.

'Excuse me,' he said, 'but I think I might know this man.'

'What do you mean?' asked Vellacott.

'Can I have permission to . . . touch him, please?'

'It depends on what you're going to do, Constable.'

'I just want to roll back his sleeve, sir.'

'Very well – go ahead.'

Colbeck, Tallis and Vellacott watched with interest as the constable rolled back the sleeve on the right forearm of the corpse. It took him less than a few seconds to reach a conclusion. He smiled grimly.

'I had a feeling it might be him,' he said.

'Who?' asked Colbeck.

'It was those broad shoulders of his, see. When I

arrested him the first time, he had his sleeves rolled up, so I saw it clearly. He had that tattoo of a heart on the right forearm.'

'Who the devil is he?' snapped Vellacott.

'It's the man we've been searching for, sir – Jim Carmody.'

'Are you sure?'

'Yes, Inspector. I'd bet anything that it's him.'

'I was told he bought a ticket to London,' said Vellacott.

'He didn't use it,' Colbeck pointed out. 'Well, Inspector, you were right about one thing. Carmody was connected to the first murder.'

'He was even more connected to the second one,' observed Tallis, drily, 'because he was the victim.' He turned to Vellacott. 'Do you see how right we were to link the two murders together?'

'Carmody was the person who provided the sleepers and the red flags,' said Colbeck. 'Having served his purpose, he was disposed of – except that we weren't supposed to identify him so easily.' He looked at the constable. 'Good work, young man. You've saved all of us a great deal of time and speculation.'

'Thank you, Inspector,' said the other.

'I think I should claim some credit as well,' insisted Vellacott. 'I was wrong about Hamer, but I felt in my bones that Carmody was somehow involved. We're not the country bumpkins you took us for.'

'This is a joint investigation,' Colbeck reminded him. 'Instead of making competing claims about who found what, we should ask ourselves a vital question.'

'What is it?' asked Vellacott.

'Where is Mr Carmody's head?'

Derek Churt was surprised when Hinton delivered his apology. It sounded sincere. At the same time, the painter still resented the fact that he had been pulled away from his work. His friends would wonder if he had done anything wrong.

'They'll want to know why the police were so interested in me,' he said.

'Tell them I just wanted to check the details in my notebook.'

'They're not that stupid, Constable.'

'Then you'll have to invent a story,' said Hinton. 'Better still, tell your workmates that I didn't believe you realised early on that Mr Hubbleday had been shot. Claim that you had now convinced me.'

'That might work, I suppose.'

'I'm sorry if I put you in an awkward position.'

'I'll talk my way out of it,' said Churt, confidently. 'Look, do you mind if I give you some advice?'

'I'd be grateful for it.'

'Be more patient. Don't ask any of us to feel sorry for Mr Hubbleday. To a man, we loathed him, and we had good cause. You don't even have to mention his name. If you want to ask about someone he sacked, try to find out what the man in question is doing now. You might get an honest answer that way.'

'Thanks, Mr Churt. Good advice.'

Surprised by the mildness of his manner, the painter looked closely at Hinton.

'Were you really set on by two men?'

'They jostled me a bit, that's all.'

'You don't seem upset about it.'

'It would take a lot more to frighten me,' said Hinton with a grin. 'I'm used to wading into a pub brawl and getting hit from all directions. What happened last night was nothing. All that those two men did was to give themselves away.'

'How are you going to find them?'

'I'm not quite sure, to be honest.'

'Who else did you speak to yesterday?'

'Nobody else but the men working in the paint shops.'

'Then one of us was involved,' said Churt, pensively. 'I wonder who it was. One thing is certain, Constable.'

'What is it?'

'I give you my word of honour – it wasn't me.'

Leeming was angry with himself. Having found and confronted Waycroft, he had allowed the man to escape. Even more embarrassing was the fact that he was knocked to the ground and left with extremely wet trousers. The one consolation was that he had a pawn ticket. He knew how much Waycroft had been paid when he handed his gun over. It would have hurt the former soldier to part with something that had sentimental value for him, but he needed the money. Leeming noted the date of his visit to the pawnbroker. It was days before the murder of the works manager. Samuel Waycroft was therefore absolved of being the killer, but he could still have aided the person who did shoot him. If he'd been completely innocent, why had he knocked Leeming to the ground and fled? He was obviously guilty of something.

His first task was to go to the police station to report the attack on him. It meant that everyone in a police uniform would be looking for Waycroft now. Leeming next paid a third visit to Lilian Kinchen's house. When he knocked on the front door, he saw a curtain twitch in the bedroom. Nobody came in response to his knock. He therefore pounded the door with his fist and raised his voice.

'I know that you're in there, Mrs Kinchen,' he said. 'Open this door, please, or I'll summon help to force it open.'

He heard footsteps coming down the stairs, then the door inched open. Lilian Kinchen peered through the crack. She had a guilty look on her face.

'He's been here, hasn't he?' said Leeming.

'No,' she replied.

'I've got a nasty bruise coming on my chin. Your brother put it there.'

'I didn't know that.'

'I think that you did. Sam realised I'd been here before. It meant this house was no longer safe for him. He'll have dashed back here to grab his things and disappear. Where has he gone?'

'I've no idea, Sergeant.'

'Then you admit that he was here.'

'I . . . didn't say that,' she gibbered.

'Sam has put you in a very awkward position,' said Leeming, adopting a softer tone. 'You have my sympathy, Mrs Kinchen. The last thing you want is to have someone like me calling here. The sooner I have a proper conversation with your brother, the sooner I'll have no need to bother you.'

She eyed him sullenly. 'You're going to arrest him, aren't you?'

'I'm afraid that I have to. And if you refuse to help me, I may have to arrest you as well.'

'What about my children?' she asked, flying into a panic.

'Oh, I won't need to arrest them. They're safe.'

'There's nobody to look after them.'

'You should have thought of that before you lied to me.'

'I haven't lied to you, Sergeant.'

'All right, let's say that you've held back the truth. Now,' said Leeming, sternly, 'do I march you to the police station or will you have the sense to put yourself and your children first?'

'I honestly don't know where Sam is,' she pleaded.

'But you can probably guess.'

'He did come here,' she admitted, 'but he was in and out within seconds. Sam hardly spoke a word to me. That's the truth.'

'I need an address from you, Mrs Kinchen.'

'What do you mean?'

'You told me that his wife and children are in Wolverhampton.'

'That's right.'

'So that's where he's probably gone.'

'Oh, I don't think so,' she said, shaking her head. 'Miriam hates him. She won't put up with him no longer. That's why she went back home.'

'What was her maiden name?'

'Bisley – Miriam Bisley.'

'And where do her parents live?'

'I . . . don't really know,' she said.

'I think that you do. Which part of Wolverhampton is it?'

'I can't remember.'

He lost patience. 'Knock on the door of the house next door.'

'Why?'

'Tell them I'm arresting you and you need someone to keep an eye on the children.'

She was aghast. 'I can't let anyone know I'm in trouble with the police.'

'Then you'll have to protect your good name.'

'Sergeant Leeming . . .'

'Give me that address, please.'

'Sam said nothing about Wolverhampton.'

'Where else can he have gone?'

'I don't know . . .'

'Maybe I'm wrong,' said Leeming, spreading his arms. 'Maybe he's nowhere near Wolverhampton. But let me tell you this. Some years ago, I was involved in searching for a killer in that town. The local police were very helpful. If you don't tell me where Sam's in-laws live, I daresay the police will find out for me. Meanwhile,' he added, 'you'll be cooling your heels in a police cell here. What's your husband going to say when he discovers that?'

Her resistance vanished. 'I'll get the address for you,' she said.

Leeming smiled contentedly. 'I had a feeling that you would.'

CHAPTER ELEVEN

Edward Tallis was glad when the body of James Carmody was taken away. Apart from anything else, it helped to get rid of the egregious Inspector Vellacott, who could not stop boasting about the fact that he had picked out Carmody as a suspect at the very start of the investigation. The superintendent was now left on his own to study the notes he had made about the latest development. When he looked through the window of the stationmaster's office, he saw that Ruby Renshaw had just come onto the platform. Tallis went straight out to exchange greetings with her.

'Are you catching a train, Mrs Renshaw?' he asked.

'No, Superintendent, I came in search of information.

Inspector Colbeck may have told you that I had another . . . intimation of disaster.'

'He did mention it.'

'Has another crime taken place?'

'Something dramatic did happen,' he told her. 'A dead body was found near the base of Worcestershire Beacon.'

'That's terrible,' she exclaimed. 'I've been praying that it was not another murder. One is more than enough. Who was the victim?'

Tallis gave her a brief account of events that morning, noting the look of horror on her face when he explained that the body had been found without a head.

'I knew that something frightful had happened, but I never thought that it would be as grotesque as that. And it was Biddy Leacock who actually made the discovery?'

'It shook her rigid.'

'That surprises me, Superintendent. She has a reputation for being able to cope with any emergency. The poor woman has had enough practice at doing so.'

'What do you mean?'

'Biddy and her sister have had a lot of setbacks. This time last year, someone tried to steal their cow. It provides their milk, some of which they turn into cheese. Luckily, the animal made such a noise that it woke them up. Biddy rushed out in her dressing gown with an old blunderbuss,' said Ruby, 'and she was more than ready to use it. For the rest of the week, it's rumoured, she slept in the cowshed with the gun beside her.'

'Good heavens!'

'Then, of course, there was that fire in one of the outbuildings . . .'

'What caused that?' asked Tallis.

'Spite and jealousy. The other donkey owners hate her because customers always turn to her first.'

'Was it a serious blaze?'

'They were able to put it out between them,' said Ruby. 'It was just a means of giving them another sleepless night.'

'Were any arrests made?'

'No, not yet. But the police are still looking for the culprit.'

'Miss Leacock looks indomitable to me,' said Tallis, 'and your information confirms it. It's surprising, therefore, that the sight of a headless corpse should unnerve her so much.'

'It's a side to Biddy that I've never seen before. She has my sympathy. However,' she went on, 'let me turn to another matter. I wondered if the inspector had given you an invitation.'

'What sort of invitation?'

'If you ask that question, then he obviously hasn't.'

'We've been rather preoccupied this morning, Mrs Renshaw, as you can imagine. Dealing with a second murder has made our task even more difficult.'

'It was only an idea, really. Perhaps it's best forgotten.'

'No, no,' he said, 'I'd like to hear what you're talking about. If my detectives were discussing me, I want to know what they said.'

'Well, it was Sergeant Leeming's idea, really. He was complaining about what happened yesterday evening.'

Tallis frowned. 'What did happen?'

'He and the inspector came to the Imperial Hotel to deliver a report of what they'd found out. You were enjoying a drink before dinner.'

'There's no law against that, is there?'

'No, no, of course not,' she said. 'But it was in a public space. Lots of other guests were there at the time. The sergeant wondered if they could persuade you to join them at my hotel instead, where they could deliver their reports in privacy.' She smiled sweetly. 'We have a wide selection of alcohol.'

'What did the inspector say to this idea?'

'He had his doubts about it. Inspector Colbeck said that you were highly unlikely to agree. I think he decided that it was a waste of time asking you.' She looked closely at him. 'Was he right, Superintendent?'

Tallis was chastened. He felt that it showed him in a poor light. Leeming's suggestion was worth considering. Tallis could easily walk to and from Ruby's hotel. Since he'd been told by Colbeck that no other guests were staying there, it meant that they could talk more freely than they had done so in the lounge at the Imperial. Tallis began to be tempted. There was something about the warmth of Ruby's smile that swept away his reservations. Having avoided women for most of his life, he had finally found one with whom he felt comfortable, even pleasantly so. She seemed to symbolise everything that was so appealing about the Malverns.

'I'll think about it, Mrs Renshaw,' he said.

'Thank you, Superintendent.' Her eyes twinkled. 'If you do come, I promise not to have another of my sensations.'

'I might hold you to that,' he said with a rare laugh.

'I'll leave you to discuss it with your detectives. Oh, by the way,' she added, 'I meant to ask you if you'd had an opportunity to look around the Priory yet?'

'Unhappily, I haven't.'

'Very few people stay here and resist its appeal.'

'I have . . . other priorities, Mrs Renshaw.'

'Since when has God's house been reduced to a lesser priority?' she asked with a note of disappointment. 'I know that you are very busy, Superintendent, but no more so than Inspector Colbeck. Yet he found the time to visit the Priory first thing this morning. It's a place that offers comfort and inspiration.'

Kneeling alone at the altar rail, Colonel Yardley was engaged in fervent prayer. It was only after several minutes that he struggled to his feet, adjusted his coat, and walked slowly back down the nave.

Alan Hinton was studying his notebook in their temporary office when Colbeck finally arrived. The constable was relieved to see the inspector.

'Ah, you're here at last, sir.'

'I apologise for my lateness,' said Colbeck. 'We had a crisis to deal with.'

'What sort of crisis, sir?'

'A second murder victim has been found.'

Hinton blinked. 'Where?'

Colbeck brought him up to date with the morning's events, explaining that a new dimension had been added to the investigation. Hinton was intrigued by what he was hearing. His own news seemed paltry by comparison.

'How have you got on here?' asked Colbeck.

'I'm working my way through that list you gave me, sir.'

'Is there anything to report?'

'There is, actually. I went for a meal at a local pub last night.'

'I hope you haven't recorded the details in your notebook,' teased Colbeck. 'All I'm interested in is information pertaining to the first murder.'

'One or more of the painters may be implicated, sir.'

'Are you certain of that?'

'It's a strong possibility.'

Hinton told him about the scuffle with the two men in the dark, and how he had wondered if one of them had been Derek Churt. After a long chat with the man, however, he had accepted that Churt was completely innocent. The painter, he recalled, had offered him useful advice on how to talk to members of the workforce.

'Churt sounds like an intelligent man,' said Colbeck.

'I think that he can be trusted, sir.'

'Can he be trusted to work with us?'

'No,' said Hinton. 'I don't think he'd go that far. He's fiercely loyal to his workmates. Also, he admitted that he had a thrill of pleasure when he realised that Mr Hubbleday had been shot dead.'

'Perhaps I should speak to him.'

'You'll put him in an awkward position if you do so. When I had him brought here, he was afraid of how his friends would react. If he's interviewed a second time, the other painters will begin to wonder what's going on.'

'Then there's a simple solution. I'll talk to him at his home. Meanwhile,' said Colbeck, 'you carry on with the task I assigned you. Work your way through those names. I need to take advice from Mr Drake about the Hubbleday family.'

'Are you going to visit them, sir?'

'That's what I'd like to do, but they may not be ready to talk to me yet. The shock of Mr Hubbleday's murder will have left them hurt and bewildered. They may prefer to mourn in private. Who knows? I suppose that Mr Drake might be able to help me. Yes, that's a thought,' he went on. 'He was a friend of the family. If I go to the house in his company,' said Colbeck, 'I might be invited inside.'

Wolverhampton was an ancient market town that had grown into a busy commercial centre. Leeming remembered it well from a previous visit. When he reached the address given to him by Lilian Kinchen, he found himself standing outside a cobbler's shop. Through the grimy window, he could see a stolid, middle-aged man, hammering nails into the sole of a boot. Leeming went into the shop and inhaled the strong smell of leather and polish.

'Mr Bisley?' he asked.

'That's me, sir,' said the man, politely. 'What can I do for you?'

'I wondered if you could tell me where your son-in-law is.'

Bisley glowered. 'Don't mention him.'

'Why not?'

'It's because he made my daughter's life a misery, that's why.'

'Then you've answered the question that brought me here,' said Leeming. 'I'm Detective Sergeant Leeming from Scotland Yard and I'm investigating the murder of the works manager at Appleby's in Oldbury.'

'That's where Sam used to work.'

'We know. He was sacked for being drunk.'

'Are you saying he was something to do with this murder?' asked Bisley, alarmed. 'No, I don't believe it. Sam is cruel, selfish and a useless husband, but I don't think he'd stoop to murder.'

'He'd stoop to anything if he was really desperate. See this?' asked Leeming, indicating his chin. 'Your son-in-law gave me this bruise. That's why I want to find him. I went to his sister's house in Tipton, and she gave me this address.'

'Lil should know better than that.'

'Mr Waycroft's wife and children are here. It's the obvious place to go.'

'Except that I told Sam to stay away for good,' snarled Bisley, raising the hammer he was holding. 'If he showed up here, I'd dash his brains out – not that he has any brains, mind.'

'Have you any idea where else in Wolverhampton he might have gone to?'

'I don't know, and I don't care.'

'Is your daughter here now?'

'Yes, she is. Why?'

'Could I speak to her, please?'

'No, you can't,' said the other, stoutly.

'Why not?'

'It's because I swore to protect her from that idiot. If you so much as mentioned his name to her, Miriam would have a fit. He treated her rotten, Sergeant. The only time she was happy was when he went off to the Crimea. Miriam was proud of him then,' he recalled. 'Sam was doing something for his country instead of going off to the pub whenever he fancied.'

'I'm surprised he had enough money to do that.'

'He didn't. That was part of the problem.'

'So how did he pay for his beer?'

'I think he turned to thieving.'

'Do you have any proof of that?'

'It was the way he sniggered when I asked him where his money came from,' said Bisley. 'Sam Waycroft should have been locked up. It's the only way Miriam would have been safe. He won't come crawling here, Sergeant. That's certain. He knows what would happen to him if he does.'

'Can I ask you to do something for me?'

'That depends on what it is.'

'If he does turn up in Wolverhampton,' said Leeming, 'tell the police. Ask them to get in touch with me at Appleby's in Oldbury. Will you do that, please? It could lead to Mr Waycroft's arrest.'

'Then I'll make sure I pass on the news,' said Bisley. 'Though there might not be much left of Sam by the time you get here. If he comes anywhere near here, it's not him you'll have to arrest – it's me.'

Harold Unwin seemed to know everyone within ten miles of the railway station. When Tallis questioned him about Biddy Leacock, he reeled off several anecdotes about the woman. Because he had an obvious affection for her, Unwin was even more well-informed about Ruby Renshaw's history. Tallis lapped up every detail.

'Did you ever come across James Carmody?' he asked.

'I knew everyone who worked on the railway around here,' said Unwin.

'How would you describe him?'

'He was a cheerful soul – always laughing. Jim was a good-looking man. He was very popular with women.'

'Was he married?'

'He wasn't, sir, but some of his women friends were.'

'That's deplorable,' said Tallis, sharply. 'The bonds of marriage should be respected. Why did Carmody leave the railway?'

'He found the work too hard. After that, he drifted from job to job. Eventually, he finished up working in a pub in Upton. It meant he had free accommodation and meals. It would have suited Jim.'

'Where did he live when he worked on the railway?'

'He rented a room in Upper Wyche.'

'Where's that?'

'It's close to the Worcestershire Beacon, sir.'

Tallis was startled. Carmody's body had been found near the village where he used to live. Before he could ask for more information about the murder victim, he heard a train approaching. Unwin moved away. He was soon welcoming the passengers as they stepped onto the platform. Tallis was about to return to his lair when he was hailed by a distinctive female voice.

'Superintendent!' she called.

'Ah,' he said, turning to see her descending on him. 'Good day to you, Lady Foley.'

'Do you have any news for me?'

'Yes, I do.'

'Good!' she said. 'Perhaps you would be kind enough to step into my waiting room. I simply must hear what has happened . . .'

Ernest Drake was delighted to have an excuse for a second visit to the Hubbleday house. On the way there in a cab, he told Colbeck about the family and how the murder victim's brother had taken control.

'It's unlikely we'll get to meet the wife and daughters,' he explained.

'I daresay that the brother will be able to answer all the questions I have.'

'Yes, he will. Reuben is very different to Cyril.'

'In what way?'

'He was less ambitious, for a start. As soon as Cyril got one promotion, he went in search of another. He was tireless, Inspector, always brimming with energy. That brought him to Mr Appleby's attention and led in due course to the position as works manager.'

'I gather that he was . . . not exactly liked by the employees.'

'Cyril spurned popularity,' said Drake. 'It was meaningless to him. Power was much more important.'

'What did he think about these excursions?' asked Colbeck.

'They were Mr Appleby's idea. Cyril was happy to go along with them.'

'But it meant that productivity would suffer every time dozens of men were taken away from the Works. In his position, I'd have resented that.'

'Cyril did have . . . reservations,' confessed Drake.

'And what about you?'

'Me?'

'What was your opinion of the excursions?'

'They kept the men happy, Inspector. I was pleased about that.'

'I don't hear any hint of enthusiasm in your voice, Mr Drake.'

'It's not for me to criticise Mr Appleby's decisions.'

'Would you be more honest if alone with Mr Hubbleday?' He saw Drake twitch as if he'd been stung. 'I'm told that you were close friends.'

'That's true. Cyril and I played chess together.'

'Who usually won?'

'He did,' said Drake, sadly. 'It was uncanny.'

'I'm not surprised that you enjoy playing chess. It's a game that would appeal to someone who spends his working day making careful calculations. From what I've heard about Mr Hubbleday,' continued the inspector, 'I'd say that he was an unlikely chess player. He was regarded as a man of action. There doesn't seem to have been a more contemplative side to him. Chess requires concentration.'

'Oh, Cyril had that, believe me.'

'Did you play for money?'

'No,' said Drake, surprised by the question, 'we played for the pleasure of it.'

'There's not much pleasure in getting beaten regularly.'

'I did have the occasional victory, Inspector,' Drake told him. 'In any case, the real treat for me was to spend time with Cyril away from the Works.' He lowered his voice. 'It's something I'll miss.'

Lady Foley's waiting room was private territory. When he went in after her, Tallis felt that he was entering the holy of holies. While she sat down, he was kept standing as he told her the latest news.

'Heavens!' she exclaimed. 'A second murder? This is intolerable.'

'I regret it as much as you, Your Ladyship.'

'How can you? Only someone who lives here can understand the horror of it all. The Malverns are known for their intrinsic safety.'

'I know. It's a privilege to be in this part of the country.'

'Then justify your presence here by making arrests,' she said, tartly.

'They will come in the fullness of time,' he promised her.

'Where are your officers?'

'Two are in Oldbury and the third, Sergeant Leeming, is in Tipton.'

'Those are places from which excursionists pour in upon us,' she said, acidly. 'We get the sweepings of the Midlands here.'

'They bring money here, I daresay. Hoteliers and tradesmen will surely welcome them.'

'Not if they only come for one day. The vast majority alight from the train at Malvern Link and walk in the hills, leaving their foul mess behind. Those who come on to this station are often in search of the Water Cure. They are rather more acceptable – and considerably better dressed.'

'I take your word for it.'

'Excursionists are nothing short of vandals. Their numbers should be controlled. You ask Colonel Yardley.

He is very eloquent on the subject.'

'I can imagine that he would be.'

She glared at him. 'Why do you say that?'

'I had the good fortune to meet the colonel,' he explained. 'He's a man after my own heart. Colonel Yardley believes in maintaining high standards in every sphere of life. It's something that I always strive to do.'

'That's very commendable, Superintendent.'

A knock on the door prevented Tallis from saying anything else. The stationmaster popped his head into the room to inform Lady Foley that her carriage had arrived. The conversation with Tallis was abruptly terminated. Rising to her feet, she bade him farewell and sailed out.

Reuben Hubbleday was pleased to see the visitors and invited them into the house. Colbeck and Drake were soon seated beside each other on the sofa. One glance around the room told Colbeck that the former works manager had been extremely well paid. The place was tastefully and expensively furnished. A piano stood in one corner. A large gilt-edged mirror hung over the fireplace. Christmas cards abounded and a little Christmas tree stood on a low table.

'Allow me to offer my condolences to you and the family,' said Colbeck.

'Thank you,' said Reuben.

'Were you and your brother close?'

'Yes, Inspector, we were. As the younger one, of course,

I was very much in Cyril's shadow. No matter how hard I worked, I could never match his achievements. His success was remarkable.'

'And well deserved,' Drake interjected.

'Yet it clearly made him enemies,' said Colbeck.

Reuben nodded. 'I'm afraid that it did.'

'Have you any idea who they were?'

'No, I haven't. We never discussed such things. Cyril liked having robust arguments with people because he always won them. I suppose that it made him feel invincible.'

'And, as a result, off guard.'

'He felt he was a match for anyone,' said Drake. 'And he was until . . . until the excursion. It would never occur to him that he'd be the victim of an ambush.'

'Whoever arranged that ambush,' recalled Colbeck, 'had no pity for the family. He informed them of Mr Hubbleday's death in the cruellest way.'

'The message pushed through the letter box was vile,' recalled Reuben.

'Do you still have it, sir?'

'No, Inspector. As soon as I read it, I threw it on the fire.'

'That's a pity,' said Colbeck. 'It might have told us something about the person who wrote it. Was the handwriting neat or was it an illiterate scrawl?'

'It was written in capital letters. It said that my brother had been killed and why he was hated.' Reuben bit his lip. 'The bad language was disgusting.'

'Who first opened the letter?'

'It was my sister-in-law, unfortunately. Dorcas was devastated.'

'I can well imagine.'

'They sent for me and showed me the letter. It turned my stomach.'

'You did the right thing,' said Drake. 'In your position, I'd have hurled it on the fire as well. The family were so lucky to have you to turn to.'

'I've moved in here to protect them, Mr Drake. If we get any more gloating messages through the door again, I'll be here to intercept them.'

'But I hope you'll hang onto them as well,' said Colbeck. 'They could provide us with evidence. Have you spoken to the neighbours?'

'No – why should I?'

'If they know you might receive unwanted mail, they could help by glancing out of their front window from time to time. Someone posted that first message through the letter box. Involve the neighbours in keeping watch.'

'I never thought of that,' admitted Reuben.

'There's a lamp not far from the front door here. Even in the dark, someone creeping up outside would be seen.'

'Thank you for the advice, Inspector.'

Reuben had none of his brother's famed vigour and self-confidence. Having spent a lifetime beside a domineering man, he was subdued and uncompetitive. Colbeck felt sympathetic towards him. He decided that Reuben was a good, kind man, thrust into a dire situation with which he was struggling to cope.

What the inspector really wanted to do was to speak to the widow and the two daughters. They would be able to provide useful information about Hubbleday's domestic life, but they were still dazed by the fearsome blow they had received. Colbeck would have to wait until they had recovered. Having learnt as much as he felt he could from Reuben, he thanked him for his help.

'It was good to meet you, Inspector,' said the other. 'As soon as my sister-in-law and nieces feel able to speak to you, I'll be in touch.'

'Thank you.'

'And before you go,' added Reuben, turning to Drake, 'I'm grateful for your offer. On behalf of the family, I accept it.'

'Good,' said Drake. 'I'll be in touch.'

They exchanged farewells with Reuben then left the house. Once alone together, Colbeck was curious.

'What was that about an offer?'

'It's a private matter, Inspector,' said Drake.

'Then I won't pry into it.'

Having asked the cab driver who'd taken them there to wait, they were able to clamber into the vehicle. As it set off, Colbeck had another question to ask.

'What is the name of the daughter due to be married?'

'Marion.'

'Who is the bridegroom?'

'It's a charming young man named Philip Wren,' said Drake. 'You may have noticed Wren's Timber Yard, the largest in the area. As the only son, Philip will inherit it one day. Cyril thought it was an excellent match and he was very difficult to please.'

'In what way?'

'Marion is a beauty. She attracts a lot of attention. If it had been left to her, she would have chosen someone else.'

'Really?'

'She has a mind of her own, Inspector. Young women are expected to obey their fathers, but Marion has a streak of independence. Her choice was John Armitage. If you'd seen them together, you'd have said that they were made for each other.'

'What was her father's objection?'

'Armitage came from brewing stock. Cyril claimed that, whenever he met the man, he had a strong whiff of beer about him. Put simply, he wanted someone better for Marion. There was a ferocious argument about it.'

'Whose side did Mrs Hubbleday take?'

'Dorcas was forced to back her husband,' said Drake. 'Privately, I suspect, she agreed with her daughter's choice.'

'So, Marion's father broke up the relationship?'

'Yes, Inspector. It caused a lot of aggravation.'

'Oh, dear!' said Colbeck. 'I have a daughter myself. Even at the age of four, Helena likes her own way. When she reaches the right age, she won't let her father dictate to her. I fancy that she'll insist on choosing her future husband, and why shouldn't she be allowed to do so?' He turned to Drake. 'Do you have children?'

'No – I'm not married.'

'Then you've escaped that problem.'

'Having seen what happened in Cyril's case,' said Drake, 'I'm very glad. He told me that Marion moped for over a year. It took time to bring her around to the idea of marrying Philip Wren.'

'What about the man she really wanted?'

'John Armitage was deeply hurt.'

'He must have resented Marion's father.'

'He did,' agreed Drake. 'John was wounded to the quick.'

Seated in his office at the brewery, John Armitage read the report in *The Times* about the investigation into the murder of Cyril Hubbleday. Grinning broadly, he reached for a pair of scissors and cut the article out.

As soon as he had delivered the body of James Carmody to the hospital in Worcester, Inspector Vellacott sent a telegraph to Birmingham. It was a summons to Dr Peck, the pathologist. The latter had responded instantly. When Vellacott later called at the hospital to see how the post-mortem was going, Peck was slightly confused.

'Mr Hubbleday was a much easier assignment for me,' he said.

'Why?' asked Vellacott.

'The cause of death was obvious. He'd been shot in the head.'

'What about Carmody?'

'I'm still trying to find out how he was killed. There's not a mark on his body. It's possible that he was poisoned, I suppose, but I've seen no indication of that so far. That brings us back to the head.'

'Unfortunately, we don't have it.'

'It's a pity,' said Peck. 'If we did, the cause of death would be apparent.'

'What do you mean?'

'He was either shot in the head or had his brains beaten out. I'm relying on guesswork here and that's very unscientific. I'm sorry, Inspector, if you want certainty, then you have to help me.'

'In what way?'

'Bring me the head and I can be more exact.'

'We've no idea where it is,' said Vellacott. 'What sort of man kills someone, then removes his head?'

'He's a collector.'

'I don't follow.'

'The person you're after enjoys killing and likes to keep trophies.'

Colonel Yardley had had a busy morning with his gun. When he got back to his house, he was able to hand over dozens of pigeons to his cook. After taking off his hat and coat, he walked to the drawing room. His wife, Charlotte, had been dozing in front of the fire in her wheelchair, but she came awake when the door opened.

'Is that you, Francis?' she asked.

'Yes, my love,' he replied, coming over to her to plant a gentle kiss on her head. 'How are you?'

'Much the same. I tire so easily.'

'You must have as much rest as you need.'

Charlotte Yardley had been a tall, stately woman when he had married her, but she had caught a wasting disease in middle age. It had sapped her energy and reduced her to a rather sad, wan, almost skeletal figure. Though her body now sagged, however, her mind remained alert.

'Have you been out shooting again?'

He smiled. 'Need you ask?'

'Why do you have the instinct to kill? You're not in the army now.'

'I'll always be in the army,' he said, proudly. 'Besides, there was a time when you appreciated your husband's marksmanship.'

'Was there?'

'I remember your delight when I came home from a hunting expedition in India. Whenever I see the trophy I bagged that day, I still feel a sense of great pride.'

He looked down at the rug in the middle of the room. Stretched out helplessly on the floor, the tiger seemed to stare malevolently back at him.

CHAPTER TWELVE

Marion Hubbleday had luncheon alone with her uncle. Her mother and younger sister preferred to have their meal served in the master bedroom. Marion was fascinated to hear about the visit from Inspector Colbeck.

'Why didn't you call me when he was here?' she asked.

'I wasn't sure that you felt able to deal with any questioning,' said Reuben. 'When I spoke to you this morning, you said that you still felt hurt and fragile. The inspector was very understanding about it.'

'What was he like?'

'He was a true gentleman in every way – polite, considerate, patient. Also, he's something of a dandy. To tell you the truth, he made me feel rather shabby.'

'Is he hopeful of finding the person who . . . ?'

'He's determined to do so, Marion. I was impressed with him. Inspector Colbeck is unlike any of the policemen we could meet around here. There's an air of quiet authority about him.'

'I look forward to meeting him.'

'Would you like me to say that you're ready to speak to him?'

'Not today,' she decided. 'Perhaps tomorrow.'

'I'll send him a note to that effect. Mr Appleby would value the opportunity to speak to you as well. He had great admiration for your father.'

'Suggest that he and the inspector come together.'

'I will. And I'm glad that you feel ready to talk to them.'

'You never know. Something I say may be helpful to the inspector.'

'That's true.'

Reuben was about to eat his breakfast when he heard the letter box opening and shutting. He went swiftly into the hall. Picking up the envelope from the floor, he opened the front door and looked out. A young man was running away down the road. There was no hope of catching him. Glancing at the envelope, he saw that it was addressed to Marion. He closed the front door and went into the dining room.

'I thought the post was delivered earlier,' she said.

'This came by hand. It's for you.'

'Let me see.'

'Perhaps I should open it first,' he said, looking at the envelope with suspicion. 'I'm not having you or anyone else in the house being upset again by a cruel sneer.'

She held out her hand. 'At least let me look at the handwriting.'

He passed it to her. 'Very well, but please don't open it.'

'There's nothing to fear,' she said, excitedly. 'I know who it's from. Oh, how sweet of him to write!'

'Is it from Philip?'

'No, it isn't. It's from John Armitage.'

Jerome Appleby looked pleased when Colbeck called on him in his office.

'You have something to report?' he asked, hopefully.

'Yes, I have,' replied Colbeck. 'When I arrived this morning, you were too busy to see me. I've had to bide my time.'

'I'm fully available now, Inspector. What's happened?'

'There's been a second murder, sir.'

'What!' cried Appleby. 'When – and where?'

'A man whom we believe may have assisted Mr Hubbleday's killer has been found dead near the base of a hill in the Malverns. He'd been decapitated.'

'Saints preserve us!'

'Inspector Vellacott took the body to Worcester Hospital.'

'Where exactly did the murder take place?'

'It was at the bottom of Worcestershire Beacon.'

Appleby was shaken. 'That's no great distance from my home.'

'It may not be a coincidence.'

'What's going on, Inspector?'

'We don't know,' admitted Colbeck. 'Our theory is that the killer made use of this man – James Carmody – then disposed of him. Perhaps he decided that Carmody knew too much.'

'But why cut off the man's head?'

'It was a means of concealing his identity. Luckily, it failed. Thanks to a constable from the Worcestershire Constabulary, we know who the victim is.'

'The killer is taunting you, Inspector,' said Appleby.

'Sooner or later, he'll do it once too often, sir.'

'What are your officers doing?'

'One of them is right here, sir, talking to people who knew the men sacked by Mr Hubbleday. They included a Samuel Waycroft. He threw a punch at the works manager when he was given his notice.'

'I remember the incident.'

'We've traced Waycroft to Tipton. Sergeant Leeming is there at this moment in the hope of apprehending him.'

'Are you telling me that Waycroft is the killer?'

'It's highly unlikely, I fancy. But he may be involved in the plot.'

Appleby plied him with more questions and Colbeck did his best to give him reassuring answers. But the fact remained that there was no positive news to pass on. When he heard that the inspector had been to Hubbleday's house that morning, Appleby pressed for details.

'How are they holding up?'

'We weren't allowed to see Mrs Hubbleday or her daughters, sir.'

'Neither were Drake and I.'

'They're being carefully guarded by Mr Hubbleday's brother.'

'Yes, I was impressed with the way that Reuben stepped into the breach.'

'At a time like this,' said Colbeck, 'the family needs someone like him. He's a godsend.' A memory nudged him. 'Might I ask you something, sir?'

'Yes, of course.'

'It concerns Mr Drake. I was astonished when he told me that he and Mr Hubbleday played chess on a regular basis.'

'Why?'

'I've learnt a lot about your works manager, most of it to his credit. But nobody even suggested that he was the sort of person who would enjoy a quiet evening at the chessboard.'

'Yes, it does seem odd, I agree.'

'How do you explain it?'

'I can only put it down to Cyril's competitive spirit. He simply had to shine at whatever he took up, whether it was bowls, darts or – in this case – chess.'

'Bowls and darts are games for men who enjoy a physical contest. Chess is a battle of minds. It's also absorbing. When he left his job at the end of the working day, Mr Hubbleday went home to an adoring family. Yet he seems to have ignored them. Didn't Mr Drake have a family of his own?'

'No, Inspector. Ernest Drake lives with his sister, a maiden lady with a sharp tongue. You can't blame him for wanting to get out of the house on some evenings.'

'His needs might be satisfied by a game of chess,' said Colbeck, 'but I find it strange that Mr Hubbleday didn't prefer to enjoy family life. It's what fathers do.'

Appleby pondered. 'I never thought about it that way,' he said at length.

Helena Colbeck was now old enough to join her mother and her grandfather for luncheon. She wore a bib and needed a thick cushion underneath her so that she could reach her food. Helena liked to wobble precariously on it between courses. Inevitably, she asked the question that was always at the forefront of her mind.

'Where's Daddy?'

'He's at work, darling,' said Madeleine.

The girl pouted. 'He's always at work.'

'It's only because he has to make money to spend on you,' Andrews told her.

'Will Daddy be here for Christmas?'

'Yes, of course.'

'He'll do his very, very best,' said Madeleine.

'What does he do when he's away?' asked the girl.

'He has a very important job, darling.'

'You always say that.'

'It's true.'

'Yes,' said Andrews. 'You should be very proud of your daddy. He helps people who are in trouble.'

'Is that what he's doing now?'

'Yes, it is.'

'Where is he?'

'We're not sure, Helena.'

'But wherever he is,' added Madeleine, 'Daddy will be thinking about you.' She looked at her daughter's empty plate. 'Have you had enough?'

'Yes, thank you, Mummy.'

'Would you like to get down?'

'Yes, please.'

Rising from her seat, Madeleine pressed a bell on the wall to summon the nanny. As soon as the woman appeared, Helena hopped off her chair and went out with her. Andrews watched them go.

'You didn't have a nanny to look after you at that age,' he said.

'No,' agreed Madeleine. 'I had someone far better – Mummy. And I feel so guilty sometimes that I can't do what she did and devote myself to my daughter.'

'You have work to do, Maddy.'

'Yes, and I love it.'

'Then you must stop worrying about Helena. I'm always here, remember. That means she has two people to look after her.'

'Three,' corrected Madeleine. 'You've forgotten Lydia.'

'She must envy you sometimes.'

'Why?'

'You have everything that she'd like, Maddy. You have a loving husband, a wonderful daughter, and a career as an artist. Her life must be so empty.'

'I don't agree. Lydia keeps herself occupied.'

He chuckled. 'I know what she'd really like.'

'What's that?'

'Lydia would like to keep herself occupied with Alan Hinton.'

'Don't be so coarse.'

'It's obvious, Maddy. She wants him and he wants her, but they live in different worlds. There's always going to be a big gap between them.'

'There was a big gap between me and Robert,' said Madeleine, 'but we found a way to bridge it somehow. Perhaps the same thing will happen to Lydia and Alan.'

'I doubt it.'

'Why?'

'You had something that Lydia doesn't have – a doting father to look after your best interests. I feel sorry for her. What she really needs is not Alan Hinton.' He tapped his chest. 'It's someone like me.'

Madeleine laughed. 'Perhaps I should hand you over to her.'

* * *

213

When the detectives met in their office at the Works, they compared notes. Colbeck was disappointed to hear that the sergeant had lost track of Samuel Waycroft and decided that it might be better to stop searching for him for a day or two.

'Sooner or later,' he said, 'Waycroft will drift back to his sister in Tipton. Let him think that you're no longer on his tail. You've alerted the local police. They can look for him. As it happens, we have a much bigger problem than Waycroft.'

'What is it?' asked Leeming.

'There's been a second murder.'

'I don't believe it!'

'The victim was James Carmody, though we were not supposed to know that.'

'What do you mean?'

'The killer had cut his head off.'

Colbeck explained what had happened and how they had retrieved the body from the Beacon. Leeming was surprised that Tallis had been involved.

'Did he really help you to retrieve the corpse?' he said.

'Yes,' replied Colbeck. 'He was prepared to get his hands dirty.'

'He usually gets other people to do jobs like that.'

'It's the first time he's been really useful since we arrived in the Malverns.'

His companions laughed. 'Did you say that to him, sir?' asked Hinton.

'No,' said Colbeck. 'Even my courage has its limitations

sometimes. Now, please tell Victor what happened when you went out for that meal last night.'

'Ah, yes. I was warned.'

After listening with interest to his account, Leeming snapped his fingers.

'That means the person we're after is one of the painters,' he noted. 'All we have to do is to root him out.'

'Easier said than done,' warned Hinton.

'Let's see how I get on with Churt,' said Colbeck. He turned to Leeming. 'He's the painter Alan picked out. I intend to have a quiet word with Derek Churt – well away from this place.'

'What am I to do, sir?' asked the sergeant.

'I'm sending you back to Great Malvern to help the superintendent.'

'Oh, no!'

'That's only part of your job. Firstly, I want you to stop off at Worcester so that you can go to the hospital. Dr Peck, the pathologist, will have been working on his second post-mortem there. Ask him what he's found so far.'

'Yes, sir.'

'Then reward yourself by going on to the superintendent.'

'He'll probably send me off to that mad old woman who treated me like dirt.'

'Lady Foley is not mad,' said Colbeck. 'It's just that she believes herself to be superior to ordinary mortals like us. Humour her, Victor.'

'I'd rather ignore her altogether.'

'What about me, Inspector?' asked Hinton.

'You carry on with what you're doing. The more we know about how this place operates, the more understanding we'll have of why Mr Hubbleday inspired such hatred.'

'What will you be doing, sir?'

'I'll be pursuing another line of enquiry,' said Colbeck. 'Until today, I thought that the most likely suspects worked for Mr Appleby. I've now come across one who has nothing at all to do with this Works.'

'Who is he?'

'John Armitage.'

Armitage was a tall, handsome, broad-shouldered young man with flowing dark hair. He had grown up in the brewery trade. Now that he was in his mid-twenties, he had moved into management. Armitage had been promoted to the position of sales manager, a role that involved travel. It had made him markedly more urbane than his friends at the brewery.

He was in his office when a youth knocked on his door and opened it.

'I delivered that letter for you, Mr Armitage.'

'Did anyone see you?'

'No, I did what you told me to do, sir. I slipped it through the letter box and ran away.'

'Well done,' said the other. 'That will be all.'

The youth closed the door and went away. Armitage unlocked a drawer in his desk and took out an album of treasured memories. When he turned to the last page, he read the sad words that Marion Hubbleday had written to him when they had been forced apart. Beside the card she had sent him was the newspaper article that he had earlier cut out from *The Times*. He felt a surge of satisfaction.

Cyril Hubbleday was no longer able to thwart him.

Victor Leeming had been warned. Before he could gain access to the mortuary at Worcester Hospital, he would first have to get past Hugo Lipton, the unctuous, self-regarding manager who had irritated Colbeck so much. It took Leeming over five minutes to shake him off and have a conversation with Montgomery Peck. The pathologist had almost completed his post-mortem and was able to show part of his report to his visitor. Accustomed to reading such reports, Leeming could understand most of the medical jargon. He was impressed by how thorough Peck had been.

'Carmody's body was found close to eight o'clock this morning,' said Leeming. 'How long had he been dead?'

'It's impossible to give an exact time, Sergeant. Apart from anything else, he'd been exposed to the elements all night. If I had to make a guess, I'd say that Carmody was killed somewhere between eight o'clock yesterday evening and midnight.'

'Nobody else would have been around at that time.'

'No human being, perhaps, but there were animals on the prowl. One of them had a nibble at his trouser leg, and I daresay other creatures had a good sniff. A death outdoors is soon discovered by animals.'

'In your report, you say that the head was hacked off.'

'Yes,' said Peck, 'a chopper or even an axe was used. It must have been a vicious attack.'

'You examined the body of Mr Hubbleday as well, didn't you?'

'Indeed, I did. In his case, I had more to work on. His head was intact.'

'What was the difference between the two corpses?'

'Mr Hubbleday didn't suffer,' said Peck. 'He was killed instantly by a bullet. Mr Carmody, on the other hand, was attacked by a sharp weapon. He'd have felt every blow until he passed out.'

'Did the same man kill both victims?'

'No, I don't believe that he did.'

'Why not?'

'Mr Hubbleday was lured into the open and shot from above by a marksman. It was quick and professional. This gentleman,' he went on, indicating the naked body on the slab, 'was punished by someone in a rage.'

'Were the two killers working together?'

'You're the detective, Sergeant. I'll be interested to hear what you discover.'

Marion Hubbleday was alone in her bedroom, holding the letter sent to her by John Armitage. Simply seeing the familiar handwriting again was a tonic to her. The warm sentiments expressed brought a host of precious memories flooding back. For the first time since she heard the news of her father's murder, Marion's spirits rose. She was so engrossed that she did not hear the knock on the front door. Shortly afterwards, footsteps ascended the stairs. When someone tapped on her door, Marion put the letter guiltily aside.

'Come in,' she said.

Her uncle opened the door. 'You have a visitor.'

'Who is it?'

'Philip.'

'Oh, I see.'

'He's hoping to have a private word with you but will understand if it's not convenient.' He could see that she was uncertain. 'Shall I send him away?'

'No, no,' she said. 'Tell him that I'll be down in a minute.'

'I will – then I'll leave you both alone.'

When her uncle disappeared, Marion took one last look at the letter then slipped it into the drawer of the dressing table. She looked at herself in the mirror and realised how pale she was. After brushing her hair, she pinched both cheeks to put some colour into her face. Marion then went downstairs and into the drawing room.

Philip Wren leapt up from his chair and grasped her hands in concern.

'How are you, Marion?'

'I'm . . . trying my best to be brave.'

'What about your mother and sister?'

'They still can't believe what happened,' she said. 'Let's sit down, shall we?'

'Of course,' he said, leading her gently to the sofa and lowering himself onto it beside her. 'I've been so worried about you.'

'It's kind of you to come, Philip.'

'My place is beside you. We'll be man and wife in the new year.'

'Yes . . . of course . . .'

Philip Wren was a slim young man of medium height with wavy fair hair that gave him an almost raffish look. It belied his character. In fact, he was subdued and serious. Marion had been drawn to him by his intelligence and his kindness. He might lack the excitement of John Armitage but there were compensations. That, at least, was what Marion hoped.

'Have any . . . arrangements been made?' he asked.

'Mr Appleby is taking care of all that.'

'What have the police said?'

'I haven't spoken to them yet.'

'Would you like me to do so on your behalf?'

'There's no need, Philip.'

'It will save you the trouble of doing so.'

'Uncle Reuben has been in touch with an Inspector Colbeck. He's come all the way from London to take charge of this case. I'm told he's very experienced.'

'Then let's hope he soon finds the blackguard responsible.' He squeezed her hands. 'I'll help you through this, my darling.'

'Thank you.'

He looked into her eyes, worried that she was not really concentrating on him.

'Have you had many condolence cards?'

'Dozens and dozens.'

'Then you must have received mine.'

'It came yesterday, Philip, and brought me such comfort.'

There was a long pause. 'What about . . . you know?'

'No,' she said, firmly. 'John has not been in touch. That's all in the past.'

He smiled. 'I was hoping you'd say that.'

Colbeck liked him on sight. John Armitage was pleasant, well spoken and open-faced. Genuinely surprised that the inspector should call on him, he invited his visitor into his office and waved him to a chair. Colbeck had long ago learnt never to trust first impressions. Some of the most charming and plausible people he had ever met had turned out to be shameless villains. Since Armitage was holding down an important job in the family brewery, however, he was patently not a career criminal. It remained to be seen whether there was any shade of darkness in his soul.

'Why have you come to me, Inspector?' asked Armitage.

'I believe that you and Marion Hubbleday were once close, sir.'

'That was long ago.'

'From what I've been told, you must have been bruised.'

'I'm a fully grown adult,' said Armitage, 'and have learnt to shrug off disappointments.'

'Being forcibly separated from the woman you loved is rather more than a mere disappointment.'

'No, no,' said Armitage, 'I agree. At the time, I was wounded by the attitude that Marion's father took. It was hurtful – both to me and to her. But time has healed those particular scars and I enjoy my life.'

'May I ask if you are married?'

'I am not, but there is someone . . . very dear to me.'

'Then I wish you both well,' said Colbeck. 'When did you first hear of the murder of Cyril Hubbleday?'

'It was not until this morning,' replied Armitage. 'In my position as sales manager, I have to travel a great deal. I've been away for days.'

'I see.'

'When I came to work this morning, a copy of *The Times* was on my desk as usual. I was shocked to read of the murder.'

'Was there no other emotion once the shock had worn off?'

'I didn't open a bottle of champagne, if that's what you mean,' said Armitage, with the ghost of a smile. 'I didn't even reach for a pint of our Best Bitter.'

'I'm sorry you find such appalling news a source of amusement.'

'You misunderstand me, Inspector. I took no pleasure in the discovery. What bitterness I felt about Marion's father disappeared long ago. My immediate reaction concerned her. I felt intensely sorry for Marion.'

'Did you convey those feelings to her?'

'No, of course not. I'm no longer part of her life. Really, Inspector,' he went on, 'I don't know who has been telling tales about me, but he or she has misled you badly. Yes, I did come close to making a proposal of marriage, and it was nipped in the bud by Marion's father because he found me . . . unsuitable. That much is true,' he conceded. 'But the notion that I've harboured dreams of revenge ever since is an insult to me. I have a full and satisfying life to lead. Why should I jeopardise it by contemplating the death of someone I have done my best to forget?'

'You haven't done your best to forget his elder daughter, I fancy.'

'Fond memories fade over time, Inspector.'

'That's not been my experience, sir,' said Colbeck, holding his gaze. 'Might I ask you a favour, Mr Armitage?'

'You can certainly ask it, but you may not like the answer you get.'

'Since you only became aware of Mr Hubbleday's murder today, you will not have had adequate time to reflect upon it. I ask you to do so at your leisure. During the time that you and his elder daughter were close, you must have had an insight into their family life. What sort of man was her father?' asked Colbeck. 'Can you imagine his upsetting someone so much that he felt impelled to strike back?'

'I can well imagine it.'

'Why is that?'

'Cyril Hubbleday took a delight in needling people. It was almost as if it was his hobby. He fawned over Mr Appleby but bullied everyone else at the firm. When the news of his death was announced, there were probably silent cheers from the workers.'

'Was he such an ogre?'

'Ask that question at Appleby's. That's where you should look,' advised Armitage. 'Search among the people who toiled under him. I venture to suggest that it's much more fertile ground for investigation than this brewery.'

'That's sound advice, sir.'

Armitage rose meaningfully from his seat. 'It was good to meet you, Inspector,' he said. 'I wish you well in your search.'

Edward Tallis was at once pleased and disappointed to see one of his officers getting off the train in Great Malvern. Glad to have someone to assist him, he was sad that it was the sergeant and not Colbeck himself. Whisking the newcomer into the stationmaster's office, he demanded his news.

'Did you arrest Samuel Waycroft?'

'I tried to, sir, but he escaped.'

Tallis peered at Leeming's chin. 'You've got a bruise.'

'I don't need you to tell me that, sir. Waycroft caught me with an uppercut. The surprise is that I still have all my teeth.'

He told Tallis about his fruitless search for the man in Wolverhampton but insisted that he would catch him in due course. Leeming then talked about his visit to Worcester

Hospital. The superintendent was interested to hear what the pathologist had said about the likely time of death. He made an instant decision.

'Let's go there now,' he declared.

'Where?'

'To the Beacon, of course.'

'Why?'

'There's still enough light for us to search the area where the body was found. I daresay we might even bump into the person who stumbled on it.'

'The inspector said it was a woman named Biddy Leacock.'

'That's right.'

'Why would a donkey woman be out in this weather?'

'Force of habit, I fancy.'

Leaving the office, they found a cab waiting outside the station and asked to be taken to the Worcestershire Beacon. As soon as they were moving, Tallis had a rare compliment to pay.

'That was a good idea of yours,' he said.

'Was it, sir?'

'Yes, it was both good and unexpected. Let's be candid, shall we? You are not exactly known for your brainwaves.'

Leeming ignored the gibe. 'What idea are you talking about, sir?'

'The one that Mrs Renshaw reported to me,' said Tallis. 'You suggested that we'd have more privacy in her hotel than in the Imperial. How right you were! Over dinner last night, I had to listen to people around me discussing their ailments and hoping that the Water Cure would get rid of them.'

'It's far too dangerous,' warned Leeming. 'Mrs Renshaw told us all about it. It's more likely to drown you than cure you. I can't believe that people pay all that money for the treatment. Oh, I'm sorry, sir,' he went on. 'Yes, I did say it would be better if we met at our hotel. The inspector agreed but thought that you'd never approve. That's why he didn't mention it to you.'

'I'm grateful that Mrs Renshaw did pass on the idea. I agree to it.'

'Does that mean I've done something right at last?'

Tallis rounded on him. 'What are you insinuating?'

'Nothing, sir – we'll be pleased to welcome you this evening.'

When the cab reached the foot of the Beacon, they got out. They began to walk up the incline. Tallis was soon puffing but Leeming was under no pressure at all. When they reached the stables, they saw someone emerging from behind the building. Biddy Leacock had lumbered into view. She sensed the possibility of customers.

'Did you want to go right to the top?' she asked.

'No, no,' gasped Tallis.

'You'd have a donkey apiece.'

'That won't be necessary, Miss Leacock.'

'Please yourself,' she mumbled and went off down the hill.

'What was she doing up here?' asked Leeming.

'Feeding the animals, I daresay. She's more interested in them than she is in her fellow human beings. However, let's carry on. There's not far to go now.'

'What exactly are we looking for, sir?'

'Clues.'

'What kind of clues?'

'We'll know that if we find them.'

CHAPTER THIRTEEN

Derek Churt was enjoying his position among the fellow painters more and more. As the only one of them who went on the excursion, he'd acquired a lustre. Whenever the murder was discussed, his colleagues always deferred to him. He had been wrong about their reaction to his interview with Constable Hinton. Instead of arousing their suspicion, it increased their respect for him because they assumed that his version of what happened on the excursion was of value to the detectives.

'I hope they never catch the killer,' said one of them.

'They won't,' said Churt.

'Why not?'

'He's too clever.'

'What makes you think that, Derek?'

'Shooting Hubb wasn't done on the spur of the moment. Planning was needed. He had to stop the train at the right place and rely on Hubb getting out to see what caused the delay. Then he had to shoot the right man from high above him, where he couldn't see Hubb's face properly. If he was clever enough to do all that,' said Churt, 'he'd be clever enough to escape. He could be a hundred miles from here.'

'But what made him want to kill Hubb in the first place?'

Churt grinned. 'Do you really need to ask me that?'

Everyone burst out laughing. They were united by their shared hatred of the works manager. Since Hubbleday was no longer prowling the place and keeping everyone under surveillance, there was a sense of freedom in the air. The working day had suddenly turned into something they could relish.

When the hooter sounded to bring their shift to an end, they set off home. Churt walked beside one of his workmates until they reached the street where the latter lived. As his friend peeled off, Churt was surprised to see his wife in the distance, waiting outside the house. As soon as she caught sight of him, Agnes broke into a trot. He lengthened his stride to reach her more quickly.

She threw herself into his arms.

'What's wrong?' he asked. 'You look so upset.'

'I'm worried, Derek.'

'Why – is there something wrong with Peter?'

'No,' she said. 'This man came to the house. He's a detective inspector from London. I was afraid he'd come to arrest you.'

'He has no reason to do that, Aggie.' He took her by the shoulders. 'Now, calm down. I've done nothing wrong.'

'I'm so frightened.'

'There's no need.'

'I mean, you've never been in trouble of any kind.'

'Leave it to me. I'll sort it out.'

Putting an arm around her, he hurried her back to the house. They let themselves in and went straight to the living room. Colbeck was kneeling beside Peter, watching the boy moving the toy train across the floor.

'Mr Churt?' he asked, looking up.

'That's me.'

'Then I must congratulate you on your eye for detail. The locomotive and carriages are beautifully made. It's no wonder that Peter enjoys playing with the train. And so do I,' he said, getting to his feet. 'I'm Inspector Colbeck from Scotland Yard, by the way. Don't be surprised at what you saw when you came in. I love trains as much as your son does.'

Churt stood there open-mouthed.

As they searched among the ferns where the body had been found, Leeming could hear the superintendent groaning every time he bent double. The sergeant straightened his back to pass on his advice.

'I think that it is time for you to retire, sir,' he counselled.

'Don't you dare give me advice,' said Tallis, shooting him a look.

'You were puffing and panting all the way up here then you started moaning whenever you bent over.'

'I have a minor back problem, that's all.'

'Retirement would cure that, sir.'

Tallis bared his teeth. 'Do you wish to remain at Scotland Yard?'

'Of course I do, sir.'

'Then stop flirting with dismissal,' warned the other. 'Shut up and keep searching. That's what we came for.'

Leeming was cowed. 'Yes, of course.'

They widened the search slightly, allowing the sergeant to put more distance between them. There was diminishing light for them to see properly but they forced themselves on. Instead of raising the prospect of retirement, Leeming decided that he should admire the superintendent for taking part in a search he would normally delegate to others. He brushed another patch of ferns apart.

'Damnation!' cried Tallis, twenty-odd yards away.

'Have you found something, sir?'

'I didn't, but my foot did.'

Leeming suppressed a laugh. 'Ah, I see.'

'I stepped into something nasty.'

'Lots of wild animals have been here – not to mention those donkeys.'

'Search in silence,' ordered Tallis, scraping his shoe

231

against a fallen branch. He looked around with dismay. 'A man was killed near here. Something must have been left behind.'

'Do you mean the head?'

'Well, he'd hardly take it away with him, would he?'

'It's possible, sir. You've forgotten that case we had in Swindon. The killer decapitated his victim then left the head in the local church.'

'Let's concentrate on the crime in front of us,' said Tallis, tetchily. 'I'm working on the theory that Carmody was executed right here.'

'There's no indication of that.'

'Put yourself in the mind of the killer. Which is easier – to bring someone to this spot, then hack him to death, or to kill him elsewhere, then drag a dead body all the way here? Think of the physical effort involved. It's not as if he could hire one of Biddy Leacock's donkeys to bring the corpse up here.'

'That's a point,' admitted Leeming. 'But why take him to this spot?'

'Carmody used to live in that village nearby. He knows this hill well. Whoever involved him in the first murder, could have arranged to meet him here. Having got Carmody to this spot with a promise of some kind, the killer silenced him for good.'

'Leaving only the body behind.'

'I still feel the head is not far away. Let's keep looking for it.'

'We haven't got much time left,' said Leeming, glancing up at the sky. 'Besides, if the head really is here, it will surely have been buried. We'd need a spade to dig it up.' He gazed around him. 'This really is a beautiful spot, sir. I can see why you wish to retire here.'

'I'm not retiring anywhere just yet.'

'You told us that you were thinking about it.'

'That decision is in abeyance,' said Tallis, sharply. 'As for the light, we've a good twenty minutes left to search the area, perhaps even more. Let's get back to it.'

'Watch where you put your feet this time, sir.'

Tallis bristled. 'Are you daring to give me advice?'

'It was a slip of the tongue, sir . . .'

Colbeck put the man at his ease by talking about his family. Churt was so pleased to hear his son being praised that he gradually relaxed.

'Do you have children, Inspector?' he asked.

'I have a four-year-old daughter. It's unusual for girls to like trains but she will get one soon. Her grandfather is a retired engine driver and he's been making one for her. He'll enjoy playing with it as much as she will. As for Peter,' he went on, 'I know what he wants to be.'

'An engine driver,' the boy piped up.

Now that Churt was less tense and defensive, Colbeck started to win his confidence. They were seated together in the pokey living room, catching a whiff of the meal that Agnes was cooking in the scullery.

'I gather that you spoke to Constable Hinton,' said Colbeck.

'That's right, Inspector.'

'He told you about the way he was warned by two men from your Works.'

'That doesn't mean they are painters.'

'Agreed, but since he only spoke to men in the paint shops, Constable Hinton felt it was safe to assume that one of them at least saw and heard him. If that wasn't the case, how would he have been recognised?'

Churt was surprised. 'That never occurred to me.'

'Someone among your colleagues has information relating to the murder of Cyril Hubbleday. I know that the works manager was loathed by all of you, but that doesn't mean you should let his killer go free.'

'No, no, I see that.'

'I'm not suggesting that one of the painters was actually involved directly in the murder,' said Colbeck, 'but he could inadvertently have given the killer vital information. The man needed to know the approximate time when the excursion train was likely to arrive at that spot on the line. Do you agree?'

'Well, yes I do.'

'The only painter who had that information was you, Mr Churt. I daresay that you mentioned the departure time of the train to your workmates.'

'Yes, I suppose that I did.'

'There's something else I'd like you to suppose,' said Colbeck. 'Someone who works alongside you might have chatted about the excursion in a pub and been overheard by a stranger.'

Churt was roused. 'You can't blame me for that, Inspector.'

'There's no reason to do so. I'm just pointing out that the man who was plotting the murder of Mr Hubbleday might have hung around groups of your workmates in the hope of picking up the details he needed.'

'How was I to know that someone would do that?'

'You couldn't possibly have foreseen it, Mr Churt. In any case, that may not have happened. It's only a possibility that I put to you. I'm simply suggesting that information you gave to your colleagues might have found its way to the killer. It might have happened accidentally,' said Colbeck, 'or deliberately.'

'What are you telling me, Inspector?'

'Remember what happened to Constable Hinton. He was warned. How would you feel if one or both of the men who jostled him worked alongside you?'

'Well . . .'

Colbeck could see that his words were having the desired effect on Churt.

'Please think about it, sir,' he said. 'Seriously.'

It was Leeming who made the discovery. Tallis had all but abandoned the search. The effort of bending and groping among the ferns had told on him. It was cold, yet perspiration had begun to dampen his forehead.

Removing his hat, he used a handkerchief to dab at his face. Somewhere in the gloom, Leeming shouted out.

'I've found something!'

'What is it?'

'I don't know yet.'

'Is it the head?'

'No, sir, it's just . . . something that shouldn't be here.'

Leeming trampled through the ferns to reach him and held up a large white rag that was badly stained. He thrust it at Tallis.

'That's blood, sir,' he claimed. 'You were right.'

'I usually am.'

'Carmody was murdered here. The killer used this rag to wipe the blood off the chopper or axe he used then he probably flung it away. Wait a moment,' said Leeming as he had second thoughts. 'Why was Carmody stupid enough to come to this spot with a man carrying a potential murder weapon?'

'It may have been concealed in a small case.'

'People don't carry cases when they come for a walk up this hill.'

'Then there's another explanation,' argued Tallis. 'Perhaps the weapon was already here, hidden among the ferns.'

'If you pulled an axe out of the ferns, I'd run away as fast as I could. Why didn't Carmody do that?'

'You're forgetting something.'

'Am I, sir?'

'The pathologist told you that a large amount of alcohol

had been found in Carmody's stomach. When his killer brought him here, the man was drunk.'

'And probably unable to protect himself,' said Leeming, trying to imagine the situation. 'Then there was the time of his death. It would certainly have been dark up here. The killer had the ideal conditions. His victim was off guard and unable to think straight. Nobody was about. Even if Carmody had yelled out when the first blow was struck, nobody would have heard him – except for those donkeys, of course.'

'This is a job for Inspector Vellacott,' decided Tallis. 'My feeling is that the head must be buried somewhere near here. We need a team of men with spades. Let's give Vellacott his due. He did identify James Carmody as a suspect. He can now have the privilege of digging up the man's head.'

Ernest Drake was working in his office when Appleby came into the room, holding an envelope.

'This has just been delivered by hand,' he said. 'It's from Reuben Hubbleday. He says that Marion feels able to speak to me and the inspector tomorrow morning.'

'That's good news, sir.'

'It is, indeed. She's a resilient young woman.'

'Both of the daughters are, but the younger one feels that it's her duty to support her mother. Dorcas is still in tears, apparently. Her whole life revolved around Cyril. The future must look empty to her.'

'The rest of the family will rally around her,' said Appleby.

'I'm sure they will. Look at the way that Reuben has responded.'

'Yes, I'd only met him a couple of times before and he always seemed rather dull to me. Clearly, I was mistaken. In an emergency, he's proving to be a true saviour.'

'I agree, sir.'

'How well do you know him?'

'I've met him from time to time,' said Drake, choosing his words with care, 'and he was kind enough on one occasion to invite me to dinner at his home. He may give the impression of being dull but he's a very intelligent man. What he lacks is Cyril's competitive spirit.'

Appleby nodded in agreement. 'It's cruel that this had to happen now,' he said. 'Christmas for the family will hardly exist. Easter will be the next casualty.'

'But that's when Marion is due to get married.'

'There needs to be a longer period of mourning. Dorcas will be in no state to watch her elder daughter taking part in an Easter marriage – and Marion herself may feel that it will have to be postponed.'

'Reuben will have to be consulted,' said Drake. 'It's almost certain that he would have taken his brother's place during the ceremony. He might recommend that it goes as planned so that it can bring some joy and relief to the family. Also,' he added, 'he knows his niece well enough to realise that Marion must marry Philip Wren sooner rather than later.'

'I don't understand.'

'Philip was not her first choice as a husband.'

'No, that's right. She had another suitor, didn't she?'

'His name was John Armitage.'

'He won't present a problem, will he?' asked Appleby. 'Cyril broke up that relationship years ago. Armitage has probably married someone else by now.'

'I doubt it.'

'Has he been carrying a torch for Marion all this time?'

'It's possible,' said Drake, meeting his eye. 'But it's more likely that Marion has certainly been carrying a torch for him.'

When he left the Works that evening, Alan Hinton was on the alert. Years of pounding the beat at night as a uniformed constable had given him an instinct for danger. On his walk to the hotel, he felt quite safe. Nobody was following him.

An hour later, when he left the hotel, he had no sense of unwanted company. Hinton did not, however, take any chances. Going into the same pub as on the previous night, he went straight through to the rear entrance and off down an alleyway. If the two men were waiting to intercept him for the second time, they would be disappointed. He picked his way through a maze of streets until he found the Seven Bells. It seemed to beckon him in. A pleasing aroma drifted into his nostrils as he entered the pub. The food smelled good and there was a choice of beer.

'Good evening, sir,' said the barman. 'What can I get you?'

Leeming looked at the names on the pumps before he decided.

'I'll have a pint of Armitage's Best Bitter, please,' he said.

The train journey to Great Malvern gave Colbeck the thinking time that he valued so much. Having worked his way through every element of the investigation, he allowed himself some time to consider his family. They would be very anxious. Christmas was getting ever closer, yet the detectives were still struggling to identify the man or men they were after. Colbeck realised that explaining his absence to a four-year-old daughter would be very difficult for Madeleine. The closer they got to Christmas, the more insistent Helena would become about having her father back in the family home. If he did not return in time, the combination of pain, fear and disappointment would ruin their celebrations.

Colbeck turned his thoughts back to Derek Churt. Had he spoken to the painter at the Works, there would have been only a slim chance of winning him over. By meeting him at his home, Colbeck had been able to disarm him. There had been an unforeseen benefit. As he played with his toy train, all that Peter had talked about was the excursion. Without asking for it, Colbeck was given a child's view of the event and realised just how much it had meant to the boy. By extension, it would have delighted all the other children as well. Appleby's kindness had provided them with an uplifting experience.

By the time he reached Great Malvern, the sky was dark, and a cold wind had started to blow. He made his way to the stationmaster's office. Tallis and Leeming had news for him.

'We conducted a search of the area where Carmody was found,' said the superintendent, 'and eventually located something.'

'I was the one who stumbled on it,' boasted Leeming.

'On what?' asked Colbeck.

'It was my idea to go there,' said Tallis, quelling the sergeant with a glare. 'What happened, you see, was this . . .'

The account was concise. Colbeck was impressed by the initiative shown by the superintendent and amazed that he had searched diligently alongside the sergeant. When they showed him the blood-soaked rag, he came to the same conclusion that Tallis had reached. It had been discarded by the killer.

'Summoning the local constabulary was an excellent idea, sir,' he said.

'They wanted to be involved in this case – so I've sent a telegraph to Vellacott. His men can bring their spades to the Worcestershire Beacon tomorrow morning.'

After he had heard full details, Colbeck turned to Leeming.

'What did the pathologist tell you?'

'He told me a lot of things, sir,' said the sergeant, taking out his notebook. 'The first thing was that, if we intend to deliver a third murder victim, he'd be grateful if it came with the head attached . . .'

* * *

Madeleine Colbeck had two guests for dinner that evening. As well as her father, Lydia Quayle had joined her. Having finished their meal, they were still seated in the dining room. Caleb Andrews was in an argumentative mood.

'Why doesn't Robert keep in touch with you, Maddy?'

'He does,' she replied. 'I had a letter from him this morning.'

'That was posted yesterday. All that he could tell you was what happened the day before that. You should be kept up to date.'

'How could Robert possibly do that?'

'He could use Alan Hinton as a messenger boy.'

'Alan is part of the investigation, Mr Andrews,' said Lydia, reasonably. 'He can't be detached from that to deliver a letter here. Suppose that you were driving a train to Birmingham. Would you think of sending your fireman back to London to tell Madeleine what time you would be home?'

'Of course not,' he said. 'A fireman is vital in a steam engine.'

'Alan is vital in this investigation.'

'I agree,' said Madeleine. 'If Robert didn't believe that Alan was needed, he would never have sent for him. More to the point, Superintendent Tallis would never have agreed with the idea.'

'I think that you undervalue Alan,' said Lydia. 'He's a fine detective.'

'Yes,' agreed Andrews, 'I know. But he could surely be spared for a couple of hours to come back here on a fast train.'

'And what about Victor Leeming's wife?' asked Madeleine. 'What has she got to do with it?'

'Estelle is as keen to get the latest news about her husband as I am about mine. Who is going to deliver it to her?'

'Robert is an inspector. He should be entitled to privileges.'

'Superintendent Tallis has a higher rank and even more privileges. If he realised that one of his detectives was sneaking back here, he'd suspend him at once. Alan Hinton's place is with the others,' insisted Madeleine. 'I'm sure that he's making an important contribution.'

'I agree with you,' said Lydia.

Andrews accepted defeat. 'It was only an idea,' he bleated.

'A very silly idea,' said Madeleine. 'I have a much better one.' She stood up. 'Why don't we all adjourn to the drawing room and enjoy looking at our Christmas tree? Let's have no more arguments about Alan Hinton. He's doing a valuable job in the Black Country. Because of him, an arrest is likely to happen sooner rather than later.'

The food at the Seven Bells was even better than he had had at the Waggon and Horses the previous night. Hinton had also enjoyed his first taste of Armitage's Best Bitter. He ordered a second pint.

Colbeck was astonished that Tallis had willingly accepted Ruby Renshaw's invitation. The superintendent came to her hotel that evening and found it warm and cosy. It was a much more suitable place for serious discussion. The three of them were in the drawing room before dinner. Tallis sipped his drink and looked around with satisfaction.

'If it wasn't for the fact that the Imperial Hotel is much closer to the railway station,' he said. 'I'd be tempted to move in here.'

'No, no,' said Leeming in alarm, 'don't do that, sir. You need to stay in a bigger hotel. It's a sign of your importance.'

'That's true.'

'We thought that the Imperial was very impressive,' said Colbeck.

'In many ways it is,' agreed Tallis.

'Then what's wrong with it, sir?'

'It's full of old people – wealthy old people, who come to be pampered. I just don't fit in there.'

'But you were talking about retirement, sir,' said Leeming. 'That means you'll spend the rest of your life among old people. You'll become one of them.'

'How would you feel about that?' asked Colbeck.

'Let's forget about my plans for the future,' said Tallis, crisply. 'I came here to lead a murder investigation that has now become far more challenging than we thought. That is all that matters to me right now.'

'Then how do you wish to deploy us, sir?'

'You and Constable Hinton must continue to search in Oldbury.'

'Am I to join them?' asked Leeming.

'No, I'm sending you back to Tipton. On reflection, I've a feeling that Waycroft may crawl back there. There's still a possibility that he was implicated in the first murder. Besides, he dared to assault you. Waycroft must be arrested,' said Tallis, 'but be more careful next time you confront him.'

'I will,' said Leeming, touching his chin.

'What will you be doing tomorrow, sir?' said Colbeck.

'First of all,' replied Tallis, 'I'll be supervising the work on Worcestershire Beacon. If they dig something up, I want to be on hand.'

'That's understandable.'

'After that, I intend to take a closer look at Colonel Yardley.'

'Yes, you mentioned his name to us yesterday evening.'

'I've learnt more about him since then. The colonel is a marksman. He wins every shooting competition that is held here.'

'What motive would he have to kill Mr Hubbleday?'

'He wouldn't be prompted by personal hatred,' said Tallis, 'because he would probably never have met the man. But Hubbleday represents all that the colonel detests. He's a close friend of Mr Appleby and leads the excursions to this part of the world. According to the stationmaster, Colonel Yardley loathes Appleby as much as Lady Foley does. They feel that he's lowered the tone of the area.'

'Mr Appleby is entitled to live wherever he wishes,' said Colbeck.

'Whoever fired that shot is determined to drive him out.'

'Is that what Colonel Yardley is trying to do?'

'It's conceivable, Inspector.'

'But how did he know at what time that excursion train would come?'

'He must have got hold of the information somehow.'

'What about the second murder, sir?' asked Leeming. 'I don't think this Colonel Yardley was responsible for that. If he wins shooting competitions, he's unlikely to hack someone's head off. He'd simply have put a bullet in Carmody.'

'He may not have done the deed himself,' said Tallis. 'Perhaps he paid someone to butcher Carmody.'

'I'm not entirely convinced that Colonel Yardley is involved in any way,' said Colbeck after consideration. 'However, I respect your judgement so he must be treated as a suspect.'

'Can you think of anyone who could rival him?'

'Yes, I can, sir.'

'Who is it?'

'John Armitage.'

Tallis shrugged. 'I've never heard of the man.'

'He was very close to Mr Hubbleday's elder daughter,' explained Colbeck. 'Marion welcomed his advances, I'm told, but her father disliked Armitage. He insisted on her ending the relationship.'

'That must have wounded her deeply,' observed Leeming.

'I think that Armitage was more than wounded. When I met him, he seemed a pleasant enough young man and claimed that he had put the disappointment behind him. I didn't believe that for a second.'

'Why not?'

'His eyes gave him away. He still has strong feelings for Marion.'

'But I thought she was going to marry someone else.'

'She was, Victor, but that was when her father was alive. Marion was due to wed someone called Philip Wren. He was her father's choice,' said Colbeck. 'The young lady is now in a position to make her own decision.'

'I still favour the colonel as our prime suspect,' declared Tallis. 'I'll make more enquiries about him.'

'My mind is turning towards John Armitage,' said Colbeck.

Leeming was curious. 'Armitage . . . that name rings a bell.'

'It's not surprising, Victor. Almost every pub in the Black Country sells Armitage Best Bitter. You must have seen the advertisements.'

'Ah, yes, of course.'

'The colonel has a more powerful motive,' Tallis contended. 'Let's not forget that both murders happened here. He could have used Carmody, a local man, to get him the sleepers and red flags that he needed. Once the man had done that, the colonel had him killed.'

'That sounds convincing to me,' agreed Leeming. 'The man you're talking about, Inspector, has no connection at all with the Malverns, and he would certainly never have met Carmody.'

'That's a good point,' said Tallis.

'It's a pity that it happens to be invalid,' said Colbeck, politely. 'The Armitage brewery provides beer for public houses in several counties. John Armitage is the sales manager. When I spoke to him, he told me that he'd been away on business for a few days. That shows you how committed he is to the task of increasing sales.'

'I don't follow your reasoning.'

'Supposing that Armitage Best Bitter is served at the pub in Upton on Severn where James Carmody worked. During a visit there, John Armitage might well have met him. If he was looking for an accessory in this area,' said Colbeck, 'then I fancy he'd have shown an interest in someone like Carmody.'

'You're taking supposition into the realms of fantasy.'

'Then perhaps we can have a small wager, sir. The stationmaster will be able to decide the winner. Mr Unwin will know what beer they serve in Carmody's pub in Upton on Severn.' He smiled. 'Are you brave enough to put five pounds on Colonel Yardley as the killer? That's the amount I'm ready to place on Armitage Best Bitter being sold at the Lamb and Flag.'

The superintendent shifted uneasily on his seat.

Before he had entered the pub, Alan Hinton had memorised the route that took him there. Even after two pints of beer, his brain was functioning well. He knew exactly how to get back to his hotel. Leaving the Seven Bells, he kept his wits about him. Though he was certain that he had not been followed, he moved with caution. There was no sense of danger.

When he reached the Waggon and Horses, he recalled the

two men who had warned him the previous evening. There was no sign of them now. Hinton walked into a pool of light from a flickering lamp and on into the darkness beyond. Then, without warning, something hard struck the back of his head and dislodged his hat.

He didn't feel the kicks and blows that followed.

CHAPTER FOURTEEN

Reuben Hubbleday had breakfast alone with the older of his two nieces. Ellen, the younger one, was still fast asleep and his sister-in-law, Dorcas, was so incapacitated by grief that she would not move from the bedroom. Marion was his only companion.

'How do you feel today?' asked Reuben, gently.

'I'm still rather numb,' she replied. 'The news about Father came as such a terrible blow for us. It's brought our lives to a standstill. I still can't believe it.'

'None of us can.'

'We're so grateful to you, Uncle Reuben. You've been a rock.'

'I've done what any brother would have done,' he said, 'and that's to offer whatever help I can, for as long as is necessary.'

'But you have your own family to worry about.'

'They understand that my place is here.' He ate a piece of toast and washed it down with some tea. 'Are you sure that you feel able to face Mr Appleby and Inspector Colbeck?'

'Yes, I do.'

'If you'd prefer to have more time, I can easily postpone their visit.'

'No, no, don't do that,' she implored.

'The inspector may put some searching questions to you, Marion.'

'Then I'll do my best to answer them. The only thing that will bring me any comfort is the arrest of the person who . . . killed my father.'

'That goes for all of us, Marion. But it's not only the investigation that you might have to discuss. Mr Appleby is insisting on paying the funeral expenses. He may ask if you wish to make any suggestions regarding it.'

'I'd rather leave that to you, Uncle Reuben.'

'What about your mother?'

'She will say the same, and so will Ellen. We just want someone to take any responsibility away from us. To be honest, I dare not even think about the funeral.'

'Then I'll discuss it with Mr Appleby.'

He buttered another slice of toast then ate it ruminatively. When he glanced at Marion, he saw that her face was blank, and her mind elsewhere. He waited for several minutes until she realised that she was ignoring him.

'Oh, I do apologise,' she said. 'That was so rude of me.'

'Not at all.'

'I keep thinking about Father and what it must have been like when . . .'

'Put it out of your mind, Marion. It's not healthy to dwell on what happened that day.' He took a deep breath. 'Why don't we talk about something else?'

'Very well.'

His voice brightened. 'Were you pleased to see Philip yesterday?'

'Yes, I was. He was so supportive.'

'He loves you, Marion and will be a good husband.'

'I'm . . . sure that he will,' she said, softly.

'Did he bring up the subject of the wedding?'

'No, he didn't, but I could sense that it is troubling him.'

'Yes, he must be wondering if it should still take place at Easter.'

'We're all wondering about that, Uncle Reuben. But it's far too early to make such an important decision. I need a lot more time to recover.'

'Then I won't press you on the subject,' he promised. 'You and Philip must discuss it in private when you both feel ready to do so. What we must do is to prepare for our visitors later this morning. Mr Appleby wants to offer his condolences to you in person. But it's Inspector Colbeck who will be asking the questions. We must help him all that we can. Without realising it, we may have information that has some relevance to . . . what happened.'

Before he had breakfast at his hotel, Edward Tallis walked down to the railway station to speak to the stationmaster. Unwin gave him a cordial welcome. The superintendent was terse.

'Do you know the Lamb and Flag in Upton upon Severn?'

'Yes, sir. I've been there a number of times.'

'Do they serve Armitage Best Bitter?'

'They do, as a matter of fact. I can recommend it.'

'I see,' replied Tallis, grateful that he had not agreed to a wager with Colbeck. 'What exactly did James Carmody do there?'

'He served behind the bar,' said Unwin. 'The manager must have trusted him because Jim was left in charge of the place sometimes. He loved the job. It really suited him because he enjoyed chatting to people. Jim was so friendly. He'd tell you his life story at the drop of a hat.'

'Would he mention his time on the railway?'

'Jim would be sure to do that, sir.'

'Why?'

'Because he was glad to escape it. He hated doing early shifts or working in the rain on night duty. A nice, warm, comfortable pub was much more to his taste.'

Tallis was about to thank him and move away when he saw a man hurrying along the platform towards him. It was one of the clerks from the telegraph station.

'There's an urgent message for you, Superintendent,' said the man.

'Then let me have it,' ordered Tallis, snatching it from his hand. He read the telegraph and blenched. 'Dear God!'

'Bad news, sir?' asked Unwin.

'I need Inspector Colbeck to see this as soon as possible.'

'Ruby Renshaw's hotel is not all that far away,' said the stationmaster, taking a watch from the pocket of his waistcoat and glancing at it. 'The next train is not due for half an hour. One of my porters can run there, deliver the telegraph and get back here well before it arrives.'

'Good,' said Tallis, handing him the telegraph. 'Send him at once.'

Colonel Yardley was reading his newspaper when his wife was wheeled into the dining room by one of the servants. He got up instantly to take over, dismissing the servant with a nod before manoeuvring the wheelchair into position at the table.

'There we are,' he said, taking his seat.

'Thank you, Francis.'

'How did you sleep last night?'

'I had difficulty getting off. I resorted to one of my sleeping pills.'

'It seems to have done the job, Charlotte,' he said. 'You look wonderful.'

She tittered. 'That's what you tell me every morning.'

'Only because it's true, my love.'

They gave their orders to the servant hovering nearby and she collected their respective breakfasts from the sideboard. Once they were left alone, they began to eat.

'I'm sorry I kept you waiting,' she said.

'No apology is needed.'

'I see that you had the newspaper to divert you. It's wonderful that we can have it delivered here so early in the day.'

'We must thank the railway for that. I know that Lady Emily opposed the notion of a railway at first, but even she has admitted that it has brought benefits. National newspapers arrive here shortly after dawn. It is a wonderful service.'

'Is there anything of interest in today's edition?'

His face clouded. 'Unfortunately, there is.'

'Oh? What's happened?'

'Perhaps you should eat your breakfast first, my love. I don't wish to put you off your food.'

'Don't be ridiculous! I may be disabled but my mind is perfectly sound. There's no need to keep bad news from me. I can cope with it.'

'This is different.'

'Why?'

'Something happened less than half a mile from here, Charlotte.'

'What was it?'

He lowered his voice. 'A second man was murdered.'

'Good gracious!'

'I knew you'd be upset.'

'I'm not so much upset as frightened. Did it really happen so close to us? I always felt so secure out here. Suddenly, I'm beginning to fear for our safety.'

'We're under no threat,' he insisted. 'It's just an unfortunate coincidence that the murder took place not far away.'

'But it's the second one in less than a week.'

'They may be linked.'

'Really?' she said. 'Why do you believe that?'

'There's no point in going into details, my love.'

'That means you're keeping something from me. I'm bound to learn the full truth sooner or later. Stop trying to protect me, Francis.'

'I don't wish to shock you.'

'But you've already done that by telling me the murder had occurred. If it was linked to the other one, it means the victim was shot dead.' She was puzzled. 'You just told me that it happened less than half a mile away. Why didn't we hear the noise of the gun? Sound carries so easily out here.'

'The victim was not shot.'

'Then how was he killed?'

He took a sip of his tea then reached for her hand across the table.

'He was overpowered,' he whispered, 'and then beheaded.'

When they got to the hospital, Alan Hinton was sitting on a chair beside the bed. Colbeck and Leeming were concerned.

Their colleague had one arm in a sling and his face was covered in bruises. Though he smiled bravely, he was clearly still in pain.

'What happened?' asked Colbeck.

'To be honest, sir,' replied the other, 'I don't know. But I was lucky.'

'Is that what you call being lucky?' said Leeming as he studied Hinton's black eye. 'Can you see properly?'

'I can now, Sergeant. When I regained consciousness last night, everything was bleary, and I was aching like mad all over.'

'Who found you?' asked Colbeck.

'That's where the luck came in, sir.'

Hinton went on to explain that he had been knocked out and assaulted while he was down on the pavement. Fortunately, the attack did not last long because someone came down the street and disturbed the two attackers. They had run away, but not before they had stolen Hinton's wallet.

'They'll be disappointed,' he told his visitors. 'There was very little money in it. And they didn't get my warrant card because I keep that in my pocket. I'd have been really upset if they'd taken that.'

'What has the doctor said to you?' asked Colbeck.

'I'm fit to leave.' Leeming laughed in disbelief. 'Yes, I know that I'm not a pretty sight, but I don't want to let you down.' Hinton struggled to his feet, wincing as he did so. 'I'm ready to return to duty, sir.'

Colbeck was blunt. 'That's out of the question.'

'I want to find the men who attacked me.'

'Leave that to us,' said Leeming. 'We admire your guts, but a one-armed detective is . . . well, not much use, frankly. You need looking after, Alan.'

'No, I don't.'

'The sergeant is right,' said Colbeck. 'First, I want to speak to the doctor so that I know the full extent of your injuries. Then you must go straight back to London. The superintendent is aware of what happened to you, and he's already sanctioned sick leave. When I have a moment, I'll send him a telegraph to tell him that the sergeant has escorted you home.'

'But I'm needed here,' argued Leeming.

'Constable Hinton has priority. Take him safely back to his lodging then deliver this to my wife, please.' Taking an envelope from his pocket, he handed it over. 'It will reach her much quicker that way.'

'Then what do I do, sir?'

'Catch the next available train back here.'

'Are you sure that Alan can't manage to get home alone?'

'I'm certain. For one thing, he doesn't have any money. The attackers stole his wallet. Help him on with his coat, Victor, while I speak to the doctor.'

'Yes, sir,' said Leeming, as the inspector went out. 'Come on, Alan. We're going home to London where you can actually see daylight.'

When Hinton tried to laugh, he felt a sharp stab of pain.

* * *

Wrapped up warmly against the cold, Ruby Renshaw arrived at the railway station. Through the window of the office, Tallis saw that she was carrying a large basket over her arm. He went out immediately to greet her.

'You look as if you're going shopping, Mrs Renshaw?'

'Yes, I like to go to Worcester market from time to time. This is my last chance before Christmas.'

'I'm sorry that I had to drag the inspector and the sergeant away from you earlier this morning. It was an emergency.'

'I know. It upset me deeply.'

'Why?'

'Because I had absolutely no warning of it, Superintendent,' she said.

'It was foolish to expect one.'

'I foresaw the first murder, and I had a strong feeling that something equally serious was about to happen. And it did. This time, however, my senses let me down.'

'Don't worry about it.'

'But I should have been able to warn my guests beforehand.'

'Your gift is obviously limited to a small geographical area. If I were you, I'd be grateful for it.'

'Why on earth do you say that?'

'Detective Constable Hinton was attacked in Oldbury,' he pointed out. 'If you could predict everything that happens there, your life would be a misery. You'd have warnings of doom from all over the Black Country – and from Hereford and beyond. How could you run your hotel if you were being warned about horrendous events further afield? They would come pouring in every day.'

'Would they?' She took time to absorb what he had said. 'I see what you mean, Superintendent.'

'You'd be like a lightning conductor on a church, feeling the power of a threatening event sizzling through your brain. I know that I was sceptical about the warnings you claimed to have received,' he went on, 'but I've been forced to change my mind. I do believe that you have a gift – but it only operates within a given area.'

'That's a relief,' she said. 'I certainly don't want to foresee a murder in Birmingham or a disastrous flood in Yorkshire. My brain can only cope with so much. Thank you, Superintendent. It was so clever of you to point it out. You've put my mind at rest.'

'I'm glad to be of use, Mrs Renshaw,' he said. 'And while you're here, I must thank you once again for your hospitality yesterday evening. You put the Imperial Hotel to shame.'

She laughed. 'What a wonderful tribute! You're so kind. Anyway,' she went on, becoming serious, 'let's not talk about me. How is the officer mentioned in your telegraph? Was he badly hurt? Will he have to stay in hospital?'

'No, he won't,' said Tallis. 'I'm reliably informed that Constable Hinton is now on his way back to London, where he can get plenty of rest.'

Alan Hinton and Victor Leeming sat opposite each other in an empty compartment. Every time the train rocked from side to side, Hinton tried to suppress a groan. Leeming was sympathetic.

'I had a real shiner like that once,' he said. 'I picked it up in a pub brawl. When I went on my beat the next day, children laughed at me in the street. I was glad when the black eye began to fade.'

'I won't have that problem,' said Hinton. 'Much as I'd like to, I can't go back to work for a while. I've got bruises all over me. It was stupid of me to volunteer to return to work. If I stayed in Oldbury, I'd be a liability.'

'Have you any idea who attacked you?'

'It must have been the two men who jostled me the night before.'

'Not necessarily,' said Leeming.

'Who else could it be?'

'A couple of thugs who spotted easy pickings.'

'No, I must have been followed.'

'Then there's a good chance we may be able to catch them.'

'Is there?'

'Didn't you tell the inspector that one of those men who gave you a warning might be a painter at the Works?'

'That's right,' said Hinton. 'He probably heard me asking for information about a man who'd been sacked by Mr Hubbleday. That's why I was confronted two nights ago.'

'And you ignored the warning. I'd have done the same.'

'I wasn't going to be frightened off by anyone.'

'That's the spirit!'

'Oh, there's something I must ask you,' remembered Hinton. 'I haven't had the chance to talk to the inspector about it. He must be more wary of Derek Churt.'

'Why? I thought the man was helping us.'

'I'm beginning to have doubts.'

'I trust the inspector's judgement.'

'Churt is a leader among the painters. That's where his loyalties lie.'

'I'm not so sure,' said Leeming. 'The inspector has won him over. Churt agreed to help us and I believe he'll keep his word.'

Derek Churt was in a quandary. When he realised that Hubbleday had been shot dead, he had been delighted. In his view, it was a fate the works manager deserved. It had never occurred to him that someone who worked alongside him might have been a party to the murder. Now that it was a real possibility, he was looking at his workmates in a different way. It made him less willing to join in the usual banter.

He was painting the door of a carriage when the man next to him spoke.

'Is anything the matter, Derek?'

'No, no, nothing at all.'

'Why are you so quiet today?'

'I had a bad night,' said Churt, manufacturing a yawn. 'I can hardly keep my eyes open.' He raised his voice so that all his workmates could hear him. 'Don't you think we should club together to buy something to go on Hubb's coffin?'

'What did you have in mind?' asked a voice. 'A pile of horse shit?'

'I have a better idea,' said Churt over the raucous laughter. 'We could get him a tall, shiny top hat with a bullet hole in it.'

The laughter swelled.

During the cab ride to the house, Colbeck was able to tell Jerome Appleby about the incident the previous night.

'Constable Hinton was attacked?' repeated Appleby.

'It could have been worse, sir. Someone happened to come along and that sent the attackers running away. Had they stayed, the injuries might have been far worse.'

'This is appalling news.'

'Even as we speak, Hinton is on his way back to London.' Colbeck turned to him. 'He may even be travelling in a carriage made at your Works.'

'I must find some way to reward the fellow.'

'He would appreciate that, Mr Appleby. Changing the subject,' he went on, 'may I ask if you ever met a man named John Armitage?'

'Yes, I did on one occasion. He was a friend of Marion Hubbleday.'

'What did you make of him?'

'He was pleasant enough and did not lack confidence. Armitage talked about his plans for the brewery when he took over the running of it in due course. He had real ambition.'

'I believe he had ambitions of another kind as well.'

'That was what upset Cyril. He didn't like the man at all, and he certainly didn't warm to the idea of John Armitage as his son-in-law.'

'That's what Mr Drake told me.'

'The problem was that Marion was fond of Armitage. She was very hurt when Cyril forbade her to see him again. I gather that there were some lively rows about it. In the end,' said Appleby, 'Marion realised that her father would never change his mind. She eventually formed an attachment with Philip Wren, whose family own the largest timber yard here. That blossomed in time and Cyril gave the couple his blessing. It seemed that life in the Hubbleday home was on an even keel again.'

'You've met Philip Wren, presumably.'

'Yes, I have. He's quiet and well-mannered. Unlike Armitage, he didn't have the gall to tell me how to run my business.'

Colbeck was amazed. 'Did he really do that?'

'Oh, yes. He had the cheek of Old Nick.'

'I caught a glimpse of it yesterday. He was brimming with self-confidence when I met him.'

'If you ask me,' said Appleby, 'Marion had a lucky escape from him. Armitage was far too fond of himself.'

Marion Hubbleday was alone in her bedroom with a small box on her knees. It was normally kept hidden in a locked drawer. She took out some letters and cards, all of them sent to her by John Armitage at the height of their romance. Marion knew that she was being unfair to her fiancé in keeping the correspondence, but she could not help it. She needed the surge of excitement that her souvenirs gave her. Devoted to her as he was, Philip Wren could not match his rival.

When she heard a cab drawing up outside the house, she looked through the window and saw Appleby getting out of the vehicle. Marion moved swiftly. After putting her treasures back in their hiding place, she locked the drawer.

Edward Tallis was grateful for the response from the Worcestershire Constabulary. Inspector Vellacott turned up at the site with half-a-dozen brawny constables, each armed with a spade. They were put to work at once, digging in the area close to where the body of James Carmody had been found. Tallis and Vellacott were not the only onlookers. Biddy Leacock was there as well, watching from a distance while holding the reins of a donkey. Her presence elicited some coarse comments from the toiling policemen.

'Has word of this reached Lady Foley yet?' asked Vellacott.

'Yes, Inspector,' said Tallis. 'I informed her in person.'

'We'll get the blame once again, I'm sure. I had better brace myself for one of her astringent letters. Lady Foley does not mince her words.'

'Tell me about Colonel Yardley.'

'Why do you ask?'

'She mentioned his name to me. It seems that they dine together occasionally.'

Vellacott chuckled. 'That's because the colonel is the only man brave enough to eat alone with her.'

'What about his wife?'

'Oh, she's not well enough to join them.'

'When I met him,' said Tallis, 'we talked as one old soldier to another. Both of us saw service in India, you see. I hated that blazing sunshine at the time, but it was better than this biting wind, I can tell you.' He turned to Vellacott. 'What's your opinion of the colonel?'

'To start with,' replied the other, 'he's a man who likes his own way. Nobody in his right mind would seek an argument with Colonel Yardley . . .'

Marion Hubbleday was astonished when she first met Colbeck. The policemen who had come to the house in the wake of her father's murder had all been alike – worthy but limited men in uniform who spoke in the local accent. She was now talking to a highly educated man, impeccably dressed, and showing great compassion towards her and her uncle. After going through the pleasantries, Colbeck had a first question for Marion.

'May I ask how your mother and sister are faring?' he said.

'They are still too dazed to speak to you,' she replied. 'Mother is in bed and Ellen never leaves her side.'

'In the circumstances, it's very brave of you to speak to us.'

'I feel that it's important to do so, Inspector.'

'Quite so.' He looked at her uncle. 'I'm not entirely

sure how much you and your niece know about recent developments.'

'We know very little,' replied Reuben. 'We've been in isolation here.'

'Then perhaps I should bring you both up to date.'

'Thank you.'

'We'd be very grateful, Inspector,' said Marion.

'I'd better warn you that some of my news may be distressing.'

'Nothing can be more distressing than what has already befallen us.' She saw his hesitation. 'Don't shy away from giving unpleasant information on my account. I'm tougher than I look.'

'I admire your attitude, Miss Hubbleday.'

'She takes after her father,' said Appleby, with a smile of approval. 'Marion has the same inner strength.'

'In that case,' said Colbeck, 'you need to be aware of two dramatic events . . .'

When he told them about the second murder, Marion was horrified and covered her face with a hand. Reuben, by contrast, gave almost no reaction. He wanted to hear the full details but, out of consideration for his niece, he did not ask for them.

'You spoke of two dramatic events, Inspector,' remembered Reuben.

'Yes,' said Colbeck, sadly. 'Detective Constable Hinton has been questioning some of the men at the Works. Since he is staying in a hotel here in Oldbury, he went for a meal yesterday evening at the Seven Bells.'

'I know it,' said Marion, blurting out the words. 'John's brewery supplies them with beer.' She felt embarrassed. 'Oh, I'm sorry to butt in.'

'That's quite all right, Miss Hubbleday. What you say is quite correct. The constable told me how much he enjoyed Armitage Best Bitter.'

'What happened, Inspector?' asked Reuben, worriedly.

'Not to put too fine a point on it, sir, Hinton was brutally attacked . . .'

Now that Tallis had seen how efficient Vellacott could be, he revised his earlier judgement of the man and adopted a friendly attitude towards him. For his part, Vellacott had accepted that the detectives had the experience needed to solve what had become an even more bewildering case. As they stood beside each other near the bottom of the Beacon, they spoke with a measure of mutual respect.

'Do you have any plans for Christmas, Superintendent?' asked Vellacott.

'Yes, I'm hoping to spend it in London.'

'What are the chances of that happening?'

'At the moment,' confessed Tallis, 'they seem rather small, but we have made some advances. The inspector has persuaded one of the painters at the Appleby Works to gather information from inside it.'

'Is he still certain that there is an accomplice employed there?'

'He is – and so am I. It stands to reason.'

'I think the killer's accomplice was Jim Carmody,' said Vellacott.

'He was certainly involved in some way and paid the price for it. I was talking to the stationmaster about him earlier. Mr Unwin told me that moving from the railway to the pub in Upton on Severn had been the making of Carmody.'

'I beg leave to doubt it, sir. Carmody never stayed long in any job. The most time he spent anywhere was on the railway – just over two years. Then he worked on a farm, he gave that up to help at a forge before trying his hand at a few other things. In the end, he finished up at the Lamb and Flag. Now and again, of course, he came to our notice. We arrested Carmody for a range of offences, none serious enough to merit a long custodial sentence, unfortunately.'

'A taste of imprisonment might have brought him to his senses.'

'He didn't possess any.'

'If he was so feckless, how did he keep getting employed?'

'It's something I'll never know, sir. Carmody was very plausible. He could talk the hind leg off one of Biddy Leacock's donkeys. On one occasion,' he recalled, 'when we thought we'd caught him poaching, he produced a witness to clear him of the charge. You'll never guess who it was.'

'Why not?'

'It was Colonel Yardley.'

Tallis was startled. 'Why ever should he stick up for Carmody?'

'He employed him when he had weekend shooting parties.'

'Really?'

'The colonel said that he was the best beater he'd ever had.'

It was a connection that Tallis would never have imagined. The man whose head they were now searching for had worked occasionally for the colonel. Tallis's suspicion of Yardley hardened. If he had needed railway sleepers and red flags, he would have turned to a man who could provide them and whom he could trust. It brought the colonel into sharper focus as a prime suspect.

'How does he get on with Mr Appleby?' asked Tallis.

'He loathes the man as much as Lady Foley and expresses his dislike in a variety of ways. If he has any sense, Mr Appleby will not read *The Malvern Gazette*. Withering letters from the colonel appear in it regularly. They attack excursionists in general and Appleby in particular.'

Before Tallis could speak, there was a shout from one of the constables.

'I've found it!' he yelled.

Everyone reacted quickly. The other policemen sank their spades into the soil and rushed over to their colleague. Tallis and Vellacott hurried in the same direction. What had been discovered, barely six inches below ground, was the top of a head. It was caked in dirt. The man who had found it got down on his knees and scooped the earth away with both hands. Everyone in the circle around him watched with fascination. When the face slowly appeared, there were cries of recognition from the watching constables.

The head was retrieved with great care, revealing dried blood. When the earth was brushed away from around the mouth, they saw that it was wide open. The lips were stained with blood. Down on his knees, the man peered into Carmody's mouth.

'His tongue was cut out!' he exclaimed.

CHAPTER FIFTEEN

Marion Hubbleday held up well under questioning and provided a lot of new detail about her father's home life. Colbeck recorded the salient facts in his notebook. Looking from Marion to her uncle, he spread his hands.

'Is there anything that either of you wishes to ask me?'

'Yes,' said Marion. 'Do you have any idea who killed my father?'

'I believe that we do, Miss Hubbleday, but we need to gather more evidence before we can reveal his name – and that of his accomplice.'

She was taken aback. 'There were two of them?'

'At least two.'

'May I ask a question?' said Reuben.

'As many as you wish,' invited Colbeck.

'Actually, it's addressed to Mr Appleby.'

'Oh, I see,' said Appleby. 'In that case, I'll be happy to answer it.'

'Has this terrible business made you think twice about organising any more excursions?'

'It's certainly thrown my plans into disarray. The Easter excursion we planned now looks to be in danger of cancellation.'

'Is that because the killer targeted an Appleby train?'

'Yes. We have to consider the safety of our passengers.'

'Excuse me for interrupting you, sir,' said Colbeck, 'but this case will certainly be solved by Easter. Indeed, it's my dearest hope that we make an arrest before Christmas. We will then have something to celebrate.'

'There'll be little celebration here,' said Marion, sadly. 'Whatever happens, Christmas Day without Father will feel . . . so empty.'

'But you'll have the consolation of knowing that the man who killed him is under lock and key and will hang for his crime.'

'Knowing that will not bring my brother back to life, Inspector,' said Reuben. 'He was a force of nature. He generated so much warmth.'

'I can swear to that,' said Appleby.

'It's been good to meet you both,' said Colbeck, looking from Marion to Reuben once again. 'What you've told me has been very helpful. We'll trespass on your time no longer.' He rose to his feet. 'Thank you and goodbye.'

'It is we who must thank you, Inspector,' said Reuben getting up. 'It's a relief to see this investigation in such capable hands.'

'Before you go,' asked Marion, 'I'd like to ask after Constable Hinton. Were his injuries serious?'

Colbeck smiled at her. 'It's kind of you to ask. Have no fears about him, Miss Hubbleday. He will be back on his feet before long. Until that happens,' he went on, 'I suspect that the constable will enjoy the services of an attentive nurse.'

Madeleine Colbeck was chatting with Lydia Quayle when a visitor called at the house. It was Victor Leeming. After handing over the letter to Madeleine, he broke the news about Hinton as gently as he could. It threw Lydia into a mild panic.

'How bad is he, Sergeant?' she asked. 'Was he able to walk properly? Did the doctor say how long he's likely to be off work?'

'There's only one way to find out,' he said.

'And how do I do that?'

'You go and ask him, of course,' said Madeleine.

'Is he well enough to see me?'

'I'm sure that he is,' said Leeming. 'When I dropped him off at his lodging, he was pounced on by his landlady. She's a dear old soul and treats him as the son she never had. Alan is in good hands.'

'I can think of a better pair,' said Madeleine, looking at her friend.

Lydia reached a decision. 'I'll go to him at once.'

'What's holding you up?'

'You'll have to excuse me, Madeleine.'

'I do so gladly. Alan really needs you.'

'I must take something for him,' said Lydia. 'He needs cheering up. What shall it be – a newspaper, a book or some chocolate, perhaps?'

'I can tell you what he would love most,' said Leeming.

'What's that?'

'A pint of Armitage's Best Bitter.'

'Victor is teasing you,' said Madeleine. 'Now off you go. Give him our love and make much of him. You don't want that landlady to monopolise Alan.'

After giving Madeleine a farewell kiss, Lydia put on her coat and hat and left the house. The others were amused by her reaction.

'Alan is in for a wonderful surprise,' said Madeleine.

'I'm glad that I could tell her about the condition he was in.'

'Seeing her will be the best possible medicine for him.' She looked at the letter. 'Do I have time to read this letter and write a reply?'

'Of course, you do. It's vital. If I went back empty-handed, the inspector would never forgive me.'

'What was that beer you mentioned, by the way?'

'Armitage's Best Bitter. Alan loved it.'

* * *

Having been born into the trade, John Armitage had come to savour the smell of beer. He always joked that he enjoyed the aroma in his nostrils because it blocked out the noisome stench that haunted the streets of the town. When he got back to the brewery, he arrived in time to see two men loading barrels onto the back of a cart. He stopped to admire their skill as they hauled the barrels up some planks with the aid of ropes.

'I used to be able to do that,' he said.

'We know, sir,' said one of the men.

'Keep at it. I've managed to find lots of new customers for our beer, so we'll be increasing our output. Thanks to me, our name is reaching new parts of the country all the time. Large numbers of people will be raising a glass of our Best Bitter on Christmas Day,' boasted Armitage. 'Our competitors can't touch us for price and quality.'

Waving farewell, he walked jauntily into the building.

After knocking on the door, Colbeck went into Ernest Drake's office. The accountant got to his feet to welcome him.

'Can I help you, Inspector?' he said.

'I hope so,' replied the other. 'Mr Appleby and I have just returned from a visit to the Hubbleday household. We spoke to his brother and to his elder daughter.'

'How are they?'

'In my opinion, Marion is bearing up extremely well. She was able to give us a lot of useful information about her father.'

'She and her sister are charming young women.'

'They're relying very heavily on their uncle.'

'Reuben has been saintly,' said Drake. 'He's put their needs before those of his own family. His colleagues at the glassworks have been very understanding. He can have as long a break from his work as he wishes.'

'He sent his regards to you.'

Drake was pleased. 'Thank you for passing them on.'

'He also made a comment that was meaningless to me,' admitted Colbeck. 'That's why I popped in to see you.'

'What was the comment?'

'He said that he was very grateful for your help and would gather all the documentation he could for your perusal.'

'Ah, yes,' said Drake, understanding. 'I know what he was talking about. Cyril had many virtues, but he quailed when he saw a list of numbers. I helped him unofficially as his accountant. Once a month, we went through his records together.'

'Presumably, his brother will take over his financial affairs now.'

'That's what worries Reuben. He has no training in accountancy. He begged me to come to his assistance.'

'And you agreed, obviously.'

'I'd do anything to help that family,' said Drake, seriously. 'There were times when I almost felt part of it. Cyril Hubbleday was my best friend.'

Edward Tallis was torn between obedience and instinct. The latest telegraph from the commissioner had been short and carefully worded. Reading between the lines, he knew that he was being summoned back to London. Yet his instinct told him that he had to stay at the helm in Great Malvern. The progress he felt they had made that morning was offset by the loss of Alan Hinton. If Tallis deserted his post, then the investigation would be weakened even more. He tried to concentrate on gains. Finding the severed head had been a welcome bonus, an achievement he shared with Inspector Vellacott. In discovering a link between James Carmody and Colonel Yardley, he had an additional reward. He simply had to act on the information.

Seated at the stationmaster's desk, he was keenly aware of the train timetable that was pinned to the wall in front of him. He leant forward to examine it.

For his second visit to the Churt house, Colbeck had changed into nondescript clothing. It made it easier for him to crouch down on the floor with Peter and play with the wooden train. Colbeck was amused by Churt's reaction when he came home from work. The painter was startled.

'Yes,' he said, 'it is me. Disguise is sometimes necessary.'

'Oh, I see.'

Agnes took her son out of the living room so that they could speak alone.

'Thank you for keeping Peter amused.'

'It was the other way around, Mr Churt. Anyway, I'm sorry to surprise you for the second day in a row. I just wondered how you got on at work.'

'It was difficult at first.'

'Why?'

'The lads know me as a chatterbox. Because I was so quiet and watchful, they wondered what was wrong with me. Luckily,' said Churt, 'I managed to convince them I'd had a sleepless night.'

'Were you able to weigh them up individually?'

'In most cases, I'd already done that. Eight of the lads I work with could be excluded straight away. They're as honest as the day is long.'

'What about the others?'

'There are three of them, Inspector. Two of them only joined us a couple of months ago so I haven't really got to know them properly.'

'That leaves one more.'

'Yes,' said Sturt, reflectively. 'Simon Wragg. He's an odd fellow, who keeps himself to himself. I couldn't fault his work. It's near perfect. However, I do remember how angry Simon was when Mr Hubbleday criticised him.'

'Why did the works manager to do that?'

'It was a habit of his. He'd pick on someone just to assert his authority. It was Simon's turn that day, and he was really hurt. That doesn't mean he'd want him shot dead,' he added. 'I can't believe he'd get involved in any kind of plot. But . . . you never know, do you?'

'Keep a close eye on him, please.'

'If there is one of the painters who had some link to the killer, he doesn't have to belong to the group that I work with. He could be with a different set. Constable Hinton spoke to all of us in turn.'

'There's something you should know about him, Mr Churt.'

'What's that?'

'The constable was attacked and beaten as he walked back to his hotel last night. He's no longer part of the investigation. Please remain alert,' said Colbeck. 'You may well be working alongside someone who took part in the assault.'

When the train stopped at Stoke Edith, the only passenger to get out was Edward Tallis. It took him time to find someone who would drive him to the house, well over six miles away. Like Leeming before him, he was impressed by the size and solidity of Lady Foley's home. It had the air of a baronial castle. Invited in by the butler, he had to wait in the hall. When he was eventually invited into the drawing room, Tallis saw that he was not the only visitor. Colonel Yardley was already there, dressed for dinner. Lady Foley gave the newcomer a polite welcome whereas the colonel got to his feet and expressed real pleasure in seeing him again.

It was ironic. The superintendent's main reason for going there was to seek information about the colonel. He was delighted to see that there was no need to probe Lady Foley for details. Tallis would be able to get them from the man himself. Offered a seat, he chose one directly opposite Lady Foley, enabling him to see once again how dignified she was. There was a kind of icy magnificence about her.

'Thank you for coming in person,' she said with effortless condescension, 'instead of sending that atrocious sergeant again. What news have you brought me?'

'You already know that a second murder has occurred,' Tallis reminded her.

'Yes,' said the colonel, 'Lady Emily was telling me about that. I trust that this is not the start of an epidemic.'

'I can assure you that it is not, Colonel Yardley.'

'Is there any connection between the two victims?'

'We believe so.'

'What new information can you add, Superintendent?' asked Lady Foley.

'The second victim – James Carmody – was not simply killed,' explained Tallis. 'He had been beheaded.' Lady Foley shuddered slightly but Yardley was unmoved. 'Earlier today, Inspector Vellacott and I watched while his men searched for the missing head. It was eventually found and dug up.'

'Why was it cut off in the first place?' she enquired.

'Conceivably, it was a form of punishment.'

'What do you mean?' said the colonel.

'There was a detail that I haven't mentioned,' said Tallis, quietly. 'Carmody's tongue had been cut out.'

Lady Foley grimaced. 'How grotesque!'

'Grotesque and quite unnecessary,' added the colonel. 'The victim was hardly likely to speak after he'd been murdered.'

'Perhaps the killer feared that his victim had already done so. Carmody's death could have been a warning to others involved in the earlier murder.' He looked at Yardley. 'Does his name sound familiar, Colonel?'

'No,' said the other, face blank. 'Should it?'

'I was given to understand by Inspector Vellacott that you once spoke up for Carmody and saved him from a charge of poaching.'

'I don't remember the incident.'

'Apparently, you employed him during shooting parties.'

'I hired lots of other men,' said Yardley with a dismissive gesture. 'You can't expect me to remember all their names. Be realistic, Superintendent. This fellow was part of the rank and file. All I needed to know about him was whether he could do the job assigned to him. What's this nonsense about a charge of poaching?'

'I was only quoting Inspector Vellacott.'

'You know my opinion of him,' said Lady Foley with contempt.

'I think that you undervalue him,' said Tallis, firmly. 'The inspector deserves a pat on the back for the way he marshalled his officers this morning.'

Her voice was cold and brittle. 'We must agree to differ, Superintendent.'

'I side with Lady Emily,' said the colonel. 'My dealings with Vellacott have left me wondering how he was promoted to his rank. If he has been telling tales about me and this fellow, Carmody, he deserves a sharp reproof.'

'Quite right, Colonel,' added Lady Foley.

'It's sheer impertinence!'

'I'm surprised that you were duped so easily,

Superintendent. A man of your experience should have recognised Vellacott's shortcomings at a glance.' Her eyes flashed. 'I expected better of you.'

Marion Hubbleday was pleased to see her fiancé arrive at the house, but the pleasure was tinged with disappointment. She had hoped for another visitor, one she still held dear. Her uncle had immediately left them alone in the drawing room. Hands clasped together, they talked in whispers.

'How are you today?' asked Philip Wren, solicitously.

'I'm still in a daze. I feel as if I'm sleep-walking.'

'That will pass, Marion.'

'I hope so. My life seems so unnatural. I find it difficult to believe that it will ever change for the better.'

'It will, darling. It must do.'

'We had visitors earlier on,' she told him. 'I was hoping that I would feel slightly better by the time they left. In fact, the opposite happened.'

'Who were your visitors?'

'Mr Appleby and Inspector Colbeck, who is leading the investigation. They were very kind to me. I was put under no pressure.'

'Did the inspector give you any news?'

'Yes, he did,' she replied, 'and it was frightening. There's been a second murder, apparently, somewhere in the Malverns.'

'A second one?' he said in alarm. 'Is it connected to . . . ?'

'The inspector believes that it may be. What's happening to us, Philip? Three or four days ago, we were the happiest family in Oldbury. There wasn't a single cloud on our horizon. Suddenly, everything started to fall apart. We don't deserve it,' she said, eyes moistening. 'It's so cruel.'

'We'll come through it,' he promised, putting an arm around her shoulders. 'Be brave, darling. Your family has had cruel setbacks, but better days lie ahead. In four months or so, when we are man and wife, everything will seem so much better. The inspector will have solved the murders and the man responsible for them will have been executed. We can all start to live normal lives again.'

'I don't think that it will ever happen, Philip.'

'Why not?'

'It's because our family has been destroyed. Whenever we get together, we'll remember this awful time when someone hated Father so much that he killed him out of sheer malice. Just think about that, Philip,' she told him. 'We loved him to distraction, but he had a wicked enemy, somebody who saw him in a different light. The killer must also have loathed us, hated the life we enjoyed and deliberately smashed it to pieces.'

'We don't know what his reasons were, Marion.'

'I do,' she insisted. 'He wanted to destroy us. Father was the first victim. Which of us will be next – Mother, Ellen, me?'

'Don't talk like this,' he said, enfolding her in his arms. 'There is hope for us. This monster will be caught and hanged. You will all be safe, I guarantee it. What would your father have wanted you to do?' he asked. 'If I know him, he'd want you to stand firm. He'd expect a daughter of his to weather the storm and bring the family together again. I can help you do that, Marion. It's our duty.'

'Yes,' she said without conviction. 'I suppose that it is.'

The first thing that Victor Leeming did when he reached Oldbury was to report to Colbeck at the Works. After handing over Madeleine's letter, he told him that Alan Hinton now had two doting females to look after him – his landlady and Lydia Quayle. They would help to speed his recovery.

'We'll have to do without him for a while, though,' said Leeming.

'He may not be our only loss, Victor.'

'What do you mean?'

'The superintendent may soon be returning to London as well,' said Colbeck.

Leeming laughed. 'That's wonderful news!'

'Is it? Yesterday, there were four of us involved in this case. At a stroke, that number will be halved. I'd call that bad news. The commissioner is bound to want the superintendent behind his desk at Scotland Yard. That will weaken our investigative power,' said Colbeck. 'We'll have to work twice as hard.'

'You know me, sir. I'm happy to toil around the clock.'

'Both of us may have to do that.'

Leeming rubbed his hands together. 'Where do we start?'

'First of all,' said Colbeck, 'I'd like to bring you up to date with what's been happening here while you were away. Mr Appleby and I had an interesting visit to the Hubbleday house.'

'I've been wondering how you got on, sir.'

'We learnt a lot from the interview. Miss Hubbleday

showed a lot of courage in speaking to us. I gathered a great deal about the family from her. There was, however, an awkward moment.'

'Was there, sir?'

'Marion suddenly blurted out the name of John Armitage and she was embarrassed by her lapse. He is obviously not a friend from the past who has drifted out of her life. Armitage, I suspect, is still at the forefront of her mind.'

'But she's about to marry someone else,' said Leeming.

'That was her father's doing. In the wake of his death, she may feel differently about the match.'

'Marion would have to rely on her uncle's advice, wouldn't she?'

'That's true.'

'He's almost certainly going to take her down the aisle in his brother's place. What sort of a man is he?'

'At the moment,' said Colbeck, 'he is holding the family together. They'd have been helpless without him. He seems like a decent, responsible man who has put them first. At least, that was how he appeared.'

'Did you sense he was putting on a front?'

'No, I didn't and that's what worries me. I can usually detect people who try to give me a false impression of themselves. I may be wrong, of course, but he'd repay study. There's something unconvincing about Uncle Reuben.'

'What is it, sir?'

'I don't know yet, but answer this question. If you were shot dead, who would be the first person to rush to Estelle's side?'

'My mother-in-law.'

'Precisely – women are so much better at offering support and solace. Why isn't Uncle Reuben's wife doing the same thing? She and Mrs Hubbleday must be very close to each other. Her place is at the bedside, providing support.'

'Yes,' said Leeming, as he thought about it, 'you're right, sir. If Estelle was suddenly widowed, she'd have her mother and her two sisters there in a flash. It's what happens to a family in an emergency.'

'Then why didn't it happen here?'

The journey back to Great Malvern station was fretful. The train was late and Tallis was forced to share a compartment with a couple of boisterous farmers whose unpleasant aroma was intensified in the small space. His mind was made up. He decided that he would not be retiring to that part of the country, after all. During the time he'd been there, its appeal had slowly mellowed. The hills were a serious problem. Wherever he went, he had to cope with steep gradients. Though he had always prided himself on his fitness, he discovered that it had limits. The search at the base of Worcestershire Beacon had left him dripping with perspiration and vowing never to do anything so careless again. The environment in the Malverns was too punitive for a man of his age and bulk.

There was an even more compelling argument against his desire to move there. Tallis felt that he would simply not have a social life. People like Harold Unwin and Ruby Renshaw had been very welcoming, but he had no wish to spend more than a few minutes with each of them. And the person who had struck him most powerfully at first – Lady Emily Foley – would never include him among her friends. Most of the denizens of the Malverns respected her and were duly grateful for her philanthropy. Instead of mixing freely with them, however, she lived in isolation and controlled everything from a distance.

Tallis was not afraid of his social superiors. On the occasions when the commissioner had been unable to attend royal events, the superintendent had deputised for him. He had felt completely at ease when he was close to Queen Victoria, and he treasured the brief conversations he had had with Prince Albert. Queen and Consort had been approachable. Lady Foley was not. There would always be a high fence around the woman, making it impossible for anyone like him to get close to her – even if he had wanted to do so.

Colonel Yardley was an exception to the rule. His jovial charm had secured him invitations to dinner with Lady Foley. Unlike Tallis, he was a man with private wealth, able to buy a large estate and rub shoulders with the leading families of the area. He possessed advantages that Tallis lacked. A future in the Malverns suddenly started to look rather bleak for the superintendent. Where would he go and what would he do all day? How could he replace the thrill of occupying a senior position in the Metropolitan Police Force? He had to be brutally honest. Retirement meant loss. He would be moving from a world where he was significant to one that deprived him of the sense of power and achievement that meant so much to him.

Tallis recalled with a shudder a period when he had been unable to perform his duties at the accepted level. Physically and mentally, he had been exhausted and compelled to take a break from work. Only the sympathy and understanding of those around him had helped him to survive.

Who would be there to provide the same help in his retirement?

Notwithstanding his hatred of rail travel, Victor Leeming had been forced to concede that it had its value. Trains had not only taken him all the way to London and back, the latest one had delivered him to Tipton station when there was enough light in the sky to convince him that it was still afternoon. He went straight to the local police station. As he entered the building, the duty officer recognised him.

'Ah,' he said, 'I was hoping that you would pop in sooner or later, Sergeant.'

'Why is that?'

'There's been a sighting of that man you asked us to look out for.'

'Samuel Waycroft?'

'That's the chap.'

Leeming was delighted. 'Good,' he said. 'I have a score to settle with him.'

When Lydia Quayle returned to the house, Madeleine could see at once that her friend was upset. She took her straight into the drawing room and sat her down on the sofa.

'Well,' she asked, 'did you see Alan?'

'Yes, I did.'

'Was he pleased to see you?'

'He was and he wasn't, Madeleine.'

'What do you mean?'

'Alan is in a terrible state,' explained Lydia. 'He's got an arm in a sling, a black eye and bruises everywhere. When he tried to get up, he was in agony.'

'Oh dear!'

'He was so embarrassed that I saw him in that state.'

'Yet he must have realised how much you cared for him, Lydia.'

'That was the other thing. For obvious reasons, we were never alone. His landlady stayed in the room and pretended that she was not there, but we could feel her presence. It was mortifying,' she went on. 'I just couldn't say any of the things I wanted to say to Alan.'

'Then you'll have to say them in a letter.'

'Going there was a big mistake, Madeleine.'

'Then I take the blame for that. I urged you to go.'

'The truth is,' said Lydia, 'that I didn't realise how much I cared about him. Yet I couldn't show my true feelings. It's a shocking thing to admit but . . . to be honest, I was glad to get out of there.'

She burst into tears and Madeleine took her in her arms.

CHAPTER SIXTEEN

Reuben Hubbleday was seated at the desk in his brother's study, sifting through a series of bills, receipts and other documents. There was a tap on the door, and he turned to see it open enough for Marion to pop her head into the room.

'Am I disturbing you, Uncle Reuben?' she asked.

'No, of course not,' he replied, closing the folder in front of him. 'Come on in. I was just sorting out some of your father's paperwork.'

She stepped into the room. 'It's so good of you to take care of that for us. Father never let any of us in here. It was one of his golden rules. He said that women never understood about money.'

'That's rather harsh.'

'There was always a wicked smile on his face when he said it.'

'Even so . . .'

She looked down at the desk. 'Are you busy?'

'Not really, Marion.'

'I wondered if I could have a word with you?'

'As many as you wish,' he said, indicating the other chair. 'Sit down.'

'Thank you.'

She took time settling herself down and seemed uneasy. Realising what she had come to talk to him about, he offered reassurance.

'Whatever is said in here is between you and me,' he promised, 'so you may speak freely. Nobody else needs to know.'

'Thank you.'

'It's about the wedding, isn't it?'

'Yes, it is, Uncle Reuben. It's an awful thing to say but . . . I'm dreading it.'

'That's because circumstances have changed so dramatically. Everything has suddenly been thrown into doubt. If you want my opinion, it's far too early to reach a decision, especially one that will have such long-term consequences.'

'I know,' she sighed.

'Give yourself time, Marion.'

'I'll try.'

'Have you discussed the matter with Philip?'

'Not really,' she said. 'I know exactly how he feels and what he wants. As far as Philip is concerned, we carry on as if nothing has happened.'

'But something *has* happened,' he insisted, 'and it's changed everything. Our individual lives will each have a massive hole in them from now on. We can't pretend otherwise.'

'I realise that – Philip doesn't.'

'The pair of you need more time to adapt to a change of circumstances. I'm not talking about days or even weeks. You need months at least to see everything in perspective. Frankly,' he said, 'I should forget all about an Easter wedding.'

'Philip has set his heart on it.'

'What about you?'

'I did the same – at the time.'

'And now?'

'It doesn't feel right somehow. I love Philip in lots of ways, but he was Father's choice, not mine. Everyone said that it was a good match, and you were one of them, Uncle Reuben.'

'I don't deny it.'

'I suppose that I just let it happen,' she admitted. 'The truth is that Father knocked all the fight out of me. I couldn't go on begging him to let me marry the man I wanted. It was . . . wearing me out. Mother took his side, of course, so there was nobody to support me. I just gave in.'

'Does Philip realise that?'

'No, I don't think he does. He'd admired me for some time and was pleased when I . . . became available.' She pulled a face. 'What a horrid phrase that is!' she protested. 'It makes me sound like a prize animal at an auction. Marriage can be such a cruel business at times.'

'You're right about one thing. In this instance,' said Reuben, 'it was partly a business decision. Philip Wren's father supplies all the timber used by Appleby's. He and your father were therefore closely linked together. It seemed natural to him that the two families should have an even deeper relationship. That's why he encouraged the friendship between you and Philip.'

'And I didn't object. Philip was a nice young man. He was kind, loving and we had some wonderful times together. However,' she recalled, 'when things became more serious, I began to have doubts.'

'Did you discuss them with your father?'

'It was a waste of time. The decision had been made.'

'And you tried to make the best of it – is that what happened?'

She nodded. 'I was ground down,' she said. 'You don't know how stern my father could be when he chose.'

'Oh, yes, I do!' he said with fierce emphasis. 'I've had a lifetime of it, Marion. I still bear the scars. You only lost one argument with him. I lost hundreds.'

* * *

In the brief time that he had become the acting works manager, Oliver Innes had quickly grown into the role. Cyril Hubbleday had always stressed the importance of being seen by employees to let them know that they were being watched. Innes took his advice. He toured the entire works to publicise the fact that he was now in charge and would not allow slacking or bad craftsmanship.

When he returned to his office at the end of the afternoon, he found Colbeck waiting to see him. His visitor waved away Innes's apologies.

'I haven't been here long,' he said, looking around. 'In fact, I've barely had time to take stock of this office. There's a marked difference between your desk and Mr Hubbleday's, isn't there?'

'He was senior to me, Inspector.'

'He made that crystal clear, Mr Innes. His desk is not only much bigger than yours, it stands near the window to catch the best of the light. You are tucked away in a dark corner.'

'I make no complaint about that, Inspector.'

'There's another key difference. You have a photograph of someone I take to be your good lady while he has nothing to indicate that he had a family life.'

'That is indeed my wife,' said Innes, glancing fondly at the framed photograph on his desk. 'Margaret is always close to me. Mr Hubbleday, by contrast, kept work and home life strictly apart. This was his kingdom. He loved being here.'

'I can well imagine it.'

'If you need to search his desk, I'm afraid that I can't help you. Every drawer is locked. Mr Drake has a set of keys, however,' said Innes. 'Speak to him.'

'Actually,' said Colbeck, 'I came in search of information about one of your employees. I take it that you keep records?'

'Mr Appleby insists on it. They're carefully stacked on the shelves behind you.' Colbeck turned. 'Were you interested in anyone in particular?'

'Yes, a man named Simon Wragg – that's Wragg with a "W", by the way.'

'Then we need to go to the far end of the bottom shelf,' said Innes, walking past his visitor. 'They're arranged alphabetically, you see.' He crouched down. 'Let me find the file for you.'

'Thank you.'

'Here we are,' he said, pulling it out. 'It's all yours, Inspector.'

Colbeck took it from him and opened the cover. 'This is neat calligraphy,' he said. 'Mr Hubbleday had a fine hand.'

'Actually, it was my job to maintain the records.'

'Then I congratulate you. It's so easy to read.'

'How long has Wragg been with us?'

'Over two years, by the look of it,' said Colbeck, studying the man's record. 'His work seems to have been up to standard and there was even a commendation from Mr Appleby last year. Except for one thing, he looks like a model employee.'

'What's the one thing?' asked Innes, looking over his shoulder.

'It's this asterisk by his name. What does that denote?'

'Ah, that was put there by Cyril.'

'I can see that it was by someone else's hand because it's so ugly.'

'It's what he called a mark of disfavour, Inspector,' explained the other. 'If he was dissatisfied with someone's work, he made a note of the fact in the records. If there was a second asterisk, it means that someone was in trouble.'

'What about three asterisks?'

'It would lead to instant dismissal.'

'Would the man in question be given no chance to defend himself?'

'None at all,' said Innes. 'He'd be escorted off the premises.'

Since there was only one asterisk beside Wragg's name, Colbeck assumed that the man had simply been given the stern warning that Derek Churt had told him about. He read the detailed account of Wragg's work over the time he had been part of the painting team there. His eye then fell on a few lines about the man's background.

'He was born at somewhere called Hanley Castle,' he noted. 'Have you any idea where that is?'

'Yes,' said Innes. 'It's not far from Upton upon Severn. I know that because, in my younger days, I played cricket there from time to time. There's a pitch not far from the Three Kings Inn. We always ended up there, drowning our sorrows because they beat us every time somehow. It was maddening.' He remembered something. 'Did I hear that you're staying in Great Malvern?'

'That's right.'

'Then you'll be going right past Hanley Castle.'

Victor Leeming had learnt from experience that Samuel Waycroft was a slippery character. He therefore bided his time until evening shadows enveloped the whole area. He had two police officers to help him. Stationing one of them at the far end of the street where Waycroft's sister lived, he took up his position at the other end. The second policeman then went up to the house, knocked on the door until the sister appeared, and asked if her brother was at home. She denied it hotly. The policeman retreated into the darkness to wait with his colleague. It was not long before a figure emerged from the house and looked up and down the street. Leeming was thrilled. They had flushed him out. Turning to the right, Waycroft trotted off down the street, unaware that the two policemen were waiting to arrest him. When he reached the corner, he saw the pair in outline and realised that he was trapped.

Before they could grab him, he spun round and sprinted in the opposite direction, confident that he could shake off the pursuit. He got within reach of the corner but no further. Leeming leapt out to block his path and pushed him forcefully backwards. He was on his quarry at once.

'Remember me?' he asked.

'Get out of my way,' roared Waycroft.

'I'm placing you under arrest.'

By way of response, the man hurled himself at Leeming, but the sergeant was ready for him this time. He punched Waycroft hard in the stomach with his left fist then used the right one to deliver a perfect uppercut to the man's chin. Waycroft collapsed to the ground in a heap.

'Now you know how I felt,' said Leeming.

When he joined them at the house that evening, Caleb Andrews was upset to hear about Alan Hinton's injuries. He pressed Lydia Quayle for details.

'How badly was he hurt?' he asked. 'Was anything broken? Will there be permanent scars? Does this mean he'll lose his job?'

'No, Mr Andrews,' she said. 'There's no question of Alan leaving the Metropolitan Police Force. He can't wait to get back into action.'

'I don't blame him. I'd feel the same.'

'Alan was keen to stay there,' Madeleine put in, 'and track down the two men who assaulted him. Wisely, Robert sent him back here to recover.'

The three of them were in the drawing room, enjoying a drink before they had dinner. There was a roaring fire in the grate and the decorations on the Christmas tree were sparkling brightly. It made Lydia feel guilty.

'It's so unfair,' she remarked. 'Here are we, relaxing in comfort, while Alan is nursing his wounds in his lodgings.

What rotten luck it is for him!'

'There are compensations,' said Andrews. 'He has two attentive ladies seeing to his every need – you and his landlady.'

Lydia forced a smile. 'He'd much rather be working on the case,' she said. 'He's like Robert – born to be a detective.'

'Is he going to be replaced?'

'I don't think so, Mr Andrews.'

'Then we might as well stop pretending that my son-in-law will be back home before Christmas. It was a difficult enough job when there were four of them. They're now down to three and that superintendent is not much use to them. They could be stuck there for months.'

'Don't be silly, Father,' said his daughter.

'It's true, Maddy.'

'You're being unduly pessimistic, Mr Andrews,' said Lydia.

'I'm just facing facts. We must warn Helena.'

'No,' said Madeleine, firmly. 'That will only alarm her. She knows that her Daddy goes to work for long periods – and that's all she needs to know. I still have faith in Robert.'

'And so does Alan,' said Lydia. 'He's certain that they'll run the killer to earth before long. They've gathered a lot of evidence between them. It's only a matter of time before an arrest is made. That's what he believes, anyway.'

'I'm not sure that I do,' said Andrews, grumpily.

'Father!' exclaimed Madeleine.

'Look at the numbers. Four of them tried and failed to solve a single murder. Three of them are now coping with two murders. All we need is for Victor Leeming to be killed and there'll be two of them coping with three murders. This case is going to ruin the reputation that Robert has built up over the years.'

'It could equally well be his finest success,' said Lydia.

'There's no chance of that happening.'

'Wait and see, Mr Andrews.'

'Robert is facing defeat,' he prophesied. 'I feel it in my bones.'

'Let's stop there,' suggested Madeleine. 'Arguing about it is pointless. We're better off enjoying our dinner and talking about something else.'

'I agree,' said Lydia.

Andrews glowered mutinously but remained silent.

Leeming was relieved to have good news to report at last. When he met Colbeck at the little office in the Works, he boasted about how he had knocked out Waycroft, then arrested him the moment the man opened his eyes. His success had, however, been edged with disappointment.

'Waycroft had nothing to do with the murder of Mr Hubbleday,' he admitted.

'Are you certain about that?' asked Colbeck.

'Yes, sir. He was very angry that someone got to kill him first. It was a crime he'd dreamt about committing himself.'

'What's happened to Waycroft?'

'He's locked up at the police station in Tipton. He'll be charged with assaulting me, and he'll be rubbing his chin ruefully.'

'In other words,' said Colbeck, 'we can eliminate him from the inquiry.'

'That's right, Inspector.'

'Then we can replace him with another potential suspect – a painter by the name of Simon Wragg.'

'What do you know about him?'

'I know the most important thing, Victor – he works alongside Derek Churt. In fact, it was Churt who drew my attention to him. Wragg is something of a loner in his group, a conscientious man who gets on well with the others but spends very little time with them away from work. Also,' recalled Colbeck, 'he had a reason to dislike Mr Hubbleday.'

He told Leeming how the man had been unfairly criticised by the works manager and how the incident had left Wragg embittered. Colbeck also mentioned Hubbleday's use of the asterisk in the company's records.

'I reckon that the superintendent does something like that,' claimed Leeming. 'The difference is that he doesn't write anything down. He keeps bad marks for each of us inside his head. From the way he treats me, I must be into double figures.'

'There are also lots of good marks against your name, Victor.'

'He doesn't seem to remember those.'

'Then we need to jog his memory,' said Colbeck, 'and the best way to do that is to make some headway in this case.'

'Are we going to confront this man, Wragg?'

'No, we'll keep him in reserve. It's more important to find the person who conceived the idea of killing the works manager. I'd like your opinion of one of the suspects.'

'Who is that?'

'John Armitage.'

'He wanted to marry Hubbleday's daughter, didn't he?'

'Yes,' said Colbeck, thoughtfully. 'And I fancy that he still nurses the hope of doing that one day.'

Alone in the stationmaster's office, Tallis went carefully through the evidence they had so far gathered. Time and again, Colonel Yardley came into his mind. As a fellow soldier, he found it difficult to believe that a man with the colonel's status and background would stoop to such a heinous crime. Yet the doubts about him persisted. Yardley had to remain on the list of suspects. The attack on Alan Hinton had been a setback but it had drawn someone out into the open. The attempt at hampering the investigation was an indication that progress had been made. While he regretted that one of his officers had been viciously assaulted, Tallis saw that it was not without its value to them. It signalled that they were closer to the culprit and his associates than they had dared to imagine.

Crouched over the fire in the office, the superintendent

was constantly interrupted by the arrival and departure of trains. There were also the frequent appearances by Harold Unwin, who came in and out on a series of errands. Tallis felt that he needed somewhere more private for his review of the case. Tempted to return to his room at the Imperial Hotel, he was about to leave when another idea popped into his mind. He smiled for the first time that day.

'How nice to see you again, Inspector,' said Armitage, shaking his hand.

'I'm glad that we caught you in time, sir,' said Colbeck.

'Oh, I'll be here for a couple of hours yet. I start early and finish late.'

'Allow me to introduce Sergeant Leeming, who is working on the case with me. He's heard compliments about Armitage Best Bitter.'

'It's true,' said Leeming. 'Our colleague, Detective Constable Hinton, had nothing but praise for your beer.'

'It's gratifying to hear that,' said Armitage, beaming. 'If he wishes, I'll be glad to give him a tour of the brewery.'

'That won't be possible, sir.'

'No,' added Colbeck. 'After enjoying a meal at the Seven Bells yesterday evening, he was ambushed by two thugs who stole his wallet and left him barely conscious.'

Armitage looked shocked. 'That's terrible news!'

'He'll recover, sir.'

'I hope that he didn't drink one glass too many of our Best Bitter.'

'His mind was clear when he left the pub,' said Colbeck. 'He blames himself for being caught unawares.'

'I see.'

It was almost as if Armitage knew that they were coming. When they were shown to his office, he was pleasant, at ease and hospitable. He even offered them a free sample of their beer. To Leeming's disappointment, the offer was politely rejected by Colbeck. The inspector began to probe.

'I take it that you know the Seven Bells, sir,' he said.

'I know all the local pubs that are wise enough to sell our beer.'

'What about the Lamb and Flag in Upton upon Severn?'

Armitage shrugged. 'What about it?'

'I understand that you supply their beer.'

'It's only one pub out of hundreds that favour the Armitage brand.'

'Have you been to the Lamb and Flag recently?'

'Yes, I have, as it happens, Inspector. I popped in there a couple of weeks ago when I was in the area.'

'Then you might have met Jim Carmody,' said Leeming.

'Who?'

'He worked as a sort of assistant manager there.'

'In the course of a normal day, Sergeant, I meet dozens of employees in the various pubs that I visit. What is so special about this . . . Jim Carmody, was it?'

'He was murdered, sir.'

Armitage's eyebrows shot up. 'Really?' he exclaimed.

'We found him at the base of the Worcestershire Beacon,' said Colbeck. 'He was concealed in a patch of ferns. To be more exact, his body was. The killer had hacked off his head.'

'It was later dug up nearby,' added Leeming.

'This is gruesome news,' said Armitage, solemnly. 'I feel for the man's family. But why are you passing on these grim tidings to me?'

'I thought you might be interested, sir,' explained Colbeck. 'You are clearly a man who takes his job seriously and who would make a point of getting to know the names of all the people with whom you do business.'

'I deal with publicans, Inspector, not with mere employees.'

'From what we've heard about him, Carmody was very gregarious. If, as you say, you went into the Lamb and Flag recently, you would certainly have noticed him. He'd have seen to that.'

'Perhaps I did,' conceded Armitage, 'but I've no memory of it.'

'Let's try another pub,' suggested Colbeck. 'Do you have any association with the Three Kings Inn in Hanley Castle?'

Armitage looked uncomfortable for the first time.

Lady Foley was a slave to tradition. Even when she dined alone, she dressed as if for a formal occasion and sat at the head of the long dining table. Four footmen and the butler waited upon her, each of them immaculately attired. Now that she had a guest in the shape of Colonel Yardley, she omitted her usual litany of instructions to her staff and engaged in conversation.

'What's your opinion of the superintendent?' she asked.

'Splendid fellow,' replied Yardley with enthusiasm. 'I spy a soulmate, Lady Emily. We are cut from the same solid English oak and our priority is service to Queen and country.'

'I applaud that, Colonel.'

'Why do you ask about him?'

'He interests me,' she said. 'Why does a man of his age and achievements bother to work for the Metropolitan Police Force? He surely deserves honourable retirement and recognition of his dedication to both army and law enforcement.'

'I couldn't agree more, Lady Emily.'

'What was his rank?'

'Tallis was a major – an excellent one, I daresay.'

'He looks and sounds as if he deserved a higher rank.'

'I'm sure that he did. He exudes a sense of authority.'

She smiled. 'One might say the same thing of you, Colonel.'

'I was born to it,' he said with a grin. 'What else could someone of limited abilities like me do with my life? The army was my natural home. When I found a dear wife who was willing to share it with me, I became the happiest of men.'

'Is the superintendent married?' Lady Foley asked. Yardley

chortled merrily. 'Have I said something amusing?'

'Tallis is a crusty old bachelor and that is not a criticism, by the way. Some of us are born to find a partner in life while others, like the superintendent, are happier to plough a lone furrow.'

'Living alone has its advantages,' she said, grandly.

'You've adapted superbly to the situation forced upon you, Lady Emily.'

'Thank you.'

Their soup was served. Lady Foley gave a nod of satisfaction. It was up to her required standard. They ate in silence for a couple of minutes then she spoke.

'Do you believe that these appalling murders will be solved?' she asked.

'Of course I do – don't you?'

'Seeds of doubt are beginning to sprout.'

'I have complete faith in the superintendent and his detectives,' he affirmed. 'They are battle-hardened veterans. Tracking down killers is what they do. There are not many hiding places in the countryside, Lady Emily. Sooner or later, Tallis will flush the villain out into the open.'

'I do hope so, Colonel.'

'He will see it as his mission.'

Edward Tallis was relieved to see that the Priory was still open at that time of the evening. Entering by means of the North Porch, he walked to the bottom of the nave and gazed towards the distant altar. A selection of candles had been lit in various places throughout the church, enabling him to see a few ghostly figures flitting about. He lowered himself into a pew.

What had begun as a Benedictine Priory was now the parish church of Great Malvern. Though he could not actually see the massive Norman pillars that held it up or the soaring magnificence of Perpendicular architecture all around him, he felt that he was in a very special place. At Scotland Yard, he was a person of distinction and wallowed in the fact. Here, it was different. He was an anonymous worshipper who felt the cleansing power of humility.

After offering up a silent prayer, he addressed the problems that had sent him there, going patiently over the information they had so far gathered and doing his best to make sense of it. He made no appeal for divine intervention. Crimes could only be solved by gathering then interpreting the relevant evidence. Tallis felt that he already had sufficient clues. What he lacked was the thread that held them together. Eyes closed and head bowed, he began to search once again through the confusing mass of information they had so far assembled. Somehow, they had to deliver the answers he and his detectives sought.

Colbeck was in search of those answers. Though the mention of Hanley Castle had startled him at first, John Armitage had recovered quickly and explained away his momentary discomfort. He had been born and brought up there until the family brewery in the Black Country had begun to flourish. They had moved house, trading an idyllic country setting for a pulsating industrial town. The boy who had romped in the Malverns was soon an apprentice at the brewery with a taxing daily round.

'It was agony at first,' he told them.

'Yet you learnt to love it,' observed Colbeck.

'I'd have done the same,' said Leeming with a grin. 'What could be nicer than working in a brewery and getting free glasses of its output?'

'There was no drunkenness on site,' Armitage told him. 'Anyone seen having a pint of beer was sacked at once. My father was very strict. I learnt to follow in his footsteps. Those who work for us have to earn their wages.'

'I gather that you once gave advice to Mr Appleby,' recalled Colbeck.

'That's right, Inspector.'

'How did he respond?'

Armitage grinned. 'He went red in the face and blustered.'

'Why?' asked Leeming. 'What did you say to him?'

'I told him the truth, Sergeant. I said that he was wrong to featherbed his workers. Sending them off on excursions was a big mistake.'

'What do you mean?'

'They'll come to expect treats as a part of their job.'

'Mr Appleby was a disciple of Robert Owen,' Colbeck pointed out. 'At his factory in Lanarkshire, Owen worked on the principle that happy employees work more efficiently. That's why he gave them additional rewards.'

'Appleby's workers are not happy – they're spoilt.'

'Yet they produce wagons and carriages of the highest quality.'

'They'd do the same without being sent on trips into the countryside,' argued Armitage. 'They're paid to do a full day's work, not to go scampering around the Malvern Hills.'

'I rather admire Mr Appleby's methods,' admitted Colbeck.

'That's because you're not a businessman, Inspector. Granted, Appleby is a brilliant entrepreneur. Look at the huge profits that he makes. But he has a fatal weakness.'

'What is it?' asked Leeming.

'He needs to be liked. That's why he wastes money on his workers.'

'I disagree,' said Colbeck. 'I think that Mr Appleby is providing incentives. It's the reason there's a long waiting list of people who want to work for him. In his own way, he's a model employer.'

'It's not a model I'd care to follow,' said Armitage, 'and it didn't find favour with everybody. I know that because Mr Hubbleday told me how much he disliked the excursions. It blurred the lines between management and labour.'

'You didn't get on with Mr Hubbleday, did you?'

'I made every effort to do so.'

'Did you have a blazing argument with him?'

'I was never given the chance,' said Armitage. 'I was simply eased out of his elder daughter's life. Marion was forbidden to speak to me, and the servants were told that I was to be turned away at the door.'

'You strike me as a man who'd fight back,' said Leeming. 'You wouldn't give up easily. It's not in your nature.'

'Quite right, Sergeant. It isn't.'

'How do you feel now that Mr Hubbleday is dead?'

'Oh, I think you're clever enough to answer that question yourself.'

'Then let me ask you another one, if I may,' said Colbeck, having lulled Armitage into a state of relaxation. 'If you were brought up near Hanley Castle, you must have known someone who now works at Appleby's.'

'It's possible,' said Armitage. 'What was his name?'

'Simon Wragg.'

'I'm sorry, Inspector. I've never heard of him.'

They both knew that he was lying.

Having chosen his hiding place, the man stayed there for over half an hour. A figure then glided past him and went to the house nearby before banging on the door with his fist. Moments later, Simon Wragg came out and the two of them went off together, chatting happily. Emerging from the shadows, Derek Churt went after them.

CHAPTER SEVENTEEN

On their journey back to Great Malvern, they had much to discuss and were grateful that they had a compartment to themselves. Victor Leeming was forthright.

'We've found the killer,' he declared.

Colbeck was dubious. 'There's insufficient evidence to justify an arrest.'

'Armitage gave himself away, sir. When you asked him if he knew Simon Wragg, he told a barefaced lie. It's the link we needed. Armitage and Wragg must have grown up together. We've been wondering how the killer got precise details about the excursion train. The answer is that Wragg provided them. He works alongside Derek Churt, the one painter who went on that trip and who admitted that he talked openly about it to the others.'

'You're assuming that Armitage is the killer.'

'It's obvious,' said Leeming. 'For a start, he had a strong motive. Hubbleday not only stood between him and his daughter, he treated Armitage with contempt. That would rankle.'

'When I first met him,' recalled Colbeck, 'I asked Armitage if he was married. He told me he was not but that there was someone very dear to him.'

'Yes – it was Marion Hubbleday.'

'Not necessarily.'

Leeming wagged a finger. 'I remember something else he told you.'

'What was it?'

'He'd been away for a few days. Part of the time, I'll wager, was spent in the Malverns, lying face down at the top of that cutting to shoot a man he loathed. That's how it happened, sir. Armitage had a strong motive and was clever enough to create an opportunity.'

'Colonel Yardley also had a motive and far better knowledge of the area than Armitage. More significantly, the colonel would have been able to recruit James Carmody to provide the railway sleepers and the red flags.'

Leeming was defiant. 'I'll stick with Armitage.'

'I prefer to be more cautious.'

'He killed someone he hated to marry someone he loved. You told me how pretty Marion Hubbleday was. It's no wonder Armitage wanted her as his wife. And she welcomed his interest.'

'Then why did she accept another man's proposal?'

'I daresay that her father bullied her into doing so.'

'She's an intelligent, God-fearing young woman,' said Colbeck. 'Once she'd made a commitment, she would abide by it. If she believed that Armitage had murdered her father, she would be horrified.'

'But she was not supposed to find out, sir. Armitage knows her far better than we do. He was acting on the assumption that – once she came out of mourning – Marion would turn to him.'

'It would be marriage built on a vile crime. I don't think that even Armitage would contemplate that.'

'In my opinion,' said Leeming, 'he'd stop at nothing. He's ambitious. When he sets his mind on something – however difficult – he'll get it. Don't you agree?'

'No, I don't.'

'What are we going to do about him?'

'Nothing at all,' said Colbeck. 'If he is guilty, we'll let him think that he's shaken us off. He'll start to relax. That's when mistakes creep in.'

'He's already made some. I think we should detain him.'

'That's going too far, too fast. Besides, we have other suspects to consider.'

'Who else is there, apart from Colonel Yardley?'

'Oddly enough,' said Colbeck, seriously, 'someone else's name has just come into my mind.'

'Who is that?'

'Ernest Drake.'

'That's ridiculous,' spluttered Leeming. 'He and the murder victim were best friends. Drake couldn't possibly have been involved in the shooting because he was in the train at the time.'

'I know, Victor. But I'm also aware of the fact that it was Drake who explained away the dead body beside the line by claiming that it was a cow that had to be shot. Apparently he was very convincing.'

'So?'

'I'm wondering if the excuse was prepared in advance,' said Colbeck. 'Drake is hardly a man you'd turn to in an emergency. He looks too meek and mild. Yet he saved that excursion by telling a lie to conceal a dreadful event.'

'Then who shot Hubbleday?'

'His accomplice.'

'Armitage or the colonel?'

'I've no idea,' confessed Colbeck. 'I'm just exploring an idea that sounds incredible. Ernest Drake is so self-effacing that he's virtually invisible. What possible motive would he have to want the works manager killed?'

'There isn't one.'

'What would he stand to gain?'

'Nothing, as far as I can see. You told me that he was almost part of the Hubbleday family. He was at their house a great deal.'

'Why was he invited there so often?' wondered Colbeck. 'Something doesn't quite ring true about that friendship. And there's another thing to consider. Drake had his own office and enough work to keep himself busy throughout the day.'

'Go on, sir.'

'Why did he have the keys to Hubbleday's desk?'

Ernest Drake waited for over an hour beyond the time when his day at the Works had ended. There were too many people about for him to make his move. Only when he was convinced that he was safe did he slip along the corridor to Hubbleday's office. Using the key, he opened the desk drawers in turn and began to take ledgers and documents out before putting them into the bag he had brought. After examining his haul to make sure that he had everything he needed, he locked the drawers, checked that nobody was in the corridor outside then headed for the exit.

Marion Hubbleday felt confused and hurt. Though he had broken up a romance that meant so much to her, she still had a duty to love her father. She had therefore been shocked when her uncle had revealed his bitterness towards his brother. There had never been the slightest sign of it before. Uncle Reuben had been a kind, generous, supportive man to Marion and to the rest of her family, accepting the fact that his elder brother made all the decisions. There had never been any dissension between the two of them.

What puzzled Marion was the fact that her uncle's outburst should come at such a time. He was sharing a house of mourning with three grief-stricken women. They relied on his support and patience and were grateful for the way that he lifted the burden of making decisions from off their backs. Marion had begun to view him as a paragon. And yet he had suddenly exploded in front of her, shattering all the assumptions she had made about him over the years. It was the look on his face that frightened her because it reminded her so much of her father. When he spat out the words, her uncle's features had twisted into an ugly scowl.

There was some relief now. He had gone back to his own family for the evening, leaving Marion to share a meal with her mother and sister for the first time since the murder. It would be something of an ordeal for her. She had already decided to say nothing about the incident because the other women would be deeply wounded to hear what had happened. How would Marion respond when the pair of them talked so fondly of Reuben and praised his virtues? She would have to bite her tongue.

Since they had been in the Malverns, Colbeck and Leeming had seen many strange sights, but none had startled them quite so much as the one that now confronted them. They arrived back at their hotel to find Tallis seated in the lounge with Ruby Renshaw and sipping a glass of sherry. It was an unexpected domestic scene. They had never seen the superintendent alone in the company of a woman before, yet he was clearly enjoying the situation. By way of a welcome, he raised his glass to them.

'Welcome back!' said Ruby, rising to her feet. 'The superintendent and I were just talking about the Priory.'

'I visited it earlier on,' said Tallis. 'I didn't realise it was so inspiring.'

'Why was that?' asked Colbeck.

'It was not for anything I actually saw because it was largely in shadow. It was because of the feelings it generated. I felt wanted – that's the only way to describe it. I felt wanted and respected.'

'Was this before or after you had a glass of sherry?' said Leeming.

'It was before, Sergeant,' replied Tallis. 'I was as sober as a judge.'

'During my time as a barrister,' recalled Colbeck, 'I met very few judges who believed in sobriety. One of them told me that he needed a stiff glass of brandy before a trial because it was the only way to stay awake.'

'That's a terrible thing to admit,' said Ruby.

'Justice moves in strange ways, Mrs Renshaw.' He turned to Tallis. 'I'm glad that you found time to visit the Priory, sir, but I'm sorry that it was in dark shadow. You saw none of its superb features, such as its medieval glass. It's among the finest in the whole country. I was also fascinated by its misericords.'

'Its what?' asked Leeming, mouth agape.

'Misericords.'

'What on earth are they?'

'The church was built as a Benedictine priory,' said

Colbeck. 'Monks had to endure long hours standing up. To offer them a degree of comfort, tiny shelves were carved under the hinged choir stalls so that they could rest against them and have some support as they stood there.'

'That's cheating,' said Leeming.

'You wouldn't say that if you had to stand for eternity during a service. Besides, misericords are not merely a source of relief for aching bodies. They are elaborate carvings that delight the eye, works of art in some cases. I could spend a whole morning studying those in the Priory.'

'Oh, no, you couldn't,' warned Tallis. 'We have important work to do first. Now then, I need to know if your day has been fruitful.'

'Then I'll leave you to discuss it in private,' said Ruby, leaving the room.

'Thank you, Mrs Renshaw.'

'What about your day, sir?' asked Colbeck.

'Disappointing.'

'I'm sorry to hear that.'

'We've had more luck,' Leeming piped up. 'We questioned John Armitage and caught him out. I think he is our man.'

'He's a credible suspect,' said Colbeck, 'but I'd go no further than that.'

'The inspector has suggested another name.'

'Oh?' said Tallis. 'Who is that?'

'Ernest Drake.'

'Surely not – he was Hubbleday's friend, wasn't he?'

'That is what we've been led to believe,' said Colbeck, 'yet his name keeps buzzing around in my mind. I can't see what he stands to gain by Hubbleday's death. All I know is that there's something about Drake that encourages me to give him a lot more attention.'

Alone in his study at home, Drake went through the ledger with an expert eye. From time to time, he tore out a page with great care and consigned it to the wastepaper basket. When he had finished with the ledger, he moved on to the collection of documents and letters that he had also taken from Hubbleday's office. Recognising his own handwriting, he tore up copies of the letters that he had sent to the works manager and tossed them on the fire. Only when they had been consumed by the flames did he go back to his desk and continue his work.

Dinner was eaten, for the most part, in silence. Marion Hubbleday was grateful that neither her mother nor her sister even mentioned Reuben. After days spent together in the main bedroom, Hubbleday's wife and younger daughter had made the effort to come downstairs at last. It was a small but important step. When the meal was over, they thanked Marion for dealing with any visitors then withdrew upstairs. Marion sat there for a long time before she heard a cab drawing up outside the house. Uncle Reuben had returned.

Jumping to her feet, she felt the urge to avoid what could be an embarrassing encounter. After taking a deep breath, however, she scolded herself for being so cowardly. The only way to resolve the situation, she decided, was to deal with it. When a servant admitted Reuben to the house, therefore, he found Marion in the drawing room. His manner was warm and friendly.

'How was dinner?' he asked.

'It went off well,' she replied. 'Neither mother nor Ellen had much to say but the important thing was that they did come downstairs at last.'

'Do they feel able to cope with a visit from your Aunt Hetty?'

'I believe that they do, Uncle Reuben.'

'Then I'll send for her tomorrow. My wife has been dying to come.'

He broke off to remove his hat and overcoat so that he could hand them to the servant who was hovering beside him. The woman disappeared and closed the door behind her. There was a long, uneasy silence.

'Why don't we sit down?' he suggested. 'We must talk.'

'Yes, I know, Uncle Reuben.'

They sat opposite other. Marion was tense. Her uncle was subdued.

'I owe you an apology,' he said. 'It was wrong of me to snap at you like that. I'm very, very sorry, Marion. Did you tell your mother and your sister?' he asked, worriedly.

'No, Uncle Reuben. It would distress them beyond bearing.'

'I'd hate that.'

'To tell you the truth, I'd rather forget the whole thing.'

'I'd hoped that you'd forgive as well as forget.'

She was firm. 'I'm not ready to do that yet,' she told him.

'Then I'm rightly rebuked,' he said, penitently. 'May I tell you one more thing about your father?'

'Not if it's to his detriment.'

'It concerns you and . . . John Armitage.'

'That's water under the bridge. Father disliked him intensely.'

'I think that he judged him unfairly.'

'Yes,' she said, 'and so do I. But it doesn't matter now.'

'Then I won't tell you what Armitage said to me.'

She was curious. 'Why should John speak to you? I don't remember his ever meeting you.'

'He wrote to me, Marion. He'd heard you say how reasonable I was, so he asked for my help. I agreed to see him but made it clear that I could not interfere in any decisions that my brother had made.'

'What did John say to that?'

'Perhaps we should leave it there?' he suggested. 'I don't wish to add to your grief. I'm sorry that I mentioned Armitage.'

'Tell me what John said,' she pleaded.

'Marion—'

'I'm not a child, Uncle Reuben.'

'Very well,' he agreed. 'He said that he loved you and would never give up wanting you as his wife.' A wan smile flitted across her face. 'Armitage seemed sincere. He spoke with great feeling.'

'Why didn't you tell me this before?'

'It was not my place to take sides. I couldn't meddle in your affairs any more than my brother would meddle in mine. In any case, I knew how upset you were at losing Armitage. It would only have hurt you even more.'

'That was very considerate of you.'

'I had your best interests at heart, Marion.'

Though she gave him a nod of thanks, she still felt uneasy in his company. At a time when she was mourning the death of her father, her uncle had shattered the image she had of him. There was no way it could be repaired quickly.

'What else did John tell you?' she asked.

'Perhaps it's better if you forget him,' he said. 'You belong to Philip now.'

'It was you who brought John's name into the conversation.'

'That's true.'

'I haven't seen him for a long time and things have . . . cooled between us. I'd just like to know what he said about me.'

'No matter how long it took, Armitage told me, he'd wait until he could marry you. It was no idle boast, Marion. He meant it.'

After brushing away a tear, she hurried out of the room.

Biddie Leacock was up as usual before dawn. After a frugal breakfast with her sister, she went up to the stables near the base of Worcestershire Beacon so that she could check on her donkeys and fill their hay nets. When she left the building, she glanced up towards the patch of ferns where she had stumbled on the body of a murder victim. The memory coursed through her mind like boiling water, making her turn in agony and bring both hands up to her skull. Until the killer was caught, visits to the Beacon would always be a source of pain for her. There had to be a way that she could help the detectives. She began to rack her brains.

Because they were not alone on the train to Oldbury, Colbeck and Leeming had to be content with their own thoughts. The inspector was asking himself questions about Ernest Drake, conscious of the fact that the man had been on excursions with Hubbleday to the Malvern Hills many times. He would have had plenty of opportunities to pick out the most suitable spot for an ambush. He could also rely on the fact that, when the train stopped, Hubbleday would jump down angrily onto the track to see what had caused the delay.

There were two problems with Colbeck's theory. Try as he did, he could not find a convincing motive that led Drake to hatch a murder plot. And he could not imagine how the shy accountant would be able to recruit a marksman to shoot someone dead. Drake and Armitage seemed an unlikely partnership. An alliance between Drake and the colonel was an impossibility.

Leeming, meanwhile, was amassing evidence to bolster his theory that the killer was John Armitage. He believed that the latter had been powered by a desire for revenge. In

Simon Wragg, he had an accomplice who could provide him with details of the time when the excursion train would reach the chosen spot. All that Armitage had to do was to arm himself with a rifle, choose his spot and fire. By the time he reached his destination, the sergeant had convinced himself that Armitage was guilty of the murder. He was young, fit, able and had known the area since his childhood. In shooting his victim, Leeming believed, Armitage had not only killed a man he despised, he had also rescued Marion Hubbleday from a forced marriage so that he could persuade her to become his wife.

During the cab ride to the Works, the detectives were able to talk at last.

'I'm having my doubts about Ernest Drake,' admitted Colbeck.

'Why is that?'

'I can't see him hiring an assassin, somehow. Then, of course, there's the second murder. How and why could he have ordered that?'

'It's not often that you change your mind, sir.'

'I haven't changed it completely, Victor. I still think we need to put Drake under the microscope. There's something about him that worries me.'

'That means I was right,' said Leeming, jubilantly. 'Armitage is definitely the killer. We should arrest him at once.'

'I'm sorry. I still believe that we need more evidence.'

'I think we already have enough, sir.'

'Then we must agree to differ.'

There was a firmness in Colbeck's voice that brought the discussion to an abrupt end. Leeming shifted to another subject.

'I've been thinking about those misery things.'

'Misericords.'

'Yes, that's right. I thought that the Benedictine order was very strict. Monks were supposed to suffer, weren't they?'

'Indeed, they were, Victor, they endured all kinds of privations. But they could hardly stand up indefinitely. That's why the misericords were carved.'

'In other words, they remained sitting down.'

'No, they didn't. Have you forgotten what it was like to be on duty at night in uniform?'

'I still have bad dreams about it,' groaned Leeming.

'You were supposed to be on foot for the whole shift,' reminded Colbeck. 'Yet I daresay that you rested against something solid from time to time or even found a low wall on which to perch.'

'We had to get relief somehow.'

'That's all that the monks were doing. They were coping with an ordeal by doing something that was midway between sitting and standing. It's a bit like the situation we're in,' Colbeck went on. 'We're trapped between doubt and certainty.'

'I'm not,' said Leeming under his breath.

* * *

Though it involved a detour, John Armitage was more than ready to make it. On his way to the brewery, he first took his horse down the road where the Hubbleday house stood. Pausing for a few moments outside it, he gazed up at what he knew was Marion's bedroom. After blowing her a kiss, he rode off at a canter.

They arrived at their office to find a letter awaiting them. Colbeck read it with mingled surprise and delight. He handed it to Leeming.

'Who is it from?' asked the other.

'Derek Churt. He's used his initiative and done us a great favour.'

'His handwriting is even worse than mine,' said Leeming as he read it.

'There are grammatical errors as well,' said Colbeck, 'but they're forgivable. Churt didn't have the advantages of a good education. What he discovered is invaluable. I thought we had no chance of identifying the men who attacked Alan Hinton, yet we now have their names and addresses.'

'Simon Wragg and his brother.' He handed the letter back. 'Who do we tackle first, sir?'

'Before we approach either of them, we'll visit Simon Wragg's home.'

'Why?'

'You'll soon find out.' Colbeck pocketed the letter. 'Let's go.'

* * *

Ernest Drake was working at his desk when Jerome Appleby came into the office. The accountant was on his feet at once.

'Good morning, sir,' he said.

'I'm sorry to disturb you, Ernest, but I need your help. It concerns the funeral arrangements,' explained Appleby. 'All that I have so far is Reuben's approval of the undertaker's I've chosen.'

'He'll need to consult his sister-in-law and her daughters.'

'That's where you come in. You're a family friend.'

'I did mention the funeral when I last went to the house, but Reuben said that it was too early to consult the women. Marion had some suggestions to make but her mother and sister will want to offer their opinions as well.'

'Could I ask you to call at the house again, please?'

'Yes, of course. I'll be glad to go,' said Drake. 'I just wish that I was able to take some cheering news with me but there's none, alas.'

'That doesn't mean the investigation has stalled. Inspector Colbeck and Sergeant Leeming are working extremely hard.'

'Then why have they made no visible progress?'

'It will come,' said Appleby, concealing his disappointment. 'Give them time, Ernest, and it most certainly will come.'

Oliver Innes obeyed his orders to the letter. Moving from one paint shop to another, he appeared to be on a routine inspection. He had a brief chat with each group of men before moving on. When he came to the team that included Derek Churt, he stopped for a couple of minutes to watch the painters at work. About to move off, he pretended to remember something and turned to Simon Wragg.

'Oh,' he said, casually, 'I wonder if you could spare me a few minutes. I've been going through everyone's work records and came across an anomaly in yours.'

'What do you mean, sir?' asked Wragg.

'Come to my office and I'll show you.'

'If that's what you want . . .'

Innes grinned. 'I'd be grateful if you wipe the paint off your hands first.'

Wragg did as he was asked, then followed Innes out.

Colbeck was waiting patiently in the office assigned to him. When there was a tap on the door, he opened it to welcome Wragg and the acting works manager into the room.

'Thank you, Mr Innes,' he said. 'You can go back to your office now.'

'I was glad to be of help, Inspector,' said the other.

'What's going on?' asked Wragg as the door was shut behind Innes. 'I was told there was a problem about my work record.'

'There is, Mr Wragg. It's come to a sudden end.'

The painter tensed. 'Who are you?'

'I'm Inspector Colbeck from Scotland Yard and I'm trying to find out who attacked my colleague, Constable Hinton. You'll remember him, I'm sure.'

'Well, yes,' said the other, cautiously. 'He came and talked to us.'

'What did you make of him?'

'He . . . seemed to do his job well.'

'Somebody thought that he was doing it too well,' said Colbeck.

He took a few moments to appraise Wragg. The latter was a tall, thin, bushy-haired man in his thirties. He seemed calm and composed. Colbeck indicated a chair.

'Take a seat,' he invited.

'Oh, thank you,' said Wragg, sitting down. 'I'd be grateful if you'd explain what I'm doing here, Inspector. I only get paid for the time I spend in the paint shop.'

'You won't be going back there, I'm afraid.'

'Why not?'

'Because I have reason to believe that you were involved in the assault on Constable Hinton.'

'That's ridiculous!' shouted Wragg. 'I never touched him.'

'Keep your voice down, please. I have excellent hearing.'

'Who told you that lie?'

'Are you Simon Wragg of twenty-two Railway Street?'

'Yes, I am.'

'And your wife's name is Nancy, I believe.'

'What's she got to do with it?'

'Mrs Wragg was much more welcoming than you are,' said Colbeck. 'When we called at the house earlier on, she was very helpful.'

'You had no right to go there.'

'I had every right – as you well know.'

'What are you talking about?'

'I'm arresting you for the assault on Constable Hinton. On the previous evening, of course, you and your brother tried to intimidate him.'

'Leave Terry out of this!'

'I can't, I'm afraid. While you and I are having this little chat, your brother is being arrested at his place of work by my colleague, Sergeant Leeming. I don't think the builder who employs him will be very impressed with Terence Wragg of fifty-two Pearl Street.'

'I swear that we had nothing to do with any assault.'

'Would you swear that on the Holy Bible?'

'Yes, I would!' asserted Wragg.

'Then you're a more wayward Christian than I thought. Your wife, on the other hand, struck me as an honest woman. When I asked her how you had spent the two evenings when Constable Hinton was accosted, she confirmed that you had gone out with your brother on both occasions.'

'Nancy lied to you.'

'She had no reason to do so,' said Colbeck. 'I asked a simple question, and I got a straight answer. Except that, in one instance, it wasn't entirely honest, but Mrs Wragg was not to know that, was she?'

'What are you talking about?'

'You told her that you had found a wallet on the pavement.'

'It's true, I did.'

'You forgot to say that you took it from Constable Hinton's pocket.'

'He must have lost it somehow.'

'Yes – moments after one of you knocked him unconscious.'

'You can't prove anything,' said Wragg, aggressively.

'I don't need to,' said Colbeck, taking a wallet from his pocket and holding it up. 'This is all the proof I require. It has the constable's name in it.'

Wragg abandoned all hope of being able to talk himself out of the situation. Leaping up from the chair, he made a dive for the door, but Colbeck was too quick for him, stretching out a foot to trip him up then standing over him.

'I'd be very grateful if you resisted arrest,' he said with a challenging smile. 'I will then have the pleasure of overpowering you and inflicting some pain on behalf of Constable Hinton.' Grabbing him by the collar, he lifted the man upright. 'What are you going to do?'

Wragg began to quail.

CHAPTER EIGHTEEN

Edward Tallis's elation was short-lived. When a telegraph arrived from Colbeck, telling him that two arrests had been made, the superintendent was delighted. His joy was almost immediately turned to despair by a telegraph from the commissioner that amounted to a direct summons. Tallis had to return to London at once. It was cruel. At the very moment when they had made some headway, he was being withdrawn from the investigation. Colbeck and Leeming would be left to soldier on alone.

While he was at the telegraph station, Tallis dispatched an apologetic message to Colbeck. He then retrieved his valise from the hotel and paid his bill. When he got back to the railway station, he told Unwin that he was off.

'We'll be sorry to see you go, sir,' said the stationmaster.

'There is a consolation. You'll have your office back again.'

'I was only too glad to be of assistance.'

'Your help will be noted in my report, Mr Unwin.'

'Thank you.'

'It made all the difference.'

'I hope that you leave with some regrets, sir.'

'I do, indeed,' replied Tallis. 'This is a beautiful part of the country, and it was a pleasure to visit it. My two abiding memories will be meeting Lady Foley and spending some time in the Priory.'

'Don't forget Mrs Renshaw.'

Tallis smiled. 'Oh, I could never do that.'

The distant rumble of a train built up to an explosion as it thundered into the station and eventually squealed to a halt. After a last wistful look in the direction of the town, Tallis got into a compartment and settled down. His work there was over.

While Jerome Appleby was pleased to hear of the arrests, he was disappointed to learn that one of the brothers now in custody had been an employee of his. He sought more detail.

'Who recruited them?' he asked.

'We don't know, sir,' replied Leeming.

'The fact is,' said Colbeck, 'that neither of them could tell us because they didn't know themselves. According to Simon Wragg, he was approached by a stranger and offered what sounded like easy money. All he was asked to do was to hassle someone and, if that failed to frighten him off, to assault him. He and his brother did that and were no doubt well paid.'

'They also stole Hinton's wallet,' explained Leeming, 'and had the small amount of money inside it. They must have laughed aloud at how simple it had all been. Luckily, one of your other painters was able to identify Wragg as a likely suspect. His instinct was sound.'

'The man deserves a reward,' said Appleby.

'He'd prefer to remain anonymous,' Colbeck told him.

'Why?'

'He has his reasons, Mr Appleby. The Wragg brothers were involved in this case but only on the fringe of it. We have still to apprehend the killer himself.'

'Do you have a suspect in mind, Inspector?'

'We have two,' replied Colbeck, 'but I won't name them yet.' He glanced at Leeming. 'If you'll excuse him, the sergeant will go off to interview one of them.'

'I send him off with my blessing.'

'Thank you, Mr Appleby,' said Leeming, heading for the door.

Colbeck waited until he had left before changing the conversation.

'I'd like to ask you about Mr Drake,' he said.

'Please do so.'

'How long has he been here?'

'Oh, well over ten years, Inspector. During that time, he's

made himself indispensable. We couldn't manage without Ernest.'

'Why is that?'

'He lives for his work,' said Appleby. 'He's the first to arrive and the last to leave. There's not much to occupy him at home, I'm afraid. He and his sister live together, though I'm told that she can be difficult at times. It's the reason he's dedicating his life to us.'

'How close were he and the works manager?'

'They were extremely close,' Appleby told him. 'Given their different characters, it's hard to believe that they would get on at all, but they did. To be honest, I've never really understood it.'

'I was told that he was like one of the family.'

'That fact has been very helpful to me. I've been able to use Ernest as a link between me and the family. In fact, he's there at this moment in the hope of speaking to Cyril's wife and daughters. He's quiet, patient and very tactful,' said Appleby. 'In many ways, Ernest Drake is a saint.'

When he got to the house, Drake was warmly welcomed by Reuben Hubbleday. Marion soon joined them and heard why their visitor had come.

'I'm not sure if Mummy and Ellen are ready to talk about it,' she said.

'We can't postpone decisions time and again,' Drake told her.

'It's not as if we'll actually attend the funeral.'

'That's true, Marion, but it would be rude not to consult you all.'

'I've tried raising the subject with my sister-in-law,' said Reuben, 'and she dissolves into tears. What you can tell Mr Appleby is that the whole family is grateful for his concern and generosity.'

'We are,' confirmed Marion.

'What about invitations?' asked Drake. 'They'll need to be printed.'

'We'll need to look at some examples of the cards first,' said Reuben. 'Then there's the problem of whom to invite.'

'I've already started to make a list,' said Marion. 'Mummy and Ellen can't even bear to look at it. But that will change.'

'Is it possible to speak to your mother?' said Drake.

'I'm not sure.'

'Could you please ask her for me?'

'I'll try, Mr Drake, but I make no promises.'

'Thank you.'

The two men watched her go and close the door behind her. Reuben sighed.

'Marion is bearing a heavy load,' he said. 'She's had to make a lot of decisions on behalf of the family and act as a kind of link with the outside world.'

'The strain is telling on her. You can see it in her face.'

'She's young enough to come through this ordeal and recover. I wish that I could say the same about Dorcas. The shock has taken years off her life.'

'There is one source of help for the family,' said Drake.

'Cyril has left them well provided for. I helped him to draft his will.'

'That was very kind of you.'

'What else are friends for? Talking of which,' he went on, lowering his voice, 'have you decided when you and I will be able to have our discussion?'

'I've been thinking about that.'

'Would you rather wait until the New Year?'

'Frankly,' said Reuben, firmly, 'I'd rather forget the whole thing. I was grateful for your kind offer but I chided myself for being such a coward. It's a duty I should take on myself, not farm it out to someone else.'

'But I'm familiar with Cyril's financial affairs.'

'I appreciate that, but I've reached my decision. If I unload the problem onto someone else, I'll feel guilty. Instead, I'll grit my teeth and tackle it myself.'

Drake struggled to hide his disappointment.

Victor Leeming arrived at the brewery to find that Armitage was in a meeting. While he was waiting, the sergeant fell into conversation with Ian Dale, the sales manager's assistant.

'I don't know Mr Armitage well,' said Leeming, searching gently, 'but he seems to be very decisive.'

'It's a gift he inherited from his father. It will stand him in good stead.'

'Why?'

'Well, he will be taking over the brewery in a few years when his father retires. Running a business successfully needs someone who has a flair for organisation and ambitions for the future.'

'If young Mr Armitage takes complete control . . .'

'Then I become sales manager,' said Dale. 'Working alongside him has been an education. I intend to build on what he has achieved.'

Leeming could see why Dale had been given his post. He was in his thirties, good-looking, educated and spoke well. He was also clearly in awe of John Armitage.

'When you take over from him,' asked the sergeant, 'will your job involve much travelling?'

'Oh, yes. Most of our beer is sold in the Black Country but Mr Armitage has made a point of reaching out beyond its boundaries. He's gone to rural parts of this county, Herefordshire and Shropshire,' said Dale, 'and is now setting his sights on Gloucestershire and Oxfordshire. Our sales are expanding all the time.'

'That must mean he's away from here for days.'

'Yes, he often stays over at a country pub somewhere – if the licensee has been wise enough to order our beer, that is.'

'Where has Mr Armitage been recently?'

'He was in the Malverns earlier this week.'

'Was it a profitable visit?'

'Oh, yes,' said Dale. 'He came back with a smile on his face. But then, he usually does. Mr Armitage can be very persuasive.'

'Has he taught you any of his tricks?'

Dale bridled. 'They're not tricks, Sergeant – he has a gift.'

Leeming asked him about Armitage Best Beer and Dale praised its qualities at length. Evidently, he had already mastered a salesman's patter. After letting him roll on for a few minutes, Leeming suddenly shifted the conversation elsewhere.

'Has Mr Armitage ever talked to you about the murder?'

Dale shrugged. 'What murder?'

'The works manager at Appleby's was shot dead.'

'Oh, yes, I vaguely remember it now. But I don't think that Mr Armitage talked about it. Why should he?'

'There was a time when he courted the daughter of the murder victim.'

Dale was astonished. 'Really? That's news to me.'

'But her father opposed the match. You must have known that.'

'Mr Armitage never discusses his private life, Sergeant.'

'Does the name of Marion Hubbleday mean nothing to you?'

'No,' said the other, 'it doesn't. But even if it did, I would not discuss the lady with you. Mr Armitage would not approve. If you have any more questions of that nature,' he added, 'you'll have to put them directly to Mr Armitage himself.'

Before Leeming could stop him, Dale spun on his heel and left the room.

* * *

Colbeck was in his office when Ernest Drake appeared. The inspector was surprised.

'I thought that you were visiting the Hubbleday house,' he said.

'I was,' replied Drake. 'I've just returned. Reuben Hubbleday asked me to pass on a message to you, Inspector.'

'What was it?'

'He'd appreciate a visit from you.'

'Did he say why?'

'No, he just wanted his request passed on.'

'How did you get on at the house, Mr Drake?'

'I'm not really sure. Mr Appleby asked me to raise the question of the funeral with the family, but Reuben was the only person willing to talk about it. Preparations must be made. We need their approval.'

'I understand that.'

'How is the investigation going?' asked Drake.

'We arrested the two men who assaulted Constable Hinton.'

There was a momentary hesitation. 'That's good news.'

'It is and it isn't. While it's good to have them in custody, it's frustrating that they were unable to tell us who had employed them. In short, we can't connect them to the person who plotted the murder of the works manager.'

'That's a shame,' said Drake.

'But we're getting closer all the time. However,' Colbeck went on, rising from his chair, 'I'll get over to the house at once. If I've been summoned, it must be over a matter of importance.'

Drake swallowed hard.

Leeming was looking around the sales manager's office when the door opened, and John Armitage burst in. He was frothing with anger.

'What the devil do you mean by asking my assistant about my private life?' he demanded. 'You had no right to do so.'

'It was only a polite enquiry.'

'That's not what he told me.'

'He misunderstood me, Mr Armitage.'

'Ian Dale is highly intelligent. He knows what he heard. You were prying.'

'It's an unfortunate habit that I have,' said Leeming. 'When I'm involved in a murder investigation, I can't stop myself asking what people like you think are intrusive questions.'

'They're not just intrusive, Sergeant. They're downright insulting.'

'I have my job to do, sir, and you have yours – at the moment.'

Armitage was stung. 'What does that mean?'

'It means that there is a question mark over your future,' said Leeming, evenly. 'Why didn't you tell us that you stayed somewhere in the Malvern Hills earlier in the week?'

'It slipped my mind,' said Armitage, glaring at him.

'You're becoming forgetful, sir. The fact that you must have known Simon Wragg also slipped your mind. You might care to know that he was arrested earlier today.' Armitage started. 'I had the pleasure of arresting his brother, by the way. The pair of them confessed to a vicious assault.'

'Why are you telling me this?'

'I want to see how many more denials I can get out of you.'

'Look,' said the other, trying to master his rage, 'let me be crystal clear with you. I had nothing whatsoever to do with the murder of Cyril Hubbleday. I admit that the news of his death gave me a fleeting pleasure, but I sympathise deeply with his family. They must be suffering terribly.'

'Their suffering will be eased slightly by the arrest of the killer.'

'You must look elsewhere for him, Sergeant.'

'Why did you deny meeting Jim Carmody?'

'It's because I took no notice of him. I did visit the Lamb and Flag in Upton, but the landlord took me straight through to his parlour. If Carmody was there, I give you my word that I was never introduced to him.'

'Your word rings rather hollow, sir.'

Armitage stiffened. 'I think it's time for you to leave.'

'But I have a lot more questions to ask you.'

'Then I will answer them in the presence of my solicitor. His office is not far away. If you wish, we can go there now.'

'No, thank you.'

Armitage grinned. 'I thought that might scare you off.'

'Oh, I'm not frightened, sir. It's just that Inspector

Colbeck is the best person to deal with any solicitors.'

'Why is that?'

'Before he joined the Metropolitan Police Force,' said Leeming, 'he was a barrister. They are a lot cleverer than mere solicitors.'

He was pleased to see Armitage wince.

Colbeck arrived for his second visit to the house without any idea of why he'd been summoned there. When he was admitted, he found Reuben Hubbleday alone in the drawing room. They shook hands.

'Thank you for coming, Inspector,' said the other.

'I was intrigued by your summons.'

'Sit down and I'll explain why I sent for you.'

When they settled down, he was unduly hesitant. It was almost as if he had changed his mind and regretted sending for the inspector. Colbeck helped him out by initiating a conversation.

'How is everybody?' he asked.

'There's been a slight improvement. I had breakfast with my sister-in-law and both of my nieces. It was largely a silent meal, but I felt we'd taken a step forward.'

'I'm glad to hear it.'

'Look, Inspector,' said Reuben, clearly embarrassed. 'I may be making a big mistake. If I am, I apologise in advance.'

'What does it concern?'

'My brother's financial affairs.'

'I thought that Mr Drake was going to help you sort those out.'

'That was my intention. I've changed my mind now.'

'Why is that?'

'Before I tell you,' said the other, 'there's something you should know. My brother and I have had our differences in the past. I accepted that he was cleverer and more assertive than me, but I hated the way that he boasted about his larger income. I and my family lead a comfortable life. That would not suit Cyril. He always had to have a larger house, more money, more importance, and more control over the rest of us. Excuse me for speaking ill of the dead but you need to know the truth.'

'Any insight you can give me is valuable.'

'The truth is that I was not looking forward to dealing with his financial affairs. I was envious. I had no wish to see just how much more Cyril earned than I did. Yet I forced myself to go through some of his accounts out of a sense of duty,' said Reuben. 'It seemed unfair to place the burden on Ernest Drake.'

'You found something, didn't you?' sensed Colbeck.

'Yes, I did.'

'What was it?'

'I'd need you to look at the evidence for yourself,' said Reuben, 'but I believe that my brother has been taking money illegally out of the Appleby coffers.'

'But he couldn't do that without Mr Drake spotting the fraud.'

'That was the other shock. According to some letters sent by Drake, he was the instigator. The pair of them took advantage of the fact that Mr Appleby trusted them implicitly. It's clear to me that they would have gone on doing so had Cyril not been killed during that excursion.'

'I'll need to see the evidence,' said Colbeck.

'I've got some of the documents here,' said Reuben, indicating a file.

'Might I examine them, please?'

'Before I hand them over, I have to ask you to be discreet.'

'I fully understand.'

'My sister-in-law has lost a husband she loved,' Reuben pointed out. 'Until he has been buried, I don't want her learning that he should have been arrested for fraud. It would kill her, Inspector.'

'Mrs Hubbleday will have to know the truth eventually.'

'I know. Luckily, from what I hear, Mr Appleby is not a vindictive man.'

'He'll be a very sobered one when he realises how easily he's been deceived.'

'Do you suppose that . . . ?'

'Yes, I do,' said Colbeck. 'He has every right to ask for the money back.'

'This is going to cast a dark shadow over the family. Like me, every one of us will feel very ashamed.'

'You also have reason to congratulate yourself.'

'Thank you.'

'What you've discovered may have some bearing on the murder investigation.'

'In what way, Inspector?'

'I don't know yet,' confessed Colbeck. 'But, if nothing else, you've confirmed some of the doubts I've been having about Mr Drake.'

Lady Foley was relaxing in her drawing room when she heard hoof beats approaching the house. Glancing through the window, she saw that Colonel Yardley had just arrived. She watched him hand the reins to the servant who ran out to greet him. He hurried in through the open front door. Seconds later, he let himself into the drawing room.

'Forgive this intrusion, Lady Emily,' he said, taking off his hat, 'but I'm the bearer of bad news.'

'What's happened?'

'Superintendent Tallis has been recalled to London.'

'But he's needed here to lead the investigation.'

'Patently, it's no longer viewed as a priority.'

'Well, it's still a priority to me,' she said, getting to her feet with controlled anger. 'I feel that I need to send a second telegraph to remind the commissioner that we expect better treatment from Scotland Yard.'

'I'm in a mood to deliver the message in person,' he told her.

'That won't be necessary, Francis. You can't go gallivanting off to London. Your dear wife needs you at hand.'

'That's true.'

'How is she, by the way?'

'Charlotte is never at her best in the mornings,' he said. 'But she'll have rallied by the time that I get back, I daresay. Like you and me, she's distressed that two people have been murdered in the Malverns in a matter of days, and yet the killer is still at loose. Charlotte is terrified.' He raised his voice. 'Enough is enough!'

On receipt of the news about the superintendent's departure, Leeming was thrilled.

'That's wonderful!' he cried. 'We've been set free.'

'It means that we'll have a heavier burden,' Colbeck pointed out.

'Yes, but we can make our own decisions now.'

'That's true.'

'Oh, I feel so much better now.'

They had met up again at their office in the Works. Colbeck was curious.

'Tell me how you got on with Armitage.'

'I'm even more certain that he's guilty of both murders.'

'Why?'

'He tried to lie his head off, sir,' said Leeming.

'I daresay that he was sparing with the truth, that's all.'

'Armitage shot the works manager then killed Jim Carmody.'

'What about the attack on Alan Hinton?'

'I'm sure that he ordered that, sir. He was probably the stranger who hired Simon Wragg and his brother.'

'Then he wouldn't have been a stranger, would he?' Colbeck reminded him. 'We found that Armitage and the Wragg brothers were born and brought up in the same part of the Malverns.'

Leeming was stunned. 'I'd forgotten that.'

'You've also forgotten to say what might have motivated Armitage.'

'It was hatred of the works manager.'

'Or love of his elder daughter, perhaps?' asked Colbeck.

'The two go together, sir. He could never hope to get near Marion as long as her father was still alive.'

'Did he mention her at all?'

'No, but then he didn't need to. As soon as I met him, I had the feeling that he was determined to win her back.'

Marion Hubbleday was locked in her room, going through the souvenirs of her relationship with John Armitage. Until her father had intervened, the couple had shared some tender moments together. She had been poised to accept the proposal of marriage that Armitage was never allowed to make. Instead, he had been dumped unceremoniously out of her life. All that remained were memories and they had started to wane. She had a new destiny now.

It was very kind of Armitage to send her a message of sympathy in the wake of her father's death. She had read it a dozen or more times. But his distinctive hand no longer had the power to stir her emotions. Marion had pledged herself to another man now. Caring for Philip Wren, she believed that her future should be with him. It would be wrong to postpone the wedding for any length of time. She felt the need to commit herself to her husband and build a new life with him.

Without even looking at them again, she knelt by the fire and fed the souvenirs into the flames one by one, firmly believing that it was the honourable thing to do.

Worcestershire Beacon was more than a famous landmark to Biddy Leacock. It was a source of money and a place where she felt happy. Having lived so close to it for so long, she dared to believe sometimes that she owned it. That gave her responsibilities. As she stared up the hill at the place where she had found the remains of a murder victim, she noticed the surrounding area. Inspector Vellacott's officers had used their spades to good effect in the search for the missing head, but they had left terrible scars behind them. The sight offended her. The shallow trenches were a sign of intruders.

Biddy ambled up to take a closer look at the piles of earth. Picking up a stone, she hurled it as hard as she could then walked slowly after it to retrieve it. Without fully understanding what she was doing, she took the stone back to the point from which it had been flung. When she hurled it again, she sent it in a slightly different direction. She plodded off to see where it had landed then returned to her base. Aiming the missile in a different direction once more, she quickened her pace and all but broke into a run.

Something deep inside her was driving her on.

Hearing what had happened during Colbeck's visit to the Hubbleday house, Victor Leeming was dazed. He sat down to clear his head.

'Can this be true?' he asked.

'I saw clear proof of it with my own eyes.'

'The works manager was stealing money from here?'

'It was all Drake's fault. On his own, Hubbleday would never have devised such a scheme. They began with small amounts then gradually increased them.'

'Didn't Mr Appleby examine the accounts?'

'Of course he did,' said Colbeck, 'but they'd been doctored by Drake.'

'But he looks as if he wouldn't say boo to a goose.'

'We've arrested two killers in the past with that same inoffensive manner. Never be fooled by the outer shell, Victor. It's what's beneath it that counts.'

'When will you tell Mr Appleby?'

'I gave my word that I'd say nothing until after Mr Hubbleday had been laid to rest. His wife deserves a period of grace.'

'The truth will destroy the poor woman,' said Leeming.

'She'll have her family around her to offer support.'

They were still in the office at the Works. Having discussed Armitage at length, Colbeck turned his attention to Reuben Hubbleday. The man impressed him.

'He's got a detective's instinct,' said Colbeck. 'As soon as he looked through those documents, he smelt a rat.'

'It goes by the name of Ernest Drake.'

'You can see why he offered to help the brother look into Hubbleday's financial affairs. Drake was eager to conceal the warning signs of fraud.'

'Mr Appleby is a brainy man. He'd have to be to make those huge profits. Why didn't he suspect that Drake was up to something?'

'The accountant was too clever. Appleby told me that Drake was a saint.'

Leeming laughed bitterly. 'Saints don't steal from their employer.'

'At least one thing has been explained,' said Colbeck.

'What is it, sir?'

'I was beginning to think that Drake was somehow linked to the murder. Clearly, he was not. Drake wanted to hide the scheme he had devised, not expose it to possible discovery. Hubbleday's death must have shaken him to the core.'

Ignoring the biting wind and the discomfort of the journey, Lady Foley sat in her carriage with a blanket across her knees. She composed the message in her head, keeping it short and incisive. The loss of Superintendent Tallis was a blow that she refused to accept. When they finally arrived at Great Malvern Railway station, she was more determined than ever to make the commissioner of the Metropolitan Police Force aware of her displeasure.

Seeing the look on her face, Harold Unwin did not even dare to speak to her. He simply watched as she walked determinedly to the telegraph station. It was evident that she had heard about Tallis's departure. Lady Foley was retaliating.

The message was sent by hand. The inspector was alone in their office with Leeming when someone from the Lamb and Flag arrived. He was a big, shambling man with a lazy grin. He handed over the letter.

'It's from the landlord,' he said.

'Then it must be important,' said Colbeck, opening it at once and reading it. 'They've found something hidden in James Carmody's room.'

'What was it?' asked Leeming.

'An expensive rifle.'

He handed the letter over. When Leeming read it, he had the same reaction. The landlord would not have sent his message unless he had reason to believe that he had uncovered something of real value to the investigation.

'Thank you for delivering this,' Colbeck said to the barman. 'The sergeant will go back with you immediately.'

He led them out of the office and along a corridor, giving Leeming instructions as he did so. When he had waved the two of them off, he turned to see that he was not alone. Ernest Drake had materialised behind him.

'Ah,' said the other, 'you're back, I see.'

'Yes, I was not at the house for long.'

'What did Reuben want?'

'He wondered if we'd been in touch with John Armitage.

As you well know, there was a time when he was close to Mr Hubbleday's daughter.'

'He was dangerously close, Inspector.'

'We've spoken to Mr Armitage more than once.'

'Are you treating him as a suspect?'

'Not at all,' said Colbeck, lying smoothly, 'but we felt that he might have information that could be of use. I said the same thing to Mr Hubbleday's brother.'

'I see.'

Drake failed to suppress a smile.

CHAPTER NINETEEN

It had been an eventful day at the railway station. The sudden departure of Edward Tallis was followed by the equally sudden arrival of Lady Foley. On both occasions, Harold Unwin had been startled. But it was the third surprise that really shocked him. Having just dispatched a train, he watched it pulling out of the station before he turned around. At the other end of the platform, a donkey had just appeared with a massive woman sitting astride it. Dangling from her hand was a fearsome weapon, caked with earth. Biddy Leacock was back.

* * *

On the way there, Leeming was able to get fuller details from the messenger.

'Where was the weapon found?' he asked.

'It was in the attic,' replied the other. 'There was a hatch in the ceiling of Jim's room. I found the rifle when I went up to get something we needed.'

'Was it hidden or just lying there?'

'Hidden. Jim had wrapped it in an old blanket.'

'What sort of a rifle was it?'

'The best that money could buy.'

'Could he have afforded something like that?'

The man laughed derisively. 'No,' he said. 'I know what Jim was paid because I'm on the same wage. He could never have bought it.'

'Then how did he get hold of it?'

'I reckon he stole it.'

'Who from?'

The man sniffed. 'That's anybody's guess.'

'Were you surprised that he might be a thief?'

'Nothing surprised me about him.'

'Why do you say that?'

'He always seemed so friendly and open,' said the other, 'but I knew there was another side to Jim Carmody. He was cunning.'

The development of the telegraph system had been of immense value to the forces of law and order. Vital information could be sent quickly. When they first arrived in Oldbury, therefore, Colbeck had arranged with the nearest telegraph station that any messages addressed to him should be sent to the Works by hand. He was in the temporary office when the latest one arrived. It had been sent by Harold Unwin and it caused an instant change of plan. Instead of remaining in Oldbury, the inspector left at once and boarded a train.

On the way to Great Malvern, he considered the position that Ernest Drake was in. The man had worked his way into a friendship with the works manager and offered him the possibility of illegal gain. Between them, the two had stolen a large amount of money over the years and kept their activities hidden. Drake believed that he was safe from discovery, but an arrest would certainly be made when the truth came out. Colbeck was sorry that he might not be there to make that arrest.

Arriving at his destination, he stepped out of the train and went down the tunnel that took him to the platform on the other side. As he came up the steps, he was met with a welcoming bray from the donkey tethered to one of the iron columns supporting the canopy. Above the animal's head was one of the brightly painted bunches of flowers at the top of the column. Colbeck paused briefly to admire its delicacy. He had not abandoned his hope to meet the sculptor at some point, but it was a treat that had to be postponed.

When he peeped through the window of the stationmaster's office, he saw Unwin bending solicitously over Biddy Leacock. Seated in front of the fire, she was in a world of her own. Colbeck let himself into the office.

'What's happened?' he asked.

'Biddy found the murder weapon,' said Unwin.

'Where?'

'She's too upset to tell me, Inspector. Let's step outside.'

They moved out to the platform and Unwin shut the door behind them.

'It's standing beside my desk,' he said, pointing through the window. 'The sight of it horrified her so much that I wrapped it up in that newspaper.'

Colbeck could see the item on the floor. Before he could speak to Unwin, the latter anticipated his question.

'I know what you're going to ask,' he said. 'How did she manage to find it? The truthful answer is that I don't know. Getting any words out of Biddy is like getting blood from a stone. She's been hunched over that fire for the best part of two hours, and her donkey has been frightening travellers.'

'You must have some idea what happened.'

'My guess is this, Inspector. She went to the stables as usual then wandered up to the place where the corpse was discovered. Biddy told me it was in a terrible mess. She'd hate that. Biddy likes the Beacon to look as it ought to. I know this sounds ridiculous,' said Unwin, 'but she really cares about it. The inside of her farmhouse is like a tip yet she wants the Beacon kept tidy. Can you imagine that?'

'Yes, I can,' said Colbeck.

'Something made her search,' recalled Unwin. 'That's all I could get out of her. Something forced her on to find that chopper, however long it took. She was cleansing the area. A murder weapon didn't belong.'

'Thank goodness she had the sense to bring it here.'

'When I brushed the earth off it, I found bloodstains. That's when I decided to get in touch with you, Inspector.'

'You did the right thing, Mr Unwin,' said Colbeck, before looking through the window of the office. 'And so did Miss Leacock.'

'What's the next step, sir?'

'I need to take a close look at what she found . . .'

Leeming was glad to get to the Lamb and Flag in search of what sounded like an important clue. He was introduced to Eric Padfield, the landlord, a chubby man in his fifties with a red face and staring eyes.

'Thank you for coming, Sergeant,' he said.

'Thank you for sending for me, Mr Padfield. Your messenger told me how he came to find the weapon. That kind of luck doesn't happen to us very often.'

'I knew that Jim Carmody had been in trouble with the police before but I took him on because he was so good at his job. He worked hard and kept his nose clean. That's all I asked of him. Then off he goes for a holiday,' said Padfield, 'and the police turn up, talking about a case of murder. I was shocked. Jim Carmody? He was no killer. That's what I told them.'

'He could still be involved in the murder as an accomplice.'

'No, I refuse to believe it.'

'Could I please see the weapon that was found, sir?'

'Yes, of course,' said Padfield. 'I'll take you up to Jim's room.'

'Thank you.'

Leeming followed him up the backstairs to the landing and went along it until they reached a room at the far end. Padfield unlocked the door then led the way in. Leeming noticed how untidy it was and how few personal possessions Carmody had. The barman had told the sergeant how much he and Carmody had been paid. He had clearly not taken the job for the money. What mattered far more to him were the free meals and accommodation. Lying on the bed was a rifle of exquisite quality. Leeming studied it with great interest, feeling it in his hands and even looking along its barrel.

'Jim must have stolen it,' said Padfield.

'Maybe,' replied Leeming. 'Then again, maybe someone gave it to him.'

'Who would do that – and why?'

'It could have been for services rendered, sir.'

'Is this something to do with the first murder?'

'It could be, Mr Padfield.' He held up the rifle. 'This belonged to someone with a lot of money. Do you remember John Armitage coming here recently?'

'Yes, I do. He stayed the night, as it happened.'

'In that case, he'd have met Carmody.'

'Met him?' said Padfield with a laugh. 'Jim spent half the evening talking to Mr Armitage. You'd have thought they were old friends.'

After an hour spent with his father, going through the latest sales figures, John Armitage retired to his office in a mood of celebration. Everything was working out to his satisfaction. The brewery had increased its profits, his father was delighted with his efforts and his private life had finally taken on a glow of anticipation. An ambition he had nursed for a long, lonely time was at last in sight of being fulfilled. All that he needed to do was to wait, watch and be ready for the moment when Marion Hubbleday realised that there was no longer a barrier to a future together with him. She could marry the man she loved. Marion would be his at last.

By the time that Leeming got back to Great Malvern's railway station, Biddy Leacock had left, and taken the strong odour of donkey with her. The sergeant handed the rifle to Colbeck with a sense of triumph.

'This is the gun that killed the works manager,' he claimed.

'Are you suggesting that Carmody pulled the trigger?'

'Why else would he have it in his possession, sir?'

'He could have stolen it.'

'That's what they thought at the Lamb and Flag. Carmody could never afford to buy a weapon of this quality. Take a good look at it,' urged Leeming. 'Didn't the pathologist tell you that the bullet was fired by a rifle like that?'

'Yes, he did,' admitted Colbeck, examining the gun carefully. 'But this is no ordinary rifle. It's superbly made. Yes, it might well have fired the bullet extracted from the works manager's head, but I'd need proof that Carmody was the marksman.'

'If it wasn't him, it was John Armitage.'

'I beg leave to doubt that.'

'He and Carmody were working together, sir,' insisted Leeming. 'The landlord told me that Armitage had spent the night at the Lamb and Flag recently. During the evening, he was seen talking at length to Jim Carmody.'

'There's a definite link between them, then.'

'I think we should arrest Armitage at once.'

'Don't be too hasty,' warned Colbeck, turning the rifle over. 'Let me finish looking at this properly. There's something I want to find.'

'What is it?'

'An indication of ownership. If I bought something as expensive as this, I'd want to mark it as mine in some way. Ah!' he went on, jabbing a finger at the stock. 'There we are.'

'Let me see.'

Carved neatly into the wood was a set of initials. Leeming's elation vanished.

'FDY,' noted Colbeck. 'With the best will in the world, we can't get the name of John Armitage out of that.' He looked up. 'This was owned by Francis Yardley.'

'But the colonel denied even knowing Carmody.'

'Wouldn't you, in the circumstances?'

Leeming sagged. 'I could have sworn it would be Armitage.'

'That's because of his underlying arrogance. He feels

certain that he will be the benefactor of Hubbleday's death, though I feel that his hopes may yet be dashed. However, we can now forget all about him and his Best Bitter. This rifle is pointing us in the direction of Colonel Yardley.'

'I suppose that it does, sir.'

'Cheer up,' said Colbeck, seeing his glum expression. 'You can have the pleasure of arresting him. Oh,' he added, reaching for the chopper, 'and you might show him this when you do so.'

'What is it, sir?'

'It's the weapon he used to kill and behead James Carmody.'

Edward Tallis was back behind his desk at Scotland Yard, controlling a variety of investigations and barking at the heels of his detectives. Though he had been upset at being recalled to London, he accepted that there was just cause for his return. A royal event was due to take place soon and Tallis was required to deploy his detectives. It meant a visit to Buckingham Palace with the commissioner, a duty that Tallis always enjoyed. Meanwhile, he was as busy as ever, breaking off from time to time to wonder what was happening in the Malverns.

'For heaven's sake, Colbeck!' he cried aloud. 'I want news!'

They had imagined that Colonel Yardley would wilt at the sight of the rifle and the bloodstained chopper. Instead, he was remarkably calm and composed.

'Yes, indeed,' he said to the detectives. 'That is my rifle. It was purloined from my collection several days ago. Thank you for returning it.'

'We're here to do more than that, sir,' said Colbeck, meaningfully. 'Do you recognise this chopper?'

'Of course not, man! If I need wood chopped, I get one of the servants to do it. I've never seen the thing before. Where did you find it?'

'It was found for us by Miss Leacock.'

Yardley snorted. 'That mad old bat!'

'The woman has been very helpful to us.'

They were in the spacious drawing room at Yardley's house. Trophies of all kinds abounded. Leeming kept looking at the tiger rug on the floor. He left the talking to Colbeck.

'You say that the gun was stolen, sir,' said the inspector. The colonel gave a curt nod. 'Did you report the theft?'

'Yes, of course.'

'I'll get Inspector Vellacott to confirm that.'

'Can't you simply take my word for it?' demanded Yardley.

'I'm afraid not.'

'Then I'll report you to the superintendent.'

'He'll be no help to you, sir.'

'Damn you, man! Show some respect.'

'I don't see anyone here worthy of it,' said Colbeck, levelly. 'You're not in the army now. You're a murder suspect and will be treated as such.'

Yardley blinked. 'What evidence do you have to support your monstrous claim?'

'We have the evidence of our own eyes, sir. When we saw that rifle, we identified it by means of the initials. It's a prized possession. A man who loves shooting as much as you do will have a gun room where you store the weapons in cupboards with stout locks. That being the case,' said Colbeck, 'how could James Carmody manage to steal it?'

'You've mentioned his name before. It means nothing to me.'

'Then you've obviously forgotten that you described him as the best beater you'd ever had. In fact, you were so impressed by him that you recruited him as your accomplice.'

'That's nonsense!'

'What we don't know is which one of you fired the shot at Mr Hubbleday. My feeling is that you were the marksman. You'd never deign to let anyone else use a gun of yours.' He saw the colonel's face twitch. 'I'm afraid that you must come with us, Colonel. You are guilty of involvement in two murders. I'm going to ask the sergeant to arrest you.'

'It will be a pleasure,' said Leeming, stepping forward.

'Wait!' pleaded the colonel, as if suddenly aware of his position. 'I must ask a favour of you, Inspector. My wife, as you may know, is a sick woman. It's likely that the news will take her to her grave. Allow me some time to speak with her alone. I need to . . . take my leave of her.'

'Ten minutes,' said Colbeck. Yardley sighed with gratitude. 'Then we will leave quietly together. I take it that you don't wish the staff to be aware of what is happening.'

'That's very considerate of you, Inspector.'

'Before you go, however, we need to know who killed the works manager. Was it you or Carmody?'

'It was Carmody,' said the other, bitterly. 'In addition to an agreed amount of money, I was forced to give him the rifle. He had always coveted it. I hated parting with that gun, but Carmody insisted. In return, he used his friendship with a railway employee to find out the approximate time when that excursion train would arrive at the spot on the line that I'd chosen.'

'Did he steal those sleepers and red flags for you?'

'Yes, he did. They were placed exactly where I told him.'

'Why did you choose that particular train?'

'It belonged to Appleby,' snarled the colonel, spitting out the name with contempt. 'He should never have been allowed anywhere near the Malverns. As for that dreadful manager in charge of the excursions, I've seen him swaggering around here with that unwanted mob of visitors as if he owns these hills.'

'How did you know that he would get out of the train when it stopped?'

'Hubbleday was the sort of man who has to be in control. That meant he would be in the compartment closest to the engine. If we could stop the train, I knew that he would jump out and demand to know what had caused the delay. When he did that, he was shot dead.'

'You had no right to order his assassination.'

'I had every right!' howled the colonel, face colouring with rage. 'Appleby and his miserable retinue of employees abuse this wonderful part of the country. Somebody had to stand up to them. They're like a plague of locusts. They swoop, they ravage, then they fly away.'

'Shooting one man won't stop excursionists coming.'

'Perhaps not, Inspector, but it will act as a warning to others. That includes Appleby,' he added with a glint in his eye. 'He won't dare to send anyone here for a very long time.'

'Why did you have to kill Carmody?' asked Leeming.

'He disobeyed my orders,' said the colonel. 'I told him to do what I asked and take his rewards. But he was greedy. Once he had a hold over me, he tried to exploit it. That was his mistake. I arranged to meet him at the Beacon to collect the extra money I'd promised. I remember his glee as he counted the banknotes,' he went on. 'What he didn't realise was that I had been to the place during the night and hid the weapon nearby. While Carmody was still giggling at what he thought was his good fortune, I knocked him senseless then hacked his head off.'

'You also cut his tongue out,' said Leeming. 'Why?'

'I'm a collector, Sergeant. I always take souvenirs of a kill. If you go to the gun room,' said the colonel, 'you'll find Carmody's tongue in a jar. He no longer has any use for it.'

'That's revolting!' exclaimed Leeming.

Colbeck checked his watch. 'Your ten minutes start now, Colonel.'

'God bless you!' He offered his hand, but the inspector refused to shake it. 'I give you my word as an officer and a gentleman that I'll abide by the agreement.'

Yardley left the room at once and closed the door behind him.

'Does he feel no shame at all at what he did?' asked Leeming.

'Apparently not,' said Colbeck. 'He's lying until the bitter end.'

'What do you mean?'

'It was the colonel who shot Mr Hubbleday. It would have been a kind of target practice to him. He'd never dare to let Carmody do something that would give the colonel so much pleasure. He was a trained marksman, remember.'

'I feel sorry for his wife.'

'So do I, Victor, but I also spare a thought for Lady Foley. She trusted him. He was even invited to dine with her. Think how she will feel when she learns the hideous truth about him.'

'I hope she never hears about the tongue in a jar.'

'I daresay it would have given him a perverse pleasure every time he saw it. Look around you,' said Colbeck, with a sweeping gesture that took in the whole room. 'This place is a museum of his victims. Apart from the tiger, he killed stags, birds of prey and many other animals.' He pointed a finger. 'Look at those stuffed fish on the wall over there.'

'I'm surprised he didn't have Carmody's head in a glass case.'

'He drew the line at that.'

'Hang on,' said Leeming as a thought surfaced. 'Who was

it who hired those two men to attack Alan Hinton?'

'We'll have to ask the colonel. He obviously paid an intercessory to find someone at the Works who would take the money and ask no questions. Wragg recruited his brother, and they shared the spoils. Don't worry, Victor. The man responsible for engaging Wragg will not escape justice.'

Leeming was about to ask another question when he was interrupted by the sound of a horse galloping away from the house. Colbeck was the first to react.

'He's making a run for it,' he said.

'What about his wife?'

'I don't think he even spoke to her.'

Running to the door, Colbeck tried to open it and found that it was locked from the other side. He used both fists to pound on the wood. The door was soon unlocked by the butler, who had a bemused look on his face.

'Where has Colonel Yardley gone?' demanded Colbeck.

'I don't know, sir,' said the other. 'He just disappeared.'

'Where is his wife?'

'Mrs Yardley is always asleep at this time of day. He'd never disturb her.'

'So much for him being an officer and gentleman,' said Leeming.

'He's fled the house,' said Colbeck. 'Where might he go?'

'I've no idea, Inspector,' said the butler.

'You must have, man. In an emergency, what would he do?'

'All I can tell you is that the colonel is very religious.'

Leeming was aghast. 'Religious?'

Colbeck grabbed him and they ran out of the door.

Ruby Renshaw had had a busy day and rewarded herself by relaxing beside the fire and taking up her knitting. In no time at all, the needles were clicking merrily away as she established a steady rhythm. Nothing else mattered to her. She was lost in a private world and making something of value at the same time. Her hands were so deft and experienced that the garment began to take shape before her eyes. Ruby felt utterly content.

The feeling did not last for long. Suddenly, she began to make silly mistakes, chiding herself and having to make repairs. Her hands lost their control and fluency. It was as if something was determined to interrupt her. In the end, she let the knitting drop into her lap and closed her eyes. The familiar sensation of dread then made her shiver. All she could do was to let it run its course.

When it finally died away, she opened her eyes and thought of the two detectives staying with her. Sympathy welled up inside her.

'Oh, you poor dears!' she cried. 'It's so unfair on you!'

Colbeck drove the trap as fast as he dared but it was no match for a rider with a head start on them. Leeming was baffled.

'Where are we going?' he asked.

'You'll soon see,' replied Colbeck.

'That butler said that the colonel was very religious. I don't see anything religious about shooting one man and beheading another.'

'The colonel has a need to confess.'

'Then why did he try to tell us a pack of lies?'

'Just hold on tight, Victor, and we may find out.'

The trap rumbled and bounced along until it reached Great Malvern. When Colbeck finally brought the horse to a halt, they were outside the Priory. Tethered to a tree in the churchyard was a stallion.

'That must be his,' decided Colbeck.

Leeming was puzzled. 'What on earth is he doing here?'

'Let's go and find out, shall we?'

After tethering the horse, Colbeck led the way to the door in the north porch. They went inside. Apart from the lone figure kneeling at the altar rail, the Priory seemed empty. Candles created small pools of light in the darkness. Colonel Yardley paid no heed to the cold or the discomfort. Lost in prayer, he was confessing his sins and begging for mercy.

Colbeck took a moment to get his bearings then left Leeming to guard the door. The inspector walked cautiously down the nave. When his eyes adjusted to the gloom, he called out in a loud voice.

'I know that you're here, Colonel, and I know why. There's no escape. Please don't make it difficult for yourself.'

'Go away!' yelled the colonel.

'I'm afraid that I can't do that, sir.'

'I need to be alone with God.'

'He may not wish to indulge you,' said Colbeck, pointedly. 'You've broken one of his commandments. Thou shalt not kill.'

'Stay away!' howled the other. 'I'm armed.'

Colbeck was glad of the warning. He crouched down as he moved forward. One of the candles beside the choir stalls was suddenly extinguished. The colonel was on the move. Another flame was soon blown out, deepening the gloom in the chancel. Colbeck crept on, trying to work out where a third candle would be doused. When it happened, it was some distance from where he had expected it to be. The colonel was nimbler than he had imagined.

'Leave me be,' warned Yardley. 'You're a stranger here. I know this church like the back of my hand. Get out while you can.'

'You would never dare to commit murder on consecrated ground.'

'I'd dare anything, Inspector.'

Another candle died, many yards from the earlier one. The tables had suddenly been turned. It was Colbeck who was now being stalked. Keeping low and as quiet as he could, he scurried into an area of the nave that had no illumination at all. He pricked up his ears for sounds of movement. None came. Instead, there was a period of prolonged silence. Colbeck was keenly aware of the danger he was in. The man he was after was an expert in the use of firearms. Colonel Yardley had a gun of some sort and would certainly use it. All that the inspector had to defend himself was a kneeler he'd snatched from its hook. It would not stop a bullet.

As he continued to creep forward, Colbeck heard a sound that he recognised. One of the seats in the choir stalls had been accidentally tipped back. The sudden bang was amplified in the huge space. The colonel had given his position away. Another sound reached Colbeck's ears.

'Keep going, sir,' whispered Leeming, from close by. 'I'm with you.'

Heartened by the sergeant's support, Colbeck went on the move again. He knew that Leeming was close enough to see and follow him. Aware that the colonel was lurking somewhere among the misericords, he remembered that they were also known as mercy seats. Colbeck resolved that Yardley would be shown no mercy. It was a concept that had never entered the colonel's mind. James Carmody's horrific death was proof of that.

When they got close to the chancel, Leeming inched forward until he was level with Colbeck. The latter was pleased to see that the sergeant had also used his initiative and grabbed a kneeler. No words were spoken. Colbeck instead resorted to touch, ordering his colleague to go down one side of the chancel while he himself went down the opposite. Off they went on their hands and knees, crawling slowly. It was too late to be afraid. There were consolations. The colonel was old. His hearing would be impaired, and his reactions would have slowed down. He might also be unaware that there were two of them. That gave them the element of surprise.

The detectives continued to move forward, both ready to startle the colonel when they worked out where he was. But they reckoned without his army experience. The bang they had heard was not a sign of his carelessness. It was a deliberate ploy to lure Colbeck towards his target. Without warning, a figure suddenly appeared in the stalls not far from the inspector.

'That's far enough,' snapped the colonel, pointing a pistol at him. 'You're a brave but foolish man, Inspector. Get to your feet.'

'I'm glad to do so,' said Colbeck, calmly. 'My knees are aching terribly.'

As he rose slowly, he knew that he would be presenting the target that the colonel wanted. There would be no time for conversation. To avoid arrest, Yardley would not hesitate to shoot. Instead of straightening, therefore, Colbeck got halfway up then hurled the kneeler at the colonel, deflecting the gun so that the bullet it fired went up into roof and bounced off the ancient stone. Before he could recover, Yardley was hit in the face by a kneeler thrown by Leeming. It knocked him backwards. Colbeck dived at him and grabbed the wrist of the hand holding the gun, dashing it against the stall so hard that the weapon was released. It fell to the floor with a thud. Leeming joined in the arrest at once. The colonel ranted and swore but he was soon overpowered by his two assailants. His wrists were handcuffed behind his back. They marched him up the aisle.

'Let go of me,' he howled.

'We can't do that,' said Colbeck. 'You have to pay for your crimes.'

'You shouldn't have stopped me. I came here to kill myself.'

'The hangman will be happy to do the job for you.'

Though she unravelled the knitting and tried to start again, Ruby Renshaw could not use her hands. They simply would not obey her. Tossing the needles aside, she lay back in her chair and wondered what sort of disaster her guests would face. A fearful shock awaited them. Confronted already by two murders, were they about to suffer a third? Or would this latest prediction turn out to be an illusion?

Colbeck and Leeming were thrilled. Their delight at the arrest, however, was punctured by the fact that the telegraph station had closed. There was no way of passing on the good news to Scotland Yard. Instead, they took the first train to Worcester and delivered their prisoner to Inspector Vellacott. The colonel's peremptory demand that his solicitor be summoned immediately was ignored. He was locked in a cell with an armed officer seated outside it.

Solving the two murders was a cause for celebration. Vellacott took the detectives to his favourite pub, and they enjoyed a drink together. Colbeck was even persuaded to try a pint of Armitage's Best Bitter.

'I felt certain that Armitage was the killer,' confessed Leeming.

'We all make mistakes,' said Colbeck. 'I certainly made my share of them during this investigation.'

'It's understandable,' added Vellacott. 'The main thing is that we caught that devil at last. The news is going to cause huge waves of disbelief when it spreads. The colonel was highly respected.'

'Nowhere more so than by my superintendent, I fear. He felt that Colonel Yardley was exactly what he appeared to be. It's going to come as a rude shock to him that a man he admired was guilty of such crimes. Your help was crucial to our success, Inspector,' said Colbeck. 'You identified Carmody as a suspect at the very start.'

'He deserved to die for his part in the first murder,' said Vellacott, 'but not in the barbaric way that the colonel devised for him. Was the murder weapon really found by Biddy Leacock?'

'Oh, yes. Her contribution was important.'

'I don't know about either of you,' said Leeming, 'but my stomach is starting to rumble. Is there any chance of food here?'

'They serve an excellent meat pie, Sergeant,' said Vellacott. 'I could be tempted by one myself.'

'Then why are we waiting?' asked Colbeck. 'Let's order three meals and enjoy every morsel of them. I fancy that we've deserved it.'

When her mother crept into the bedroom to check on her, Helena Rose Colbeck was fast asleep. Madeleine adjusted the blanket slightly then planted the faintest of kisses on her daughter's head. On the bedside cupboard was a framed photograph of Colbeck. Madeleine adjusted the angle so that it would be the first thing that her daughter saw when she opened her eyes. Hoping for her husband's early return, she left the bedroom noiselessly.

It was late evening when they finally got back to their hotel. Ruby Renshaw was relieved to see them. She rose to her feet at once.

'I expected you much earlier,' she said with a note of reproach.

'We've been celebrating, Mrs Renshaw,' said Colbeck. 'We lost track of time, I'm afraid.'

'Our work here is done at last,' explained Leeming. 'We made an arrest.'

'I'm glad to hear it, Sergeant, but you may be delayed here even longer.'

'Why?'

'I had one of my sensations earlier on. It ruined my knitting.'

'But you told us that your predictions rarely come close together.'

'I was wrong,' she said, anxiously. 'I'd stake everything I own on it that something nasty is going to happen tomorrow.'

'I knew it,' said Leeming. 'The superintendent is coming back.'

'Listen to Mrs Renshaw,' advised Colbeck. 'I believe that

she can see into the future. We should be very grateful to her. If we might face a dire tomorrow, there's only one thing we can do.'

'What's that, sir?'

'We leave at once. If we hurry, we might just catch the last train out of here.' He turned to Ruby. 'Please excuse our abrupt departure. Staying in your hotel has been a pleasure, but your warning is timely.'

'Go,' she urged. 'Go while you still can.'

They reacted with speed, rushing off to their respective rooms to gather their belongings. Less than ten minutes after arriving there, they were taking leave of her and heading for the station. The first flakes of snow were already falling, and a wind was whipping them up. It suddenly seemed much colder.

'That's the disaster Mrs Renshaw predicted,' said Colbeck as the snowfall quickened. 'This is going to fall throughout the night. If we'd stayed until the morning, we might have been marooned here for a long time.'

Leeming was disturbed. 'What about Christmas Day?'

'Our families would have spent it without us.'

Madeleine Colbeck was awakened not long after dawn by the squeals of delight from her daughter's bedroom. She got up and rushed to see what had caused such pleasure. Helena was standing beside the window with the curtains drawn back.

'Mummy!' she cried. 'Look at the garden. It's all white.'

'Goodness!' explained her mother, gazing out. 'We've had snow.'

Madeleine was conscious of the fact that it was the first time in her life that her daughter had seen snow. She was so happy to share the moment of discovery with Helena. Three or four inches had fallen during the night and carpeted the whole garden. Madeleine knew at once what her daughter wanted. After dressing her quickly, she went to the main bedroom and put on her own clothing. The two of them then rushed downstairs to put on coats, hats and gloves before going out into the garden.

Helena was beside herself, running around the lawn to leave a series of footprints then scooping up some snow to examine it. Her mother could not resist making a snowball and throwing it gently at Helena. The girl laughed merrily. Though she could not mould a snowball properly, she could still hurl handfuls of snow at her mother. Pretending to be beaten back, Madeleine covered her head with her arms. It was an exciting new game for Helena, and she relished it.

When they eventually stopped to catch their breath, they saw Caleb Andrews emerging from the house, hours earlier than they were expecting him. Helena immediately gathered up some snow to throw at her grandfather, but he was in no mood to play with her.

'I've brought bad news, Maddy.'

'What sort of bad news?' she asked.

'Do you remember Billy Phelps?'

'Yes, of course,' she said. 'He lives around the corner from you.'

'I'd told him about Robert's latest case, you see. Billy knocked on my door when he came off the night shift at Euston. He warned me that snow has played havoc with the train timetable. It's not too bad here but, the further north you go, the worse it gets. Billy has heard that whole stretches of the line are under three feet of snow.'

'Oh, no!' said Madeleine in alarm.

'We may not see Robert for Christmas, after all.'

'Play with me, Grandpa,' said Helena, tugging at his coat.

'Yes, all right,' he promised, giving her a hug. 'Shall I make you a snowball?'

'Please . . .'

Breaking away from them, Madeleine tried to absorb the news. Her husband was well over a hundred miles away in a place that might well be in the grip of bad weather. Snow was a plaything for their daughter, but a disaster for Colbeck. It would hamper his work and might keep him in the Malverns for days on end. Fighting to hold back tears, she went into the house, wondering how she could explain to Helena why her father was not there on Christmas Day.

When she went into the hall, however, she heard a key being inserted in the lock. The front door swung open to reveal Colbeck, weary, dishevelled and soaking wet. She flung herself into his arms.

'You're back!' she cried.

'Only by the grace of God,' he cried. 'Victor and I spent

most of the night sleeping in a train that was held up by a snow drift. We had to walk part of the way back then managed to find a stretch of line that had been cleared. No matter,' he went on, smiling. 'I'm here, that's the main thing.'

'Come into the garden and see Helena and my father.'

'Why is he here so early?'

'He came to warn me that you might not be back for days.'

'I'm not only back,' said Colbeck, hugging her. 'I'm home to celebrate a white Christmas with my family.'

EDWARD MARSTON has written well over a hundred books, including some non-fiction. He is best known for his hugely successful Railway Detective series and he also writes the Bow Street Rivals series featuring twin detectives set during the Regency; the Home Front Detective novels set during the First World War; and the Ocean Liner mysteries.

edwardmarston.com